Burn My Letters: Tyranny to Refuge

Burn My Letters: Tyranny to Refuge

© Ruth Bonetti 2016 - First edition.
© 2018 Revised second edition.

Published by Words and Music, QLD

ISBN: 9780987544223

National Library of Australia Cataloguing-in-Publication entry (pbk)
Creator: Bonetti, Ruth, author.
Title: Burn my letters: Tyranny to refuge / Ruth Bonetti.
ISBN: 9780987544223 (paperback)
Subjects: Finns–New South Wales–Fiction.
Dissenters–Finland–Fiction.
Genealogy–Fiction.
Finland–Politics and government–Fiction.
Dewey Number: A823.4

Photo credits: Eric Back; Ruth Bonetti; Brunswick Valley Historical
Society; Migration Institute of Finland.

Burn My Letters: Tyranny to Refuge

Ruth Bonetti

tycket vara bra åtgång, ty perso-
ner flytta hit från Öykahusten.
Brän upp denna lapp lika-
som alla mina bref, ty icke
vill jag att ni skall spara
dem!

'Burn this piece of paper, just as all my other letters, I do not wish for you to keep them!'

'But what mother, who knows she will not see her son again, could do that? Sanna hid them in the family Bible.'

For my sons, Paul-Antoni, Simeon and André.
May the knowledge of your forebears enrich your lives.
My Finnish family; thank you for sharing your treasure trove of letters and
documents, and for welcoming me into your fold.

'Let us not become weary in doing good, for at the proper
time we will reap a harvest if we do not give up.'

Galatians 6:9 (NIV)

Author's Note

We view history through variegated prisms. Inevitably, oral history invites contradictions. This book relies on archival letters and documents to sift truths from myths. In chronicling this story, I have interwoven research with imagination. Information gaps were filled with suppositions based on verified facts.

My quest has been to look under the surface of dates, actions and events to find the persons and motivations that propelled them–to put flesh on bones. Thus, imagination put words into mouths but I could often draw on actual words from letters to give voices authenticity.

I am indebted to Gretchen Back-Storvist and Pia Storvist who helped me translate Karl Johan's letters from 'old Swedish' filtered through Munsala dialect. Sometimes these have been pruned without ellipses for easier reading, and turned into dialogue to minimise italics.

To the best of my extensive research, the basic information contained in the book is true and sometimes corrects fallacies of dates and details contained in early documents that have been subsequently repeated.

For example, early sources assert that Anders Back 'visited both sons' in Australia. Shipping records show he brought Wilhelm and two other lads, departing from Hangö on 26 November 1902. Wally Holm, an otherwise reliable source from a 40-year friendship with his uncle KJ, said that Anders Back brought out eight lads with Wilhelm, but shipping records show only two Swedish names. Some early sources confuse dates and ages (e.g. that KJ fled in 1896 when he was aged 18, but shipping records and notes in the family Bible prove otherwise). The story of KJ's escape over the Monäs Pass is oral history backed by some academic supposition, possibly confused with a story about Erik Johan (Ny)Holm twenty years later.

The name of KJ's friend who gave his passport is unknown, but Mats Backlund was chosen as in July 1903 KJ wrote: 'I'm sending £20 to Backlund for travel money. I would like to give him £21 for the first month as well as food if he should like to come. If not, you can keep the money.' This might imply that he was a close friend, and also shows KJ's generosity.

KJ gained his seaman's ticket on 7.6.1898 so it is a reasoned interpretation that he worked his way as crew. The captain's name and nationality are invented as are details of the voyage. The phrase 'he took a shine to KJ' is passed down as oral history, also that he suffered sea sickness and vowed 'I never come back, I don't like to go over the sea if I don't see the land, I don't go over so wide water that I don't see the land.'

Rolf Back quoted his words at Suez 'If they take me I swim to shore and take my chances with the Arabs'. Hugo Holm said he swam to shore to escape.

KJ wrote for Munsala Village News, was spokesperson and chairman of Munsala Youth which presented dramas, skits and songs. Two events have been merged in this book: Munsala Sockens notes a presentation on January 1897; apparently it caused sufficient uproar to warrant mention. After KJ left Finland, police stopped a similar a performance on 5 February 1901 (Runeberg's Day, a national day) as being too nationalistic.

Conversations and points of view are of course imaginary; the genres of magical realism and creative non-fiction have widened horizons for me to better understand my ancestors and heritage.

Preface

When Ruth Bonetti first described her heritage to me, a journey I share, I was convinced this book must be written. She has shown me drafts during its progression that prove this true. As an author used to reading manuscripts, I was bowled along by this evolving tale.

Ruth Bonetti's lyrical style evokes the feeling of a saga. She captures the voice of the Finnish emigrants, drawing on fascinating letters to bring the characters to life with magical realism. Her 'conversations' with the characters are utterly enchanting and an absolute joy.

This intriguing story, the historic letters and descriptions of her own journeys to Finland show Ruth's rapport with Finnish ethos, enterprise and a finely tuned sense of its culture.

There is much written about migration to America but almost nothing about that to Australia. Ruth Bonetti's book fills a gap.

Those who seek their roots will identify with her sense of heritage, passed from generation to generation, even at the opposite ends of the world.

Sandy McCutcheon
Novelist
Awarded Kalevalan 150 -Vuotismitali
Helsingissa Kalevalan Paivana 1985

Main Characters Family Tree

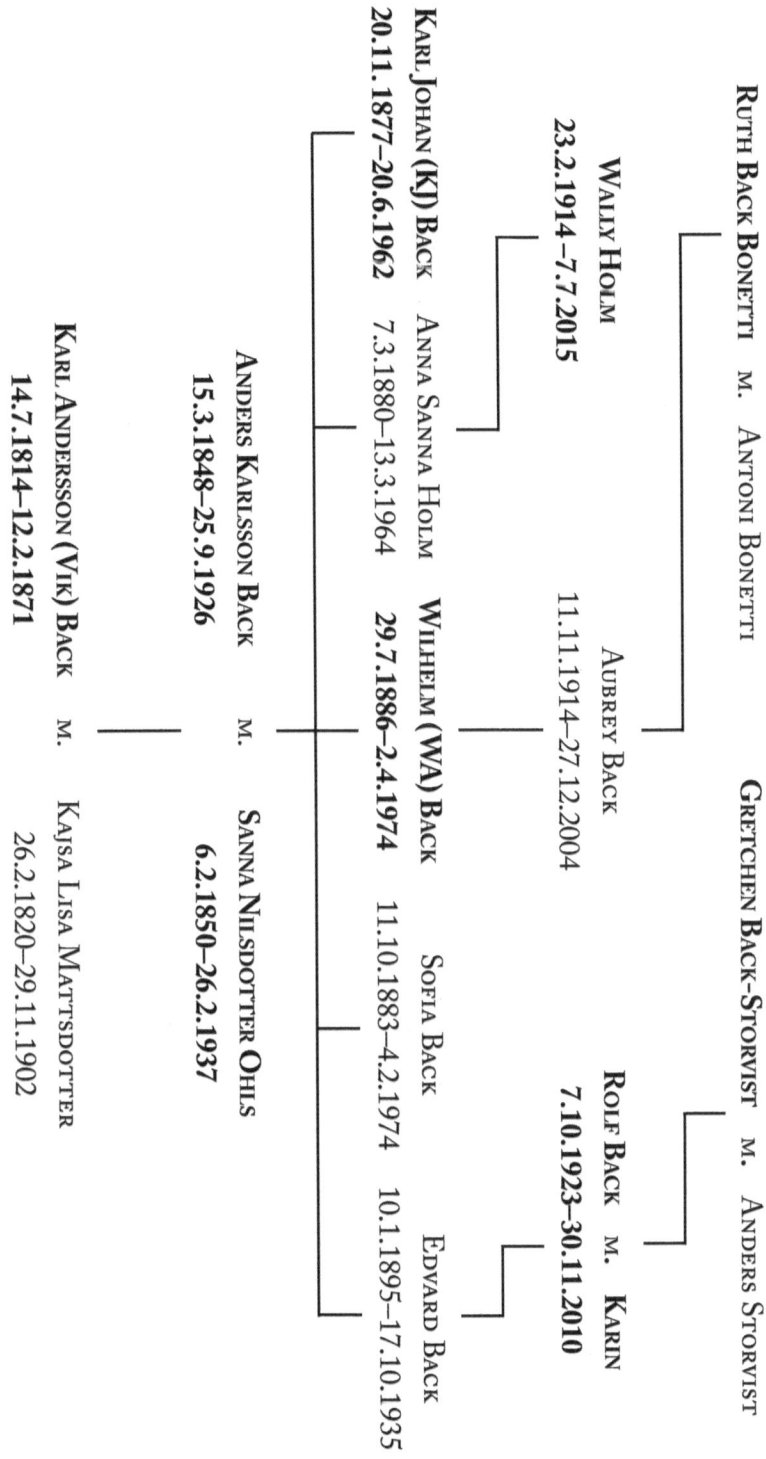

Ruth Back Bonetti   m.   Antoni Bonetti

Gretchen Back-Storvist   m.   Anders Storvist

Wally Holm
23.2.1914–7.7.2015

Aubrey Back
11.11.1914–27.12.2004

Karl Johan (KJ) Back
20.11.1877–20.6.1962

Anna Sanna Holm
7.3.1880–13.3.1964

Wilhelm (WA) Back
29.7.1886–2.4.1974

Sofia Back
11.10.1883–4.2.1974

Rolf Back   m.   Karin
7.10.1923–30.11.2010

Edvard Back
10.1.1895–17.10.1935

Anders Karlsson Back
15.3.1848–25.9.1926

m.

Sanna Nilsdotter Ohls
6.2.1850–26.2.1937

Karl Andersson (Vik) Back
14.7.1814–12.2.1871

m.

Kajsa Lisa Mattsdotter
26.2.1820–29.11.1902

Contents

The Frozen Highway

I must draw the songs from Coldness,
From the Frost must I withdraw them.
Kalevala

Where do we come from?
Who are we?
Where are we going?

My journeys to discover my heritage have woven circles around the globe. Through bleak, interminable Scandinavian winters, I imagined my Finnish Swedish forebears' reactions to glaring sun and Australian horizons. My grandfather Wilhelm Anders Back sent home photographs of his orange tree laden with golden fruit grown in lush volcanic earth around the Byron Bay hinterland. Of bananas growing rife like weeds around the verandah of his home. Such exotic fare was unknown in Finland around 1900.

What events propelled three siblings to seek haven in the Great Southland? They were refugees from the oppressive Russian occupation of Finland. Especially Karl Johan Back, the older brother who was tracked by military police at Suez. Why? Surely there were other young men to conscript as cannon fodder. Why did he write home saying 'burn my letters' and live his life as a hermit on hilltop eyries? Was his eye ever open for possible pursuing Russians? Why did he never return to Finland?

Let me take you on my discovery of the story, beginning in December 1976. Then, a homing bird, I embarked on a voyage tracing my heritage to Finland, Granddad's birthplace.

~

'Go forward.'

The voice of my Granddad spoke straight to me above the bugle calls of white Whooper swans whose wings creaked like sailcloth in the Arctic gusts.

1

How could I imagine what lay ahead, when we drove onto the ferry? Its engines revved to forge a passage from Sweden through the ice across the Gulf of Bothnia.

That four–hour crossing would propel me on a journey that has taken half my lifetime and which drew me back a century to my roots. This was no mere tourism, camera at the ready. I would soon meet relatives whose features were uncanny replicas of my Australian family. I would come to nestle amongst them in between my own migrations around the globe.

Yet back then, my spine prickled with presentiment.

~

The past drew me onward like a magnet to the land of the northern lights, its force invisible and mysterious. Feeling like a figurehead on a Viking prow, I leant forward on the rail to immerse myself in rosy sunlight as it flung diamonds across the ice.

I shivered as our ship crunched through blue–white ice walls. It was anticipation more than the cold fingers of Baltic drafts. My fur–lined hood rebuffed the chill winds.

The propellers churned out a glistening cascade of bubbles, each a prism of iridescent light. They shimmered like the froth of Byron Bay surf back home, reminding me of sun–bronzed beaches and summer holidays on the other side of the world.

A trail of sluggish water that followed the boat froze again into blobs. We passed islands encrusted with fir trees like frosting on cakes. Alongside, fishermen on skis drilled holes to dangle their lines. As I watched, snippets of family lore crackled through my memory; did an ancestor take the assassin of a Russian official to safety by sleigh over this frozen highway? And didn't I hear that Great–uncle Karl Johan Back escaped on skis across the gulf in 1899?

Huddled behind a bulwark to block the wind, I gave my face up to the sun. As I squinted into its kaleidoscope brilliance, I heard the thrust of Karl Johan's poles, saw him glance behind for pursuing Russians on frothing horses. Mist circled him as he gasped each breath. Damp from his nose and eyes froze solid onto his scarf. That was what kept him moving, those icicles. His mind thrummed.

I must escape those military police.

With each thrust, even as his energy waned, Karl Johan focused on the pale light behind the mist. In it he pictured flowers, golden like the sun, growing wild and free: fragrant orchids in a profusion of exotic palettes and textures. Parakeets, like those in that book his father Anders found, painted

2

in all shades of the rainbow. And the 'jackass' bird that laughed just for the joy of the summer. A land of warmth and riotous colour beckoned.

His eyes watered from the strain of searching out the stronger ice. Patches thinned as the warmer Gulfstream air swept through. Every last sinew of strength strained. He had been on skis since he could toddle but he was slight of build. He flagged. His arms and thighs wobbled with weariness.

Pappa's book also showed snakes and man–eating crocodiles. Better a quick death in icy water rather than such a fate.

Why push beyond endurance to an uncertain future?

Just as Karl Johan flung aside his poles and collapsed on the ice, the heavens turned on a spectacle. Light swept across the dome above; an arc of emerald tinged with silvery hues danced around him, spiralled, then faded.

Aurora Borealis, named after the Roman goddess of dawn. Herald of a fresh beginning.

If he could but endure, new life awaited. His Pappa talked of the Promised Land. But Karl Johan dreamt of *Lintukoto*—that warm, paradise haven where birds nest at the edge of the sky's dome. A place to rest his wings at the bottom of the globe, far from the Russians.

Karl Johan crawled onto shaky knees and thrust his poles back into the ice. He stretched, unlocking the stiffness in his calves until they creaked in protest, then propelled forward through the whiteness, on and on. A jetty told him he had reached land near Umeå in Sweden.

My vision faded and I was left wondering if my sketchy information was a myth. Could a man really ski so far? A desperate one might. Was it in winter that Karl Johan fled? Or had he rowed across the Gulf of Bothnia under glaring sun, his hands chafing from the oars? He would have then fled south through gold–leaf birch forests. How long would it have taken? Why did the Russians pursue him?

One sentence from my upbringing lingered: 'Granddad and his brother Karl Johan migrated to escape conscription into the Russian army.' Our family story resonated with those words: *escape conscription… escape the Russians*.

Cold War novels and films fed my imagination. But I knew little more. Now, Umeå was to be my home for the next two years. I felt squeamish to live near Russia, our family's traditional foe. Tales of invasion twisted through my dreams.

I was on the brink of realising a lifetime's longing to uncover secrets of my family's past.

The ship's intercom directed us back to our car to disembark at Vaasa. We shook our heads at the gypsies who tried to cadge a lift; the women a flurry of multi–coloured, multi–layered petticoats, the men in purple boots.

Our car skidded onto Finnish land, a place of yet more slippery whiteness. It was a moment to savour: I had completed the full circle of my ancestors' migrations to Australia. Against a pink haze of snow, spruce trees waved their arms in welcome. I had come home.

That overwhelming sense warmed me like coffee down a chilled throat.

Looking Back – and Forward

I am driven by my longing, and my understanding urges
That I should commence my singing and begin my recitation.
I will sing the people's legends, and the ballads of the nation.
Kalevala

Extraordinary providence brought me to live in northern Sweden directly across the Gulf of Bothnia from the Finnish village where my grandfather was born.

My husband Antoni drove me north through a hazy gloom to Jakobstad (or Pietarsaari) where we hoped to meet Finnish family. As the songs of our land wove through my mind and heart, I began to understand that magnetic pull of the north.

Fir trees blurred through the wintry landscape. The fuzz of sun was low at two o'clock, almost lost to the horizon; the day was reluctant to eke out more hours of light. Our windscreen wipers chased snowflakes aside, each mesmerising swipe taking me back into my past.

Did destiny select me to explore this part of my heritage? Our family tree remains verdant with relatives, any of whom could have been chosen.

Perhaps the answer could be traced to my childhood in the sixties. I grew up in the Australian outback, but our family often drove a thousand miles south to holiday with relatives near Byron Bay in Northern New South Wales.

A Queensland child, I supposed all New South Welshmen 'talked funny'. I was further confused to hear they migrated from Finland and yet spoke Swedish.

My generation learned no Swedish. Yet I have been told that, aged six, I chatted with Granddad's sister Anna Sanna. She spoke little English and I knew no Swedish! Somehow we communicated despite the language barrier.

A recorded interview from 1960 shows that after almost a lifetime in Australia Granddad's English was fluent. However he still confused 'what' for 'that' and made plural 'peoples' and 'advices.' His speech was coloured with words that I later realised were Swedish or adaptations of it, like 'drinka kaffee' then 'vaska diska' (wash the dishes). When I came to learn the language I discovered he'd invented others. The word *congerichuchin* for a get–together still lives in family usage. Little wonder that it was typical of my family to play with words.

When I began to research the family story, Granddad cast the longest, most impressive shadow, the epitome of the migrant made good. A self–made millionaire, Wilhelm Anders Back, anglicised as WA, Will, or Billy Back, was 'Australia's Richest Finn', as proclaimed in a Finnish magazine article.

He loved posing for photographs: a studio portrait that graced our piano back home showed his beaming round face in round spectacles. In my memories, my grandfather always wore a suit, even in sweltering outback summers. So I was surprised when cousins sent me photographs of him boating and swimming in his black bathers.

My information about Granddad's older brother Karl Johan was scant: a brief outline in a historical society pamphlet and his two books. One photograph showed a dapper twenty–something man, a book in hand, orchid in the buttonhole of his frock coat and a potted plant at his elbow. Sensitive eyes reflected depths of thought and experience.

My Uncle Eric in his memoir dismissed him with a mere page.

The family spoke little of Karl Johan except to write him off as an eccentric black sheep. Tagged with the words 'pacifist' and 'socialist', he was lost behind the comet swathe splashed by his younger brother, Wilhelm.

I had a misty memory of Uncle Karl Johan from my childhood visits. He lived in a shack festooned with ferns, pink Maiden's Blush, orchids and grape vines. We peeped through a window. It was crammed to the ceiling with books and newspapers. There was a pulley to lift his bed when these piles threatened to overtake it. Cousins whispered that they were hustled away when great–uncle KJ (as he was known) ran out in the nude to chase the birds from his grapes.

Prolific white hair grew out of his ears. An ink spot on his finger reminded me he was a real live author. A voracious reader and scribbler of poems, I had been electrified to hear my compositions read on the *Argonaut's Club* radio program, the highlight of country afternoons. But I gathered that my family didn't set much store by KJ's writing and free-thinking philosophy. He was too unconventional for them. Instead they prized Granddad's business acumen as the sixteen-year-old emigrant turned millionaire.

While Wilhelm built mansions in Mullumbimby and Brisbane, KJ lived in various shacks, cabins and timber cottages in the Byron Bay hinterland. He published his sweeping world vision out of '*Poets Corner*', Post Office Box 4, Mullumbimby, Australia. Did he sell many books from this safe haven in the 1920s?

A decade after settling in Australia, KJ was a successful landowner and employed many fellow Finns on his banana plantations. He owned various properties and cottages. But he was easily distracted from his crops and fruit trees into cultivating orchids, writing poetry and solving the financial ills of the world—after his brother rescued him from bankruptcy in 1928.

These brothers were like two sides of a penny; one the multi–dealing capitalist; the other a socialist, dreamer and visionary who published books in a language he'd learned from a dictionary during his voyage to Australia.

Wilhelm developed farms and housing estates in Northern New South Wales and Queensland. An early photograph of Granddad's land shows a hill stripped down to sad tree stumps; he loved burning them in bonfires. KJ built and operated cedar mills yet wrote in 1900 of the need to retain forest against future land erosion. Yet, like all settlers he cleared land, and produced a bumper crop of corn that set the locals agog in 1902. But in return he planted abundant trees, bananas and all kinds of fruit.

I shared his passion for the earth and its produce.

And Karl Johan was a self–published author. That encouraged me in my writing path.

I last saw Granddad when he presided as patriarch at my own wedding.

Wedding in the Hills

Whatever is one's lot in life,
A lucky man is he,
Who has a true and loving wife…
Who shares his sorrows, hides his faults,
And wraps his thoughts in love.
K. J. Back, *The Concentrated Wisdoms of Australia*

If we were superstitious, the omens might have halted my marriage.

The heavens opened, emptying out a deluge worthy of Noah's time. Cyclone Pam, the third in three months, had crossed the coast at Coolangatta near Binna Burra, just where we planned to marry three days later on a mountain top in the open air—if all the road landslides were cleared.

A torrent of water buffeted our little red Volkswagen. The windscreen wipers made frantic but futile swipes. Defiant of black skies, we pushed on in a car painted with hippy flowers, nostrils and nose hairs. We plodded north from Sydney to Brisbane, a city already sodden and putrid from its record–breaking floods of late January 1974.

The sullen weather seeped inside; tension and exhaustion erupted into bickering. We were tempted to call it off and turn back.

Brisbane had the stink of debris and mud piled up in battered houses. Mounds of riverweed and flotsam lay engorged on the riverbanks. We could implement Plan B: to hold the ceremony in a small wooden church at Beechmont.

But joy came on the morning of the wedding. The road up the mountain was clear. Despite threatening skies, the sun sparkled on raindrops and the golden splashes of Regent bowerbirds' wings. Rainbows shone blessings through mist in the first fine day since the floods. Breezes frolicked around ladies' dresses—and threatened to steal the marriage certificate, held by a pebble on a table overlooking the cliff.

We revelled in the surrounding richness for all the senses; beauty displayed in rainforest trees festooned with ferns, staghorns and orchids; the fragrance of rain on volcanic earth. Hopkins' poetry extolled the grandeur of God. Music flowed from a string quartet, from recorder and tabor. Kookaburras and parrots laughed with us; brilliant kingfishers flashed from trees. A male whipbird's crack, followed by his mate's chuckle played out their perpetual domestic exchange.

God smiled on our union. Uncle Eric recorded it with his movie camera.

We were so engrossed in our idyllic ceremony and celebrations that family had to hint that it should end. Tradition dictated they shouldn't leave before us, but no one wanted to brave the mountain descent after nightfall. Jokers had wrapped the VW in toilet paper; stones rattled in the hubcaps and into the brake linings. Angels protected our drive down the steep mountain bends but the brake repairs hurt our budget.

As it is the world over with weddings, we had eyes only for each other. Our thoughts were focussed on the two of us: our future and our plans to travel the world. I little thought that, as we said our vows, Granddad relived his own with Christina Hart. But two weeks before, missing his soul mate of sixty–two years, he wrote us a reflective letter:

> As I look back now on our marriage at Mooball on the 4th November 1908, I can remember it as plain as if it were yesterday. The wedding was in our new home that I had finished only a few days before, and the Minister from Byron Bay came by train to perform the ceremony.

Was it mere timing that I, of myriad grandchildren, received such a personal letter in which he opened his heart and inspired other couples in the generations since? That vista across the valleys of the Lamington Plateau and the New South Wales border must have sparked in Granddad flashbacks of his early settler years and courtship just over eighty kilometres away.

> We had only one visitor with us, a Percy Smith from Sydney who was working for me on the farm, but there was my brother KJ Back and the Hart family. We had a very nice wedding breakfast and as the southward train was leaving at four o'clock everybody was off the place and we just sat down and looked around.

His letter described how he surprised his bride with the gift of a piano—her family were musical—and he'd then phoned to engage a teacher. They knelt at the bedside and asked God to protect and guide and bless them through their lives.

And we certainly asked for some material blessings that in the eyes of the Lord were very small and he blessed us with very much more than ever we contemplated or asked for. If you take God into your partnership I am sure it will be even better than what you anticipate.

Did this letter pass some mantle to me as family chronicler so I would be drawn full circle north to live near Granddad's birthplace? I didn't know then that I had trod a first stepping–stone along the path to live in Sweden, and uncover the family's story. There I would imbibe the landscape, culture and historical events that shaped our ancestors.

I would learn the music of our heritage—even source bridal marches from the family village of Munsala to play at my niece Laura's wedding. When she married at Byron Bay lighthouse, a hundred years after Granddad arrived there, I felt the prickles of synchronicity. At their reception in nearby Bangalow, sunlight streamed in making a halo around the bride through the restaurant window.

At Ruth and Antoni's wedding.

Outside, a mere twenty metres away, was the railway station where WA Back—Laura's great–grandfather—arrived on 17 January 1903 to forge his new life in Australia.

On my own wedding day, Granddad beamed in delight, encircled by his prolific family. He said grace before our smorgasbord banquet of seafood, meats, salads and tropical fruit. There was little time for conversation.

If I could go back to that special day, I'd take Granddad aside, maybe after the photographers fussed over seating us for the family group photo. I'd ask him:

Granddad, I wish you'd tell me more about your upbringing in Finland—our heritage. I have no idea what it means to be Finnish, or Swedish, or whatever we are.

I imagine his voice, with its lilting accent:

Our family came from the west coast of Finland what was colonised by the Swedes and retained Swedish language and culture.

–So, how was it, coming as a lad to the other side of the world? Leaving your family, making a new life? Weren't you afraid, deep down? (I shiver now to imagine the sense of abandonment as his father left him to return to Finland just two weeks after their arrival.)

–*It helped that my father brought me, and that Karl Johan forged the path ahead of me.*

–I feel an affinity to the 'black sheep writer' but I know so little. Do tell me more.

–*Why would you want to know about him? He was an idealist. His farms failed.*

–He was the epitome of the refugee boatperson, who escaped an oppressive regime.

–*And who caused risks for all the family in the process.*

–How, Granddad?

–*We don't speak of that. No more congerichuchin.*

–Granddad? Please stay. I am determined to learn more.

–Granddad? I'm not letting you off so lightly.

But my grandfather died two weeks after our wedding. Destiny would bring me full circle around the world to reconstruct KJ's story and find the answers to such questions.

To a wider world

Our character is the combined work of Nature, of our ancestors, their lives and surroundings, and of our own lives, thoughts and surroundings.
K. J. Back, *The Concentrated Wisdoms of Australia*

Six months after our wedding, we set off to see the world, starting with a lean student existence in London.

When Antoni was offered a position as concertmaster of a Swedish opera orchestra we felt like birds released from their cages. We shut the door on our dank basement flat, murky with navy blue and bottle green wallpaper. Its sole, grilled window looked onto a brick wall that Antoni whitewashed in a futile search for light.

We shipped our possessions and stowed the overflow in plastic garbage bags on our hire car's rickety roof–rack. With London's fumes and endless sprawl of redbrick and stone terraces behind us, we dumped the bags on Felixstowe dock and Antoni returned the car, sprinting back seconds before the ship sailed.

We threw a halfpenny overboard as a defiant gesture to our hungry experience. Goodbye England, we're off to join an orchestra in Sweden.

We were too exhausted to enjoy the anticipated sauna and smorgasbord dinner.

At Gothenburg a bemused customs official waved through our plastic bags topped with a pot–plant. We turned our next hire car towards the far north town of Umeå via Stockholm, driving through trees and trees and trees. An occasional little *hus* was wooden, painted Falu red with white trim around doors and windows. Autumn light shimmered on russet and gold birches; sunsets mirrored and multiplied on lakes.

Sweden's open spaces, high sky and crisp air rejuvenated our spirits, jaded by London's glowering drizzle. Stopping on the way for a *värdshus* lunch of prawn and egg on rye bread, we were impressed that public telephones functioned without thumping. The amenities were spotless—and free!

Stockholm's maze of freeways and unfamiliar signage baffled us. We attempted a phone call to our host Carl–Axel, for directions. 'Where are you?'

'Jag vet inte—I don't know... 'was a phrase we soon learned.

Our hosts tracked us down and took us into their home to acclimatise for a few days. Their toddler granddaughter Lisa peeped at me behind her fingers, bemused at my limited response of *'Ja, ja, nej'* and my rash attempt to read her a picture book in Swedish.

Straight highways drew us north, closer to our new home. Carpets of crumpled leaves, brilliant gold and copper and bronze, were a painter's delight. Dusk faded into dark. Hypnotic snowflakes bounced off the windscreen.

On our first morning in Umeå we opened the hotel shutters to a magical swathe of brilliant snow that shrouded houses and frosted the cars. It changed trees into grotesque mythical shapes. In that one instant we understood the genesis of trolls.

Snow fluttered from the sky in the next weeks. Other days it sheeted down. We plugged into the car park electricity and set the timer to warm the seats for the morning—after we brushed powder or scraped ice from the windscreen. We learned when it was safe to take the shortcut across the frozen river—rather than the bridge—according to textures of snow–thaw–slush–refreeze–ice–frost.

After London's dank housing, our airy and clean apartment was bliss. White painted walls, white snow-painted fir trees outside the wide windows. Our spirits lifted and sang.

New friends invited us on St Lucia Day, December 13, to drink coffee and mulled wine served by girls in white dresses. They attached candles in their hair and sang carols.

Graders cleared snow each morning. Cars changed to steel–studded tyres (*vinter dek*) but skidding round corners was the best entertainment going for the local hoons. People scooted along the ice on a 'spark'. At country village concerts I was bemused to see them lined up outside like tethered horses in a Wild West movie. We had brought our tandem bicycle across from London and rode it all year round, snow or dry.

My eighteen-year-old brother Rodney joined us for our first 'white Christmas'—the interminable black nights explained those candles on Christmas cards—then we set off to find our family roots in Finland. He sported Viking-like earmuffs, his wool coat befitting the son of Queensland sheep graziers. They would be stifling in the heat and swatting pesky flies at the other end of the world while we huddled our fingers into mittens and pockets.

As our car neared Jakobstad we stopped at a service station for directions to my relatives' address. My father's cousin Rolf had not responded to letters; perhaps they didn't arrive, for in my extravagant adoption of all things European I decided our name, Back, deserved an umlaut. After all, most Finnish words are peppered with several. A sweep of the pen changed it—until corrected—to 'Bäck'.

Door knocking proved fruitless. Neighbours dismissed our basic Swedish, and answered with Finnish torrents that defied phrase books. We repaired to a hotel to thaw over bowls of pea *soppa*. A man walked in and looked around. It was Rolf. No words needed to be spoken, we knew each other. Rolf was a mix of my uncle's nose, my brother's chin, and his hair fell like Dad's. We laughed and chattered: 'You look like Aunt Sofia! She died two years ago ...'

'And Gretchen [Rolf's daughter] is the spitting image of my cousin Dell, back home.'

These were uncanny likenesses at opposite ends of the world, springing from roots and genes, which, I would discover, traced back half a millennium.

On this, my first of many visits to my Finnish family, I felt like a migrating bird flown over the Milky Way, the path of the mythical birds in the *Kalevala*, home to roost. The family warmed to my halting Swedish and barrage of questions. Over many decades they hosted generations of fly–in–fly–out relatives from Australia for the tour of the Munsala church, cemetery and farmhouse. Everyone would return home after posing on the settee under the photograph of their great–grandparents.

But I fossicked under the surface, researched Finnish history, interviewed historians, authors and genealogists, and sought to understand their lives and culture. I became so tenacious in my search for answers, that they nicknamed me 'Rut med krut' (*Ruth with gunpowder*).

The love between us continued to deepen from the time of this first delighted welcome. On subsequent visits the family gave me folders of letters, and helped me translate the old Swedish and local dialect. One summer they took me to the forest to spend a night in the red–timbered '*stuga*' cottage my great–grandfather built.

Unveiling our heritage developed from a passion to—some might say—an obsession. I longed to know the people who bred us. To dig deeper. As the spring thaw releases the frozen earth, so bedrock emerges. I sifted truths from myths to learn how my ancestors responded to occupation and oppression. This knowledge of my roots came to change my life.

Finding Ancestors

Let us now begin our converse,
Since at length we meet together,
From two widely sundered regions.
Kalevala

In Munsala village cemetery, the snow lay metres thick. A chill wind blew red onto our cheeks. Rodney sank knee–deep into a snowdrift. His savings didn't stretch to winter boots so he wore gumboots with several pairs of thick wool socks.

Rolf shares documents with Ruth

'There are your great–grandparents.' Rolf pointed to a massive headstone inscribed Anders Back and Sanna Back who died in 1926 and 1937. Listed lower were two infant children, Nils and Johanna, who died a month apart in

1892 as well as their daughter Sofia who lived to the age of 91. Her funeral was two months before my Granddad's in 1974. Above loomed the dark spruce trees that their eldest surviving son, KJ, planted before he escaped.

I had no idea why he fled. I had yet to learn that this small village was once a hotbed of radical activists and intellectuals. My boots sank into fairy-tale snow. Its fluffy prettiness covered a bedrock of history. After the thaw, I would dig out the past exposed by the glare of midnight sun.

Snow packed into Rodney's gumboots, freezing his socks solid. As the anguish of his toes sharpened, we retreated to Rolf's cottage and a bucket of warm water to thaw our feet. Rodney retrieved ten toes—intact—from the boots. It took an hour for feeling to return to mine—in winter boots.

Rolf's wife Karin revived us with warming *kaffee* and *bullar* (buns).

'*Tack så mycket*, Karin.' (Thank you.) How wonderful to speak with my relatives in their language, albeit with grammatical mistakes. What providence to learn the language of my ancestors.

When I arrived in Sweden with a phrasebook and three words of Swedish—*ja*, *nej* and *tack*—I discovered more words were familiar. Back home, over the family breakfast table we'd ask, 'please pass the *smör*' not realising that Granddad had brought the Swedish word for 'butter' into common usage.

I told my relatives of settling into life in Umeå, and how I'd polished enough Swedish sentences to phone the local *Musikskolan* and offer my clarinet teaching services. The director answered in unintelligible floods of words. Blink. *Långsamt, tack*. (Slower, please.) Stig said in careful English that they would welcome my teaching and he would show me the 'Red Willage'.

It transpired that this was a cheerful Falu red—like most north Scandinavian houses—villa in the centre of town. It had airy studios, a library and a kitchen for brewing the many cups of strong coffee that help Swedes function through long winters.

Before my first day's lessons I asked a colleague to write down various words I might need: breath, tongue, fingers, thumb, lips, mouthpiece, reed. My trepidation on meeting the first student relaxed for she was shy but pleasant. She played competently but with little expression. 'Let's make some interesting dynamics,' I suggested.

Swedish children start English lessons at eight years so this fourteen-year-old understood, even though she was shy of speaking.

'Do you know what *forte* means,' I asked? '*Ja, ja, fort.*' We tried very fort and not so fort, and not fort at all, with little difference to her musical expression until she departed in polite bewilderment.

It was best for my morale that I only discovered at the end of the day that *fort* means *fast*, not loud.

Most Swedes speak fluent English, which they're keen to practise. So teaching youngsters gave me scope to develop my vocabulary. My students and colleagues must have suppressed giggles over my mistakes, but were too polite to correct me. The lunch table was a constant guessing game as meanings emerged from the flow of burble: burble—*fisk*—ah, they're fishing—burble, burble *båt*—in a boat. Each day more words slotted into my language jigsaw. Watching the news, there was a disaster somewhere, but where? Though it was therapeutic to be oblivious of details for a while.

After several months of a crash course in Swedish by osmosis, I knew the challenge of picking up a new language word by word. I was intrigued that my great-uncle KJ learned English well enough to write and publish books in his second language.

'Did he speak some English before he left Finland, or did he learn it along the way?' I asked my relatives.

'He learned it on the boat, picked it up. How long have you lived here, and you speak our language?'

A month. Immersion helped and I love the challenge of communicating with people in their own language.

But I couldn't write a book in Swedish.

I imagined Karl Johan scribbling out a list of words to practise on his fellow travellers on the ship, adding to it each day. As I had done.

'You are similar to him.' This seed sowed deep; later, KJ's example sustained me through my own struggles to bring books to their fruition. I read his letter of 1901 in which he advised brother Wilhelm:

> *To learn English would be a better pastime than riding a bicycle and would be good for when you come here. For example, if you learn seven words each day (that isn't much) it would become over two thousand words in a year. When you understand so many you could almost begin reading books.*

My relatives warmed to me and to my efforts to communicate in flawed Swedish. They entrusted to me parish records dating back to 1550. Karin gave me a photocopied file of twenty pages of close written names.

'Our records start with Olof Olofsson Ohls, a soldier mentioned in 1577 in Sweden. Perhaps he was born around 1550. There are fourteen generations to yourself.'

Within a few minutes my family perspective deepened by four centuries. Australians think even one hundred years is ancient! My head was spinning as I scribbled notes and drew arrows to branches of interlocking families.

What sort of people lived behind those names? What resilience and determination drove them? How did they cope with the harsh winters? How did they recover when battles were fought over their land? How did they strive to hold their country safe from invasion? Did they resist the Russian occupation, fight in the snow during the Civil War, the Winter War, the Continuation War?

The Finnish word *sisu* intrigued me, one that is not easily translated, except as 'determination' or 'guts'. To not give up against impossible odds. I sensed that my ancestors were rich with *sisu*. And that these relatives had more respect and sympathy for KJ's ideals than for his brother WA's capitalism. It seemed that the northern family took the opposite view to that of our Australian perception of the 'black sheep' in the family.

Decades later I deciphered my notes and drew a family tree. The recent generations were the hardest; it was a challenge to fit Wilhelm Anders Back's prolific descendants onto the large page. He and his brother Edvard, Rolf's father, carried the line forward.

Granddad's elder brother KJ did not marry. I wondered why. With so many men slaughtered in the world wars, some bereaved spinster might not have overlooked his eccentric ways. Did I hear some mention of a widow with a brood of offspring? Did he so grieve a sweetheart left behind, that he remained a bachelor by choice?

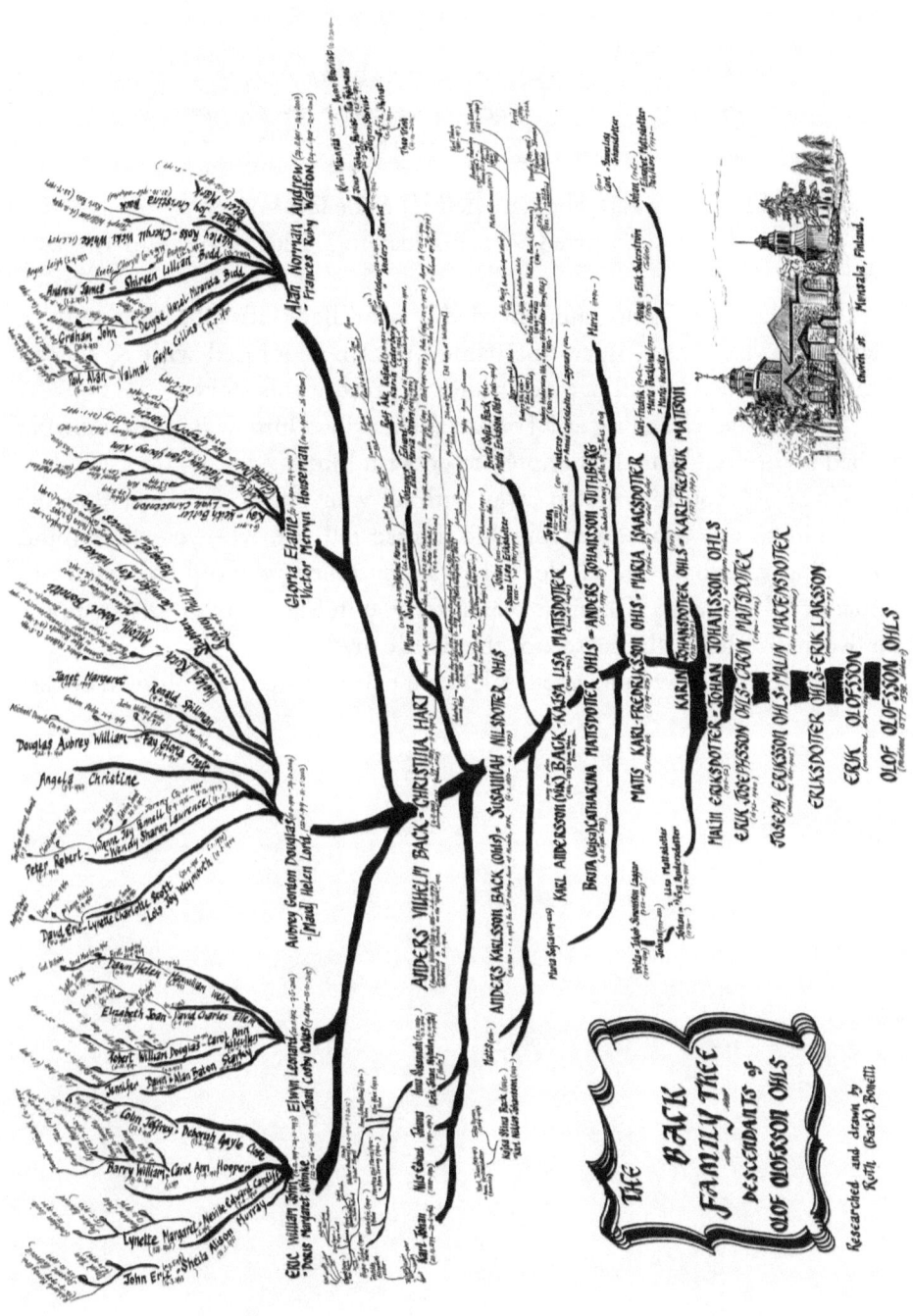

THE BACK FAMILY TREE and DESCENDANTS of OLOF OLOFSSON OHLS

Researched and drawn by Ruth (Back) Bowett

19

Yet in his 1918 book, *The Concentrated Wisdoms of Australia*, Karl Johan wrote:

> *Remember, whilst you are cursing your luck because, as it seems, your dreams of love are not to be realised, there are thousands of good girls pining their hearts away for someone to love.*

Rolf told of a woman who accosted KJ as he left home.

'A sticky beak, who pried into his leaving?' I ask. Rolf said it was a girlfriend.

This was Sofia who later married Viktor Bäck after bearing him an illegitimate daughter. (Since this name might be confused with KJ's sister Sofia, I've decided to call her Kerstin for the rest of this story.)

I picture her clutching at KJ's coat, as she willed him to stay, yet knowing he had no option. Was she tempted to go with him?

Uncle KJ, you hibernated away with all your books and I was too shy as a child to ask you about your life. Please tell me, KJ—you don't mind me calling you that? We all do. You're a storyteller; why did you flee from Finland? Why did the Russians search for you in Suez Canal? Did you pine for 'Kerstin'? The truth please, not the family myths.

I needed to know more about KJ. What better source than his own books?

Karl Johan The Author

When I go to my house and look across the paddock, which is the only fruit of my labour and all I can show for the whole of my life as a tribute to civilization, there sits the laughing jackass in the weeping willow. Such is the mixture of life in Australia.

K. J. Back, *The Concentrated Wisdoms of Australia*

I pulled out my copy of *The Concentrated Wisdoms of Australia*. The red bound cover is ornate, the title framed with leaves in which a kookaburra sits, eying trees and rolling grass.

The spine bears the text: '*By the man who Challenges the World in Literature.*' On the front cover, under his quote, '*Even our sorrows are mixed with joy,*' he reinforces that the book includes, '*A Challenge in Literature; Australia against the World for the Laureateship of the World.*'

What a grand gesture! I opened it to the Preface. This dedicates the book '*to the whole of humanity*' and gives a thumbnail portrait of a man who wore patched pants, a battered felt hat and Blucher boots without socks:

> *The one who is to bear the blame for this book is a man generally known as the Philosopher, looked upon as a person of little or no importance—*

No importance? You were Australia's first Finnish author.

> *He is a bachelor, tall and thin, with hollow cheeks and somewhat past middle age, one who lives by himself in a bark–hut on a river bank where he is often seen fishing and where he strips himself once every day, winter and summer, for a swim in the river.*

Did your skinny–dipping scandalise the locals? It's the norm to a Finland–Swede.

> *—I am not ashamed of my body and nor should others be.*

21

–Pardon? (For a moment I thought I heard KJ's voice.) You were the original Byron Bay hippie, KJ. I imagined his snort.

–I have been called many names in my life, but this I never heard before. My eyes skimmed further along the page: '*He is an uneducated man. He does manual labour at the rate of one day a week, and spends the remainder of his time in thinking and study. He is therefore not an idler, nor does he think anyone has any right to be.*'

But what was this competition? I flipped through to the chapter titled *Challenge in Literature*. First he counters those who criticise Australian literature:

> *One of those was a German count, whose name I had long since forgotten and will probably never hear of again. He wrote in his book about the unintelligent, yellow–skinned, monkey–faced Australians.*

The publication date was 1918. So KJ was responding to anti–German propaganda during World War 1 when locals eyed with suspicion any who spoke with a foreign accent. Many 'aliens' were interned. KJ wrote in umbrage against a British woman who belittled Australian poets. He defended a population of only a few millions and a history of little more than a century. It had produced no Shakespeare. 'Nevertheless, we have a fair amount of local poetry, and it cut me to the very heart to see the same ridiculed.'

So KJ, you made a challenge offering £500 prize money—a fortune in 1918. You put up the money yourself—or hoped to win it? During the war, while others threw grenades, you waged a battle of words!

–Yes, I am a pacifist—but a pen–fighter. I prepared to enter into a literary contest against any man or woman that the world can produce—

–I'm glad you included the women. Australian women got suffrage before most countries, in 1901 and first voted in 1902. Finland was soon after, in 1906. The first European nation to do so. So Google tells me.

–Open to all races, all nations and languages. (Who is Google?)

–Such vision!

–Who are you? (I imagined blue–grey eyes piercing through me.)

–I'm Ruth, your great–niece, Aubrey's daughter. WA was my grandfather.

–And you're a writer, you say? Not rich, like others of Wilhelm's tribe?

–What would you expect—you are a writer. We eat well enough. KJ, please help me; how do I write a book when I don't know the whole story?

–Write, Ruth. For your sons and for the generations to follow. People who little know the strength of heroes flows in their veins. As we read in the heroic poems of Kalevala–

–Like *Beowulf,* is it? Most of my generation haven't even heard of *Kalevala*—the *Land of the Heroes.* A decade ago I knew nothing of this heritage.

–The Russians banned Kalevala *but Herr Svedberg risked his life to teach it. In our stone schoolhouse the porter warned by a signal of knocks when school inspectors visited so we could hide the book under a floorboard. These invaders inspected our school textbooks and made us strangers in our own land, unable to read our own epics!*

–Kalevala tells of a competition in song between Väinämöinen 'old and steadfast' and the 'meagre youth of Lapland'—now I understand where you got the idea to put out a *'Challenge in Literature'.*

–Russians have long memories. One can never be safe anywhere in the world from their net. Besides, I felt myself truly Australian. My books showed my patriotism when foreigners were viewed with suspicion.

–I admire that you dared to self–publish, KJ. It's a difficult road. (I wondered if he covered costs. How many copies did he print?)

–Two hundred of my first book, five hundred of the second. (So he heard my thoughts?) *I adapted my second as* The Royal Toast *in time for the Prince of Wales' visit to Australia in 1920.*

–You hoped for royal patronage, or at least publicity?

–I presented a copy bound in Moroccan leather. This dedication – is it not fine?

On behalf of the people of Australasia and by the powers that providence has invested in me as writer, I am dedicating these compositions to His Royal Highness Edward Albert Christian George Andrew Patrick David, Prince of Wales and Earl of Chester, Duke of—

–Printing and shipping cost a pretty penny, surely? Your nephew Wally Holm told me you walked back from Sydney, 800 kilometres. Your corn bag sack was heavy with books so you made a wheelbarrow.

–*What is distance for one who has crossed the world? Traversed frozen seas on skis?*

The Treasure Trove

...In the same spirit as you would part from your best brother, who is setting out for the North when you are leaving for the South, well knowing that, as you have different destinations, it is utterly impossible to travel the same road.
K. J. Back, *The Concentrated Wisdoms of Australia*

During a later visit to Finland my second cousin Gretchen helped me translate a treasure trove of family history—four buff manila folders of letters. There was one for each emigrant; my grandfather Wilhelm Anders Back, his brother Karl Johan and their sister Anna Sanna—and one for the brother Edvard who came so close to joining them.

Granddad's missives detailed wool clips, droughts, land sales and prices per acre. Anna Sanna wrote little Swedish so her daughters penned her letters. The thickest pile was from KJ and gave intriguing glimpses of his struggles, plans and pleas for his family to join him.

A theme recurred, even decades later: fear of capture. One letter from Bangalow, New South Wales, dated 1900 struck me, filled with the loneliness of the settler adjusting to the far end of the world:

> *Write and tell something about the garden, it's the thing that I love most at home. I miss when the hanging birch blow thistledown in spring.*
>
> *Yet I will never go back to Finland.*
>
> *Please send some cherry stones as a memory, and seeds from berries and trees. Don't tell anybody; perhaps they could gossip. Burn my letters after you read them.*
>
> *Adieu and live well, from your son and brother, K.J. Back*

'What parent can burn letters from a son in exile, a son they know they may never see again?' I asked Gretchen as we paused in our translation.

Snippets were cut from some pages but were otherwise preserved.

'His mother Sanna hid them in the family Bible.'

In the family farmhouse in Munsala I was drawn to the family Bible. It was bound in brown–tooled leather and clasped with a heavy lock. Inscriptions show three children died before KJ became Sanna's eldest surviving son. Death had dogged Sanna's life. At twenty–seven she gave birth to KJ and later endured six more confinements. When her youngest child, Edvard, was born she was forty–five.

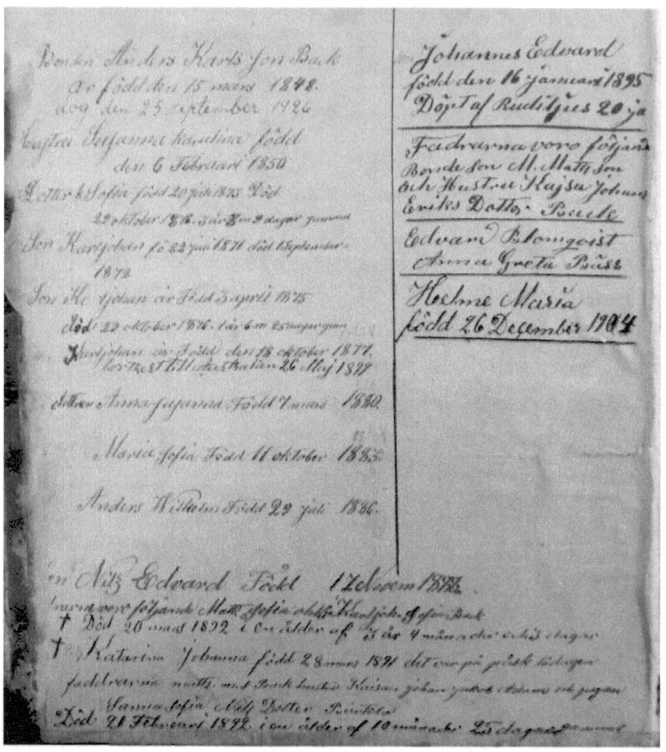

Stark black ink notes revealed that two dead brothers held the name of Karl Johan before it was given to KJ after his birth on 18th October 1877. Another two children died on the same day, 29th October 1876; two more a month apart in 1892.

Did having an earlier dead sibling of the same name, just like the painter Vincent van Gogh, inflict on KJ a life of guilt or depression? Was his sister Sofia, a strong woman, shaped by her earlier namesake? Did she fight against the soul that predeceased her?

KJ, a sensitive young man, would have been aware of his mother's moods. He was born under this shadow that skulked unsaid but could have been read

26

in his parents' eyes.

How did you feel, KJ, walking in the footprints of those others ?

—I plodded along the trail left by two little ghosts. I pretended to be strong. Mamma quaked if I developed a sniffle and dosed me with castor oil.

—That's tough, to carry the grief of dead siblings all your life!

—Many children died in infancy. Diphtheria was rife, and scarlet fever, croup and cholera. It was common to reuse names: Karl was Pappa's father. And the name Johan was for his brother.

—Expectations weighed hard. Didn't your parents lay a burden on your shoulders?

—They never spoke of those lost children but I knew their minds. I was blighted with the name of my dead brothers. Always I lived with the sense that two other spirits hovered at my elbow, answering when our name was called, moving with my feet to the barn or to the hay field. Those spirits were all I could not be. I had no will to live in another skin.

My mind buzzed with my newfound ancestors. I imagined KJ as a baby, rugged up under furs on a sled his father towed, or tottering on skis. What a contrast to my sweaty childhood in the Queensland bush.

As an adolescent, the sensitive KJ might have struggled against such expectations. KJ, please tell me the story of your early years.

Once upon a time

Life is but one continual school, which opens at the cradle and closes at the grave.
K. J. Back, *The Concentrated Wisdoms of Australia*

Once upon a time in the far north reaches of the world, a lad called Karl Johan lived in Munsala, a village in Ostrobothnia. He dreamed of far horizons. He longed to escape the humdrum of herding cows and milking, his hands raw from chilblains in the draughty barn.

Back Family, ca 1880
L-R: Karl Johan, Anders Back with Wilhelm, Sofia, Sanna holding Nils Edvard,
Anna Sanna

His father, Anders Karlsson Back, expanded their farmland and forest through dint of blisters on his hands and well–worn boot leather—and those of his sons and daughters. All were busy with the endless round of hay harvests and milking and potato planting. They shore sheep with simple shears; the girls' hands flew at the spinning wheel and loom during long winter nights. Anders directed the children through a military exercise of tasks and begrudged time frittered away with a book.

The Back house and barn near Munsala church.
Photo courtesy of Migration Institute of Finland.

The people of Munsala struggled to grow potatoes and hay in poor soil and marshland. The church and state commandeered the most fertile land. The great famine of 1866–1868 imprinted thrift on Mamma; when crops failed in 1891 and again in 1902 she baked famine bread, adding fir bark, chaff, heather seed and mountain ash berries to the last morsels of rye. This didn't stop bellies growling. Children begged for food in the village.

Funeral processions often passed by their farmhouse near the church. Mamma comforted mourners with what passed for coffee. Did some leave cholera germs on the cups? KJ lost a young brother to such a scourge; and as for little Johanna, Anders' delight … guilt hung heavily upon him all his life, as sharp as the day they laid her in the frozen earth.

—*Yes, your ears prick, Miss Nosey. Don't push me. You'll hear more when I can face it.*

As the eldest, KJ carried a double burden: that of his parent's expectations but also their hopes foiled by the deaths of two earlier siblings. Anders had little patience for his son's sensitive nature. This dreamer was happiest with a pen in his hand, rather than milking a cow. The more Anders demanded the more irresolute was KJ's response.

Perfectionist standards tied him in a bind of panic, afraid to move for fear of taking the wrong step. To his father's eyes, his mother (Sanna) mollycoddled him. Her sharp eyes noted every sneeze, slouch of tired shoulders or sigh.

Sanna stood up for her eldest son. 'Anders, he has created a fine kitchen garden. He reads and writes better than most.'

'Never mind education,' Anders said, 'the foremost need is to feed the family and work for their future.' Especially in such troubled times.

The small village of Munsala became a nucleus of intellectualism after Anders Svedberg began his elementary school a few miles from the village in 1862. A son of farmers from the nearby hamlet of Storsved, he had little opportunity for schooling except from his father's library. Yet he was determined to make education accessible to young people and began teaching while in his teens. He published his first book aged 20 and was appointed to the parliament (Diet of Estates) soon after. He contributed articles to leading newspapers.

The cream–painted wooden two storey building was the first elementary school in Swedish–speaking Finland. It grew to become a focal point of education and culture for the whole country. When KJ was born in 1877 it was well established and also trained teachers and adults.

When Pappa did release KJ from the farm work of hoeing potatoes and haymaking, Herr Svedberg noted how quickly KJ learned. He absorbed the standard issue of school books and in elementary school read Topelius' *Song of Our Land*. Then he devoured the secondary school text *Tales of Ensign Stål* by Runeberg that was to become the Finnish creed. Svedberg lent him challenging philosophers, geography and history. KJ's father eyed *The Iliad* and Socrates with distrust. 'Why would you want to waste your time with such notions, when the Good Book has all the wisdom you'd need for a lifetime?' Yet Anders himself liked to read about Napoleon and that big battle in Jutta near Nykarleby when the French hostilities spread to Finland and Sweden in 1809.

'You have a bright future, Karl Johan,' Svedberg said. The words gave heart to a lad conscious that he frustrated his father—who raged when the boy would let go of the cow teats to scribble a sentence in his notebook.

Herr Svedberg paid a visit to Anders. 'This lad has much intelligence, Kyrkback' (so Anders was known, due to his position as churchwarden). 'He has a great facility for writing. He possesses original thoughts and the powers to solve issues. An education for Karl Johan would repay you well.'

They thought the lad was milking, but he sneaked to the parlour window to hear his father berate the schoolmaster for 'putting fancies into his head' and 'distracting' him from important farm work.

'Karl Johan has a butterfly brain; it is unlikely he would complete such qualifications.' Anders showed Herr Svedberg to the door, so suddenly that KJ had to scuttle from his hiding place. Few ever won an argument with Anders Karlsson Back.

But when KJ was 12 years old, his mentor died young. He buried his nose in the books Svedberg had given him to hide his red eyes. The void was filled by parliamentarian Jakob Näs, who fostered debating societies through the local youth group.

KJ was lucky to escape chores a few days in the month for schooling. He would have despaired except for the books that found their way into a secret store in the attic. These opened vistas that he longed to explore.

Questions and Discoveries

O Lord, have mercy on the child,
Who suffers for his father's sins,
Whose blood is tainted and defiled
Before his own career begins.
K. J. Back, *The Royal Toast*

Exploring the family village of Munsala, my mind buzzed with new stories of my ancestors. A sound roused me from my absorption—the resonant tolling of the church bell. It swings in the tower that stands adjacent to the church, as so many do in Scandinavia so that the weight of snow doesn't damage the building.

Funeral of Anders Karlsson Back, September 1926.

Black–clad mourners carried a coffin down the hill from the church to the cemetery. I followed the black–shrouded party, then sat under the spruce trees KJ once planted. How many of my own forebears were carried down that same path? The church bell evoked ancestors and loved ones lost to centuries of conflicts, invasions and occupations. It signalled the collective grief of Civil War, Winter War, Continuation War and Lapland War. I resolved to learn more about the hardships and struggles of my forebears, so far from my peaceful homeland.

Inside the red–timbered Munsala farmhouse that my great–grandfather Anders Karlsson Back built, I looked closer at the dates in the family Bible. Now I understood why Sanna had such sad eyes. Simple arithmetic revealed the truth of the shameful secret of Sanna's first child, conceived out of wedlock. Let us imagine how that age-old dilemma played out—all the more intense for small village gossip and religious strictures. As I stared at a photograph of my great–grandparents, I imagined her guilty turmoil.

Sanna's father died when she was only nine years old. He had lost his spirit after his wife gave up her own struggles a year before. So Sanna had no parents to host a wedding under a homestead bridal canopy. Did Anders' father refuse to have any part of it so the couple must ask the priest to marry them in the church?

'The Ohls family is beneath you, Anders. We Backs are the cream of the neighbourhood.'

'True, I bring little dowry as my sisters are many, but you forget the high reputation my family had,' Sanna burst out. 'Our house graced the neighbourhood, with its colonnades. The Ohls farmlands and forests once stretched wider than yours—until you benefited from my parents' death and bought our land. We were too young to resist your offer.'

She would regret such outspoken words, but once out there is no recalling them. Anders' father spluttered and threatened in an ugly rasp, 'How dare you speak with such impudence, Susanna Carolina Nilsdotter Ohls?' His face turned a mottled colour, like autumn moss. He struggled to draw breath.

Bitter tears streamed as Anders gave her shoulder an awkward pat. 'Hush, Sanna,' he muttered, 'this makes it worse. Dry your eyes and go home. Let me talk this through.'

Anders' father, Karl Andersson exploded, 'Do you dare to accuse me of stealing your family's land? I gave a fair price. You and your sisters and that lazy brother were glad enough to be rescued from the poorhouse when your crops failed—doubtless for lack of attention. Your brother cannot settle to an honest day's work.'

'Pappa, he and I were in the same confirmation class; he is a good man.

Restless, perhaps; he longs to see the world instead of milk cows.'

Sanna cried, 'My brother did his best; he was but ten years old when Pappa died.'

'If you marry this woman you are no more my son!' Karl Andersson roared loud as a bull. 'I abandon you to your fate.'

Anders shrugged. 'I can't leave Sanna to fend for herself. We'll make our way together.'

'I will not bless this union, as long as I live.' Blood washed his face a deeper shade of red; so dark it was almost purple. Anger choked his heart and exploded through his veins. He crumpled at their feet, just fifty–six years old. Anders' father was dead.

So it was that Anders laid his father in the grave nine days before he pushed open the heavy wooden church door for his marriage. With no hope for a fine wedding, no organist was hired. No village fiddler led guests to celebrate with nuptial porridge and dancing. Sister Lena urged Sanna to wear their mother's high spangled bridal crown, as she had dreamed of during courting days. Sanna tried it, peeping in the mirror to see herself framed in its glory. She nearly fainted from the sheer size of it.

Sanna's heart was heavy enough without this reminder of the wealth their family enjoyed in the good times before their parents died. Then creditors trundled away ploughs and tools, cattle and pigs. But the orphans clung to the crown, a keepsake of the mother who left too young a happy marriage and eight children.

There was no such display at the brief ceremony; Sanna's thickened waist already fuelled tittle–tattle. They repeated their vows at the altar with just two witnesses, Lena and her husband Mats. Sanna swayed, sensing another presence behind. She snatched a glance into the Back family pew, expecting to see the man who would have been her father–in–law, if he had not rejected her and abandoned his son.

Sanna's neck prickled. She saw again his sharp eyes disappear under bushy eyebrows as if he frowned to see her join the family he had just left.

Her voice so choked that the priest waved an impatient hand to repeat the vows.

That was her first inkling of a spirit of death. She felt a malevolent ghost lurk as she climbed the stairs to bring broth to sustain her mother–in–law, Kajsa Lisa Matsdotter. She had taken to her bed and showed little interest in the marriage that had triggered her husband's demise.

Sanna wondered that some *hamingja* slipped across the edge of her sight when she went to the barn to collect eggs, or to milk the cow. Had this familial guiding spirit turned malevolent because of their sin and thrust her into a destiny of doom? She heard that to see one's *fylgja* boded ill, an omen of one's death. In the event it would not be her own passing, but her son's.

Sanna pushed her qualms deeper. No sense to disturb a new husband with fey glimpses. Until the deaths that followed soon after.

That ruckus was all for naught! What dull irony it was. The baby that hastened their marriage and triggered Karl Andersson's death had also died. Just fourteen months old, enough to learn to chatter and toddle. The parish records inscribed it as 'unknown sickness' though the herbal woman muttered about scarlet fever.

Anders hammered the infant's coffin. Each blow struck needles into Sanna's temples—and worse into her heart. Pain choked body and mind. She muffled sobs through the long endless nights, for fear of bringing more recriminations. There is enough pain to bear the loss of a child without adding a husband's anger. But her grief did not go away. It could not be contained in the dark silences of night. Sanna crept out to the privy to weep her heart dry of tears—until the next night. Deep in his sleep—how could he sleep?—Anders neither heard nor thought to look for her.

Sanna endured that first death with as much resolution as any bereaved mother can. She was no stranger to death; it stalked her since taking her beloved parents. But what loving God could snatch from her two more children, and on one day? Five years later her second son, also called Karl Johan, died of measles, and shared a coffin with his three–year old sister Kajsa Sofia. The hardest wrench for any mother is to wash a tiny body for the last time, stroking every crease of chubby flesh, every dimple. But two babies—what agony.

Sanna railed at God, 'Why are you so cruel to me? Was my sin so great that there is no forgiveness?'

'Hush, Sanna,' rebuked her mother–in–law. 'Or you will bring even worse punishment on your head.'

Worse? What could be worse than to lay two children in the cold earth on that bleak autumn day? The next year was a silent one. No laughter or children's chattering, no babies' cries. Their house was an empty shell.

Until Karl Johan was born a year later—the son who did live, but would leave. For fifteen years Sanna hoped that avenging angel was appeased. Yet it hovered. It swooped again.

Dark Days of 1892

You who expect the child to be a man, what would you expect a man to be?
K. J. Back, *The Concentrated Wisdoms of Australia*

In the Munsala farmhouse the kitchen and pantry are little more than an alley. I imagined kneading dough on the small table, cooking on the wood–burning stove. Kettles line a small cupboard, a pantry is crammed with plates and jugs. This was the scene of a crucial blight on KJ's life, the terrible accident of 1892. He was fourteen—a vulnerable enough age without an added load of guilt. As a mother of three sons, I know the turbulence of the mid–teenage years. It is a difficult passage for boys: not quite man, often still child. Hormones buffet them.

Sanna was to grieve for yet more children. Was there an epidemic a month after the accident: measles, diphtheria or whooping cough? Yet for both children the parish records note 'unknown illness.' KJ's sister Anna Sanna shared an even darker memory with her daughters, who told me. Little Johanna died on the 21st of February, aged ten months. Her three-year-old brother, Nils Edvard followed just a month later on the 20th of March. Was KJ so traumatised that he held himself responsible, even if other causes took Johanna? A sensitive lad, already carrying the weight of other dead brothers, might shoulder this guilt all his life.

I tossed during a sleepless night, agonising at the thought of the sheer horror that KJ must have felt. How could he cope with the guilt? Did his father lash out at him, blame his son for the death of his most treasured child? There was a personality clash between father and son: they were opposites, like apples to lingonberries. To whom did KJ then turn?

–KJ, what happened?

He and Anna Sanna were charged to mind the younger children while their parents were out. It was the anniversary of their marriage—perhaps they ate supper with Sanna's sisters.

—In that hellfire kitchen, my vision blurred from steam and tears. Johanna screamed as I flung cold water over her flailed red skin; I ran to scoop a pail of ice and fashion a clumsy bandage around her arms and face. I called for help.

'Son, what happened?' Pappa flung off his snow–speckled coat. 'Anna Sanna makes no sense for sobbing.'

'It's Johanna.' I stuttered. I gulp but a lump blocks breath and speech.

'Where is she?' He pushed into the living room. A sodden, whimpering bundle of bandages lay huddled on the divan.

'I tried to cool her but she pushes the bandages away.'

'She's burned! Stupid boy, hold the lamp closer. What have you done? Hush, Johanna my love, I'm not angry at you.'

'It was an accident, Pappa. Johanna crawled close by my heels; we collided. Oh God help me …'.

Anna Sanna pulled at her father's sleeve, 'She was so quick, we did not see her underfoot as we lifted the kettle of broth from the fire.'

'You promised to put Johanna to bed hours ago.' My ears resounded with Pappa's loud fury as much as the boxing they took.

'We did; she climbed out of her bed. The kettle slipped in my hands.'

'Pappa, don't blame KJ!' Anna Sanna begged, '…it was my fault also that she stayed awake. I begged KJ to teach me to read—'

Anders snorts, 'Madness! A woman needs no schooling to marry and raise sons.'

'You refused my pleas to attend the Svedberg school. KJ is a good teacher; we were engrossed. Johanna wanted to listen.' She blinked swollen eyes.

'Bah! School? Your place is in the house.'

'But I want to learn; KJ taught me letters enough to read a story, Johanna loves them.'

'You frittered away time reading stories and kept Johanna out of her safe bed?'

Anders thumped at the table in anguish, then drew a ragged breath, lowered his voice.

'Run, Anna Sanna, and cool these bandages in the snow outside. KJ, keep out of my sight until Johanna heals or I'll thrash you for the fool you are.'

But Johanna did not recover. Our chubby sister was laid in the frozen earth, alone and cold in the dark she always dreaded.

Only Anna Sanna met my eyes. But she refused reading lessons after that. Her interest died along with her sister.

Pappa would not forgive me, so why would the Almighty?

~

I was quiet for a moment in the wake of KJ's self–recrimination, imagining him wound in this web. How could he put his life together again?

–KJ, parish records show that you missed communion between first December 1985 and 8th August 1897. Your first communion was 24th June 1894, when you were—let me do my sums—seventeen. Did you travel? Or maybe you avoided church?

–*What son of the churchwarden could play truant from services?*

KJ had reason, for he felt sick to the marrow. It was agony to sit captive in those hard pews, fearful that the words that frothed in his head would escape in a rush: 'What loving God would allow me such torment? Why am I condemned for an accident? I loved my sister just as much as you.'

If only he could escape!

'Let me join Erik Johan Nyholm in America,' KJ begged. Nine years older, he had lived at Damskata, a little over a kilometre away. Since immigrating in 1888 to the Californian red cedar forests, everyone had heard of his exploits, as letters were shared around the village. His younger brother and KJ shared bottles of *brännvin* before he sailed to America to join Erik Johan.

Decades later, at the other end of the world, KJ would still hear the roars of condemnation. In his nightmares, the priest thundered from the pulpit, 'Do you smell the smoke, the burning? Hellfire awaits you, Karl Johan Back. The God Almighty will open that great book on the Judgment Day and read your transgressions.'

Anders nods, his lips compressed into a hard line, eyes cold with contempt.

'Yes, Karl Johan, you will be judged.' KJ pushes hands against his ears, but still their jeers echo in the valleys of his soul.

~

I began to understand the melancholy that seemed to cling to KJ.

1892 must have been a dark year for all the family. Black clouds oppressed their spirits. Sanna had little will to tend the family or kitchen. The cooking and milking fell to Anna Sanna and Sofia who was little more than a child herself.

I imagined the scene as Sanna crouched by the empty wooden rocking cradle, the same one Anders' own father, Karl Andersson Back, had crafted. It was as well no child lay in it when Sanna took to rocking it wildly, as she riled at God. 'Why did you take my babies from me?' she shrieked, while the children peeped from behind the big stovepipe, clutching its warmth for reassurance. 'You took my own parents. Without their guidance, how could I avoid falling into such mistakes?'

In a pit of despair she was silent for days on end, not speaking to her husband or children. She huddled in her shawl, singing a lullaby that chilled Anders' blood as she ran a finger along the cradle's brightly painted flowers.

It was times like that Anders could not find pleasant words for their eldest living son. Karl Johan was a sullen and intractable lad. Anders tried to exercise Christian forgiveness but his patience was short. They all struggled with their demons.

Anders pored over the Book of Job, looking for some clue as to how that man kept his faith. All his sons were taken from him, and in one fell blow. He ached over the loss of his beloved Johanna. Anders had called her his little Easter lily–of–the–valley, for she was born on Easter Saturday. Her name meant '*God is gracious*'—a bitter irony.

Since that dreadful month in 1892, all were numb and distraught. Both Sanna and Anders blamed themselves for the deaths of their children, especially the first. Did shame also kill Anders' father, Karl Andersson Back? He could not bear to see his son joined with a pregnant woman. He condemned his own son to the pit, called him a 'useless good–for–nothing Godless wastrel.'

Those words were scalded into Anders' ears and heart even decades later. He attempted to disprove the words; sure his father looked down from heaven and noted every move. He drove himself beyond endurance and expected the same from his family.

~

Ah, so that is the sense of it.

–Does it put a different complexion on his insistence of high morals, KJ?

– *Pappa was quick to point fingers at our transgressions, while guilty of iniquity himself. And now I see why Mamma felt that God took her babies as punishment. I failed to measure up against those dead children. I was not worthy to father any myself.*

School and Youth Group

Your mind is a gun. Your book is the trigger, which, used the proper way, will set off the gun—let us hope you will hit something good. Some men are only wasting ammunition, whilst with others it seems to click every time.
K. J. Back, *The Royal Toast*

My cousin Gretchen showed me the Svedberg School, innovative in Ostrobothnia. Its founder Anders Svedberg so inspired KJ that it is possible he was drawn to similar people throughout his life. He paid tribute to one in the Preface of his book *The Royal Toast*:

> *The one who is to act as a father for the Royal Toast is a Public School Teacher in one of the country schools. He is a man of some considerable mental abilities, well up in years, and he looks even older than he really is… He is attentive to his duties, and he believes in giving all their due. He does not, however, always receive his due, for he is over-worked and under-paid, and as a consequence his health is none too good. He has given the whole of his youth and manhood to his country and to humanity.*

In Jakobstad library I found a history of Munsala Parish, *Munsala Sockens*. A skim-read of a paragraph about K. J. Back revealed little information.

Gretchen and I visited Birgit Dahlbacka, the genealogist who had the parish records on microfilm in her home. She gave me handwritten pages that traced my ancestors back to the 1550s.

'I looked in *Munsala Sockens* but couldn't see much of interest,' I said.

Birgit reached for her copy and turned to the page about KJ. She pointed to the initials I'd dismissed.

'Uf!' she exclaimed to my blank look. 'It's short for *Ungdomsförening*, the local youth society. KJ was its chairman or president, and for them he wrote, acted and directed plays and comedies. There's a mention of problems with a performance in January 1899. KJ was still in Finland then.'

'Police closed down another in February 1901, on Runeberg's Day, for being too nationalistic.'

So although he had left Finland by then, was this typical of what he produced while leading the organisation? Was he a rabble–rouser, using his position to incite rebellion against the Russians?

What events might have spurred his activism?

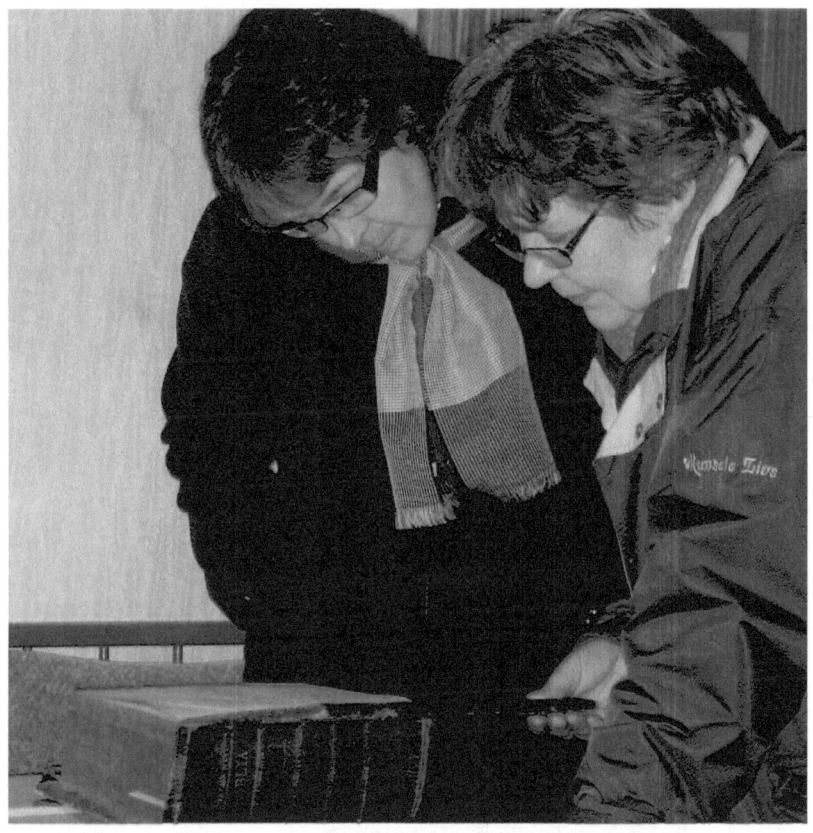

Gretchen and Birgit check the Back family Bible for hidden letters.

K J was determined to emigrate and pricked his ears at news of relatives and friends who travelled afar. 'How I wish to join Erik Johan Nyholm in American logging camps,' he sighed, 'He makes good money sharpening saws.'

'I could not bear to lose a son over the oceans, I have lost enough to the grave,' sniffed Mamma into her kerchief. Anders patted her shoulder and glared. Bristling through his sharp eyes was the reminder of Johanna, whose death he blamed on Karl Johan.

'Don't bother your mother with such talk, you useless dreamer. I wish

41

you would put the same energy into the fields.'

Sanna reminded him that 'The potato patch KJ tends at Tjiitiika supplies our needs through the winter.' Anders admitted Karl Johan's cherry trees bore well. Though he wondered that his son planted spruce trees at the family plot in the cemetery 'so some memory of me remains here after I am gone.'

'Son, you are too young to consider a voyage to America, even to Sweden.'

That spurred KJ into action. In the summer of 1898 he gained a seaman's ticket to sail across the Gulf of Bothnia, back and forth to Sweden.

But it was little used. More work fell to him as the eldest son when Anders became engrossed in his extra duties as churchwarden. He prepared before services and liaised with the priest Gustaf von Essen and the organist.

Munsala church was huge for such a village. The plans had been confused with those of Nykarleby, a larger parish. It was finished in 1635 after a hundred years of work given by the farmers of the village in their spare time.

The furlong of path from their house to the church was well worn. Anders endured the fussy quibbles of Priest von Essen, whom many villagers eyed with distrust as a foreigner. His campaign to ban schnapps at wedding festivities met with resistance. Boys in his confirmation class retaliated with a ditty:

> Essen is a pig who drinks only wine,

> Sweet wine juice gives to Essen force to smite boys as they go in school.

Never mind his German name. Some said that he was a Russian sympathiser, like the priest in Jakobstad, Johannes Arvonen.

Anders interrupted. 'Mind your mouth! As a person of authority, a priest must stay onside with the invaders. Loose talk could endanger our whole family. I blame the influence of Herr Svedberg for your rash words. And Jakob Näs. He encourages this by training your youth group in debating.'

Even Anders did not realise the extent of the dangers KJ's words would bring on them.

In 1896 there was sporadic talk of migrating. Anders wrote letters for information. As a Grand Duchy under Russia, Finland enjoyed relative peace at that time so emigration papers were stalled. When the Russian occupation tightened with the appointment of Governor Nikolai Bobrikov, Anders sought the Lord's leading. Which country would be best for his sons? America would have racial problems; the wealth mined in South Africa might tempt young men into loose living.

Events intervened which were to carry KJ across wider and rougher seas—the Russianisation of Finland would, in its own way, become a ship that would bear him to another hemisphere.

KJ's intelligence and perspective of the world had flowered under Herr Svedberg's tutelage. His next mentor, Herr Näs, recognised his talent for writing and steered it into action through the activities of the Munsala Youth Movement. Here KJ thrived. His early skits developed into cutting social satire. He was dramatist, actor and director. Anders complained at the hours KJ spent in the parish hall preparing some play or concert.

'But, Pappa, I help the youth around here. If they are occupied, they are less likely to skol *brännvin* and chew snuff behind the cemetery.'

Anders could not fault such logic. He muttered against Herr Näs for channelling his son into unproductive 'time–wasters.' Yet Anders had supported his son when Gustaf von Essen suggested KJ might be better employed distributing temperance booklets.

'Father Gustaf,' Anders said, 'Youth must be encouraged in useful pastimes. The devil puts idle time to mischief. Karl Johan is a quiet and deep–thinking young man. His talents could inspire other lads; who better than my son to act as a leader?'

The Munsala Youth Group attracted higher numbers than those in other communes. The quiet dreamer developed into an articulate young man, with a passion for social justice. At first he kept his thoughts to himself, for fear of ridicule. But Russian strictures and the Censorship Bill were the flashpoint which sparked his ideas. He used Bible verses against the evil Russians, comparing them to the Roman occupiers of Jerusalem.

KJ kept an alert eye out for repressive authorities. The priest lurked in the vestry during meetings, keeping guard. When KJ leapt to his feet in the church itself, even during services, von Essen warned Anders that his son put them all at risk. He confronted KJ, jabbing at his chest. 'Mind your mouth, young firebrand.'

Munsala folk viewed each other with suspicion, and muttered that von Essen passed information to officials. Was it a coincidence that when Mats Klockars 'liberated' his horse one night from 'safekeeping' in the Russian quarters, the Russians were led straight to Klockars' barn to retrieve it—and fine the rightful owner? How could strangers know the fields well enough to head straight for the hiding place in the forest at Lillbacka?

Still rankling from the rebuke, KJ wrote a satirical song for the Runeberg's Day celebrations of 1897. In this he played a priest whose gait and pompous puffing of chest resembled von Essen. His dramatised character led a posse of Russians through the woods, pointing out forests and pastures. He sang a hymn turned into a satirical song about Klockars, which everyone knew meant a cantor in the church. He was subtle, but the audience took his meaning.

Had von Essen seen the satire and recognised himself in the character in a white stringy haired wig? Little escaped the priest.

Backstage, Anders roared threateningly. 'How dare you ridicule the man of God—and he is my employer! You risk my position and the safety of our family.'

'If my production alerts you to the underhand ways that our priest makes his nest soft, it achieved its purpose.' He reached for his coat. 'You are blind. You work hand in glove with him. I plan to leave as soon as I can.' KJ's words were as chilly as the icicles that hung from the barn in January.

'How would you manage that? You have no finance; you cannot afford to buy your own farm without my help. You look to me for every crust of bread.'

Anders slapped him. Yes, KJ was a grown man. But the Good Book says, 'Spare the rod and spoil the child' and he still lived under Anders' authority.

Anders placed a hand on his son's shoulder. Stiff as iron, KJ flinched and thrust it away. 'Somehow I will escape from your rule. It is as loathsome as the Russians'.'

'Listen! Yes, the Tsar's powers are intolerable. But making yourself conspicuous to the officials is dangerous. They possess all the power. You might be whipped in the marketplace or sentenced to hard labour in Siberia. What man has returned from that fate?'

This inflamed KJ's anger. 'If we do not speak out against evil, we are mere puppets, Pappa.'

'You know the danger if your ridicule of authority is heard.' Anders pointed through the window to the switching post where prisoners were led in clanking chains and shackles, tied and flogged.

KJ snorted like a frisky horse. 'How can I respect a man who sidles up to the Russians like some slimy snail? Where does von Essen find the money on a priest's stipend for that fine wine he drinks? As payment for his underhand dealings?'

'Von Essen has a German name: he is no Russian.'

Applause from inside the hall marked the end of Mats Backlund's performance. He romped off to change his clothes, saying, 'Your turn, KJ, they're loving this.' K J donned a Russian cocked hat.

A door slammed. Heavy boots clomped into the hall. Voices roared: 'This is anarchy. It must cease. Handcuff those actors. And their leader who wrote this drivel!'

Anders pushed his son behind the cassocks and barred the vestry door.

During the next week KJ hid in barns, moving from one to the next. Anna Sanna and her friend Kerstin Mattsdottor took hard bread and dried fish to him. The family put out the information that KJ had gone to Vaasa to obtain his seaman's ticket—as he would later do in June of 1898. For months he was on the run, until other events overtook him.

Life in Scandinavia

The aspirations of a great man are like the horizon, one will never reach any closer to it, but the higher his aspirations are the further he reaches.
K. J. Back, *The Concentrated Wisdoms of Australia*

Back in Sweden, Antoni and I settled into the northern city of Umeå, well away from the tourist track. People were keen to know these exotic Australians and help us integrate. Like the couple who offered to drive us to the Lapp winter fair in Jokkmokk to hear stirring folk music.

But the hefty cover charge was beyond our budget. Drunk people scraped away on violins in the corridors of a school while equally drunk people danced. They wore red and yellow embroidery over blue costumes and ornate headdresses.

Once we had bought our thick warm mittens, birch carving and a reindeer horn butter knife, there was little to do. We sat around for eight hours in temperatures around –15 degrees. We had only eaten a snack and everything closed at 8 pm but people took surreptitious swigs from whiskey bottles.

The wife—let's call her Agneta—disappeared into the Lapp party and became entangled with a muscular Lapp. Her husband nursed a bottle of spirits outside. A sober Antoni was to drive us back to our hotel 40 kilometres out of town. Heavy hints got us all into the car at 1:00 am, along with a couple of drunk Lapps.

They discussed us in Swedish, but we could understand. Agneta had spent the day showing off her foreign friends but never introduced us to anyone; we felt like animals in a zoo.

While our hosts slept off their hangovers next morning we hitchhiked into Jokkmokk, and met up with friends whose parents welcomed us and cooked food for our rumbling bellies. They restored our spirits—and faith in Swedes.

It made a good dinner party tale; how we hitch–hiked above the Arctic Circle.

Aussie guests landed on our doorstep just after our travels had depleted our cash. The refrigerator was bare except for a dubious slab of lutfisk cod. How to make it edible after the usual evil processes of salting and soaking in lye? I wrinkled my nose and procrastinated. Knowing tourist budgets, how could I ask the friends to take us out to dinner? Margaret resorted to hints of reading my recipe books. There was no other choice: the smelly cod.

We spent a dark winter week above the Arctic Circle, rehearsing the Kiruna amateur orchestra for a concert. They responded well to encouragement. And as is the custom after a day's rehearsal we all said, '*Tack för idag.*' (Thanks for today.)

On our free days we drove west on the 'Blue Way' to Norway. Vegetation thinned out to bare snow, reindeers and weird sky. We felt as if on the moon, or the top of the world. Huge mountains were wild and breathtaking. We drove back into the tundra by the birch lined 'Silver Way.'

The concert was well received. Used to formal performance dress in London and Australia, I donned a floating gown for my conducting debut. The bemused players wore jeans. But Swedes were too polite to divulge their thoughts. As usual, people said '*Tack för konserten*'—a useful phrase if performers botched. One chooses to not notice.

We were invited back for a similar week the following summer. To 24-hour light and a view of midnight sun from the top of the hill.

Antoni and I played a chamber music concert in the Lapp village of Fattmomakke in western Sweden, 60 km from Norway as the crow flies. We stayed in a log cabin hotel beside lakes and waterfalls. The absorbed audience in a small church consisted of tourists as the Lapps had headed north. Locals were outside getting drunk, as many Swedes do on Midsummer. Huge and hungry mosquitoes distracted me as I played.

My work with *Regionmusiken* involved a week's stint of changing the guard ceremony at the palace during the summer. As the first foreigner and only the second woman to take part, I was vetted in top echelons for terrorist connections or explosives expertise. My colleagues exaggerated my amount of marching experience; I was vague, as it was nil. At the first band rehearsal I was placed in the front row, but new vocabulary and the moves baffled me. I was relegated to the middle and encased in forties–style grey baggy trousers and espaliers instead of a skirt. After two rehearsals we caught the train to Stockholm. My eyes feasted on green grass for the first time in nine months. Once I mastered the steps, the gig was a breeze—a daily short rehearsal, marching through the streets and over the bridge, up the hill to the castle.

After the first day, the leader told me that he was pleased and was surprised when he heard of my inexperience—but stressed the need to stay in step, whatever happened. Next day I did everything wrong, but so did others. There were changes as we went along about which march to play next, so I got out of step. As I was changing the music on the lyre, the bottom joint of my clarinet fell onto the street. I snatched it back on and kept going. It was a quick save from the only woman and first Australian. The person who wrote in the newspaper that this was the best march ever in memory did not notice.

We stayed in a five star hotel, courtesy of the king. For four days we played a few marches, then dispersed to enjoy the rest of the day exploring the winding cobbled streets of *Gamla Stan*. My music opened doors to Swedish life and culture; I was a player in its ritual rather than taking tourist snaps of the ceremony.

But I longed to explore my heritage further. It was time to revisit Finland and see it lush with summer foliage.

~

Bubbles of foam shimmered and frothed around my ship as it crosses the Gulf of

Bothnia. A rosy haze of sun vied with still crisp air. Research bustled in my head.

If we were back in the year 1900, that yacht sailing close to shore might hide weapons and propaganda under ropes in the hold. Perhaps it would belong to activist Konrad ('Konni') Zilliacus? From exile in Stockholm he printed the newspaper *Fria Ord* ('Free Speech') to circulate and incite against the Russian rule. Women hid thin rolled papers in their petticoats.

My mind carried me back to the turn of the twentieth century when Russification threw coils of restriction around the Finns and tied their tongues by insisting they speak Russian. The Board of Censors checked their words and suppressed many newspapers. Out of such repression sprang resistance. KJ must have been in the thick of it.

Why else would Russian military police go so far as Suez to trap him?

Let us follow that yacht... But with care, for this was a dangerous mission; lips were tight about the planned time and place to deliver the cargo. This boat heads north from Vaasa to the smugglers' havens of sheltered coves.

It would be death for anyone who dropped idle information that might sabotage the operation. Even wives would not know details, in case of betrayal and torture.

In the haze and daze of long summer nights there were few hours when the watchful sun allowed shelter of darkness. Then the activists received a coded signal. It was time to collect the cargo. A flotilla of small craft embarked from surrounding villages to meet the yacht.

The inlet was shielded by shadowy spruce trees and a rowan hedge near the octagonal manor house at Udden. There, Betty Hällsten, wife of the District Prosecutor in Gamlakarleby, hid political refugees in her cellar. The Hällsten porch gave a clear view of intruders. This made an ideal meeting place for activists. Her cellar stored propaganda leaflets and weapons that the local cell of radicals distributed into surrounding hamlets.

The yacht set sail back for Sweden with two blacklisted radicals hidden in wicker baskets topped with ropes and sails.

The Russian *Ochranen* police patrolled the waters of the Gulf of Bothnia.

Passive Resistance

The whole world seems to be in an unhappy state and it is the same way in our area.
K.J. Back letter, 12 September 1909

I have learned more about Russian occupation, how the west coast of Finland was a hub of Finnish resistance. This escalated after the Tsar refused to receive that five–hundred man delegation who bore the petition of half a million petition signatures. His dismissive '*I certainly cannot receive them...though I am not angry with them*' inflamed resistance all the more.

In the summer of 1899, journalist Konrad ('Konni') Zilliacus submitted a second petition to Tsar Nicholas II demanding a constitution. This International Cultural Address was ignored, like the earlier one. Konni used it as propaganda to his advantage when he displayed its return through all of Finland. Farmers gathered by railway lines to cheer and wave its progress. He succeeded in publishing protests in 500 international newspapers to make a cause célèbre of the Finnish plight.

A second Language Manifesto increased oppression, making Russian the official language of administration in Finland.

–How did such repression impact on your life there, KJ?

He is silent. I can only guess.

One fact has been passed down for generations in my family: the Russian military chased KJ, sought him in Suez. Why? Historians and family agree with me that other young men could be conscripted in the place of anyone who escaped. There was a rush of migration between 1899 and 1905. At its peak in 1902, the year Granddad emigrated, 23,000 emigrated. So, why did Russians chase Karl Johan Back?

KJ described himself as a pen–fighter, so he must have been involved in writing propaganda. Was he involved with the radicals who would form a movement called 'Munsala Socialists'?

Around the turn of the century, a Swedish speaking liberal and a social democratic party were formed. Returning emigrants from America were vocal in local affairs. They brought with them festering ideas about class struggle, trade unionism and pacifism. They felt alienated by the dominant and rigid Lutheran church and its patriarchal pastors, the Sunday Schools and sewing circles. Socialist groups livened villages by sponsoring dances and dramatic groups. But puritanical priests gave short shrift to intellectual and pacifist ideas, they denounced free love and anarchy.

The secret society called Kagal was a hive of resistance against the oppressive Russian government. Its leader, Leo Michelin, wrote a people's address to the Tsar and gathered an astonishing half million signatures. Even in these days of social networks covering the globe it would be a formidable figure.

Rather than scale back oppression, the Tsar gave Governor General Nikolai Bobrikov unlimited power as dictator over the Finns.

That night as I closed my eyes, I took KJ to task:

–KJ, I have been reading your letters, you crafty devil—

–I am not a devil, I repented, I said the sinner's prayer before I died—

–I'm closer to finding evidence of why the Russians chased you. Radical resistance?

–The more radical youth groups were in western towns like Vexala and Hirvlax.

–But they're near Munsala, yes? And what is this Munsala Socialism? Denis Rundt's thesis Munsala Radicalism—I needed help to translate that!—quotes the half–joke that, in Munsala, even the grass is red.

–That movement formed after I left the country. It was stronger during later decades of the Winter war and Continuation War.

–But you associated with many who would go on to form it. Am I correct?

Munsala was a hub of intellectuals: Judge Hällsten and his petite wife Betty who hosted soirées for cultural leaders; schoolmaster and journalist Anders Svedberg, Jonas Castrén, professor of literature, and poet Arvid Mörne. Discussions raged when Nikolai Bobrikov was appointed Governor General in autumn 1898, and resolved to Russianise the Finns. He fractured the relative peace of Finland's Grand Duchy under Russia.

Next year, 1899, came the shock of a coup d'état February Manifesto. Tsar Nicholas II broke his coronation vow to retain Finland's freedoms enjoyed for 90 years. Instead he overrode the Finnish parliament with a manifesto that asserted Russian rule and violated their constitution. This Russification of the first era of oppression dictated that the Lutheran church, already vulnerable to Pietist and Baptist popularity, must bow to Russian Orthodox religion. Russian language, currency and stamps must be used. Some Finns refused to put any stamps on their letters at all, preferring to pay a fine of double the usual cost. The artist Akseli Gallen-Kallela designed a fake 'stamp of mourning' which depicted the Finnish lion on a black background.

In a volatile country, the flash points were the decrees that made Finns subject to Russian military service and censorship of the press. Both threatened Karl Johan Back.

Let us eavesdrop on possible reactions at such a secret gathering in early 1899.

Suppose Fru Hällsten called on her distant relative Kerstin to augment her ranks of servants. They served jugs of coffee, gingerbread, and meals of potato and perch caught from the water nearby. Sometimes she took the girl on visits to Helsinki and Vaasa where Kerstin's youthful looks were useful and her ears were open to the plans whispered by the men around the docks. There too, Kerstin would meet women who forged the path to suffrage, like Tekla Hultin, who became one of the first female doctors, and Rosina Heikel and Lucina Hagman who in 1892 formed the *Unioni* and the Martha Organisation.

After clearing tables, Kerstin lingered in a corner and absorbed the discussions long into the night. She heard ideas brought by men who returned from work in American mines and forests, bringing in their trunks books by Marx and Engels. They often quoted their mentor, the schoolmaster Svedberg who died—too young, from a heart attack—in 1889. He was a strong advocate of social justice and women's inheritance rights.

Parliamentarian Jakob Näs, who hailed from Monäs, filled the gap left by his death. He laughed to tell how while in Helsinki for a meeting of the Diet, he ridiculed Governor General Bobrikov to his face.

'Bobrikov speaks only Russian, so he had no idea that I lampooned him, otherwise I would be dead now.'

As the guffaws died, Konni said 'We have one advantage now that he has made Russian our official language. He cannot speak Finnish or Swedish—nor do his judges and officials who replace those thousands of sacked civil servants.'

Fru Hällsten added, 'I hear Bobrikov asked how long it would take for Finns to learn Russian. Someone told him that Finns and Swedes had lived together for over six centuries and still only ten percent of Finns spoke Swedish.'

'But I worry that he censors the press,' frowned Konni as the laughter died. 'I may be unemployed soon. Minister of War Kuropatkin told Bobrikov that nine out of ten newspapers should be banned. And he called the *Nya Pressen* "Finland's reddest newspaper" so we are top of the hit list.'

Indeed, the Tsar signed decrees that Bobrikov could revoke newspapers and that printing presses must get a Board of Censors permit to print papers. Soon, Bobrikov took control of censorship by establishing an Advisory Committee on Press Affairs. Thus the Board of Censors was relegated to the status of a mere post office. The manifesto forbad 'needless consideration of the conscription issue in newspapers' and inappropriate criticism or headlines hostile to Russia.

Karl Johan edged his chair closer to the fireplace. He squirmed, for he was just that age for conscription. 'We will fight back all the harder against his bans on free speech and assembly. He will regret those commands to censor our words.'

'You are one of our best debaters, young man,' Näs nodded. 'A credit to the youth group. But take care, for even passive resistance is dangerous.'

Konni Zilliacus jabbed a finger. 'Then we must also prepare for *active* resistance.'

'Careful,' Näs warned. 'The *Ochranan* secret police have ears everywhere. In Helsinki Cossacks on horseback break up peaceful demonstrations with their whips.'

KJ rushed to ask, 'But if the Russian police don't understand what people say or write—they will not be caught?' He preened. 'Isak Sikström edits our handwritten newspapers. In one, I called the Tsar the Grand Perjurer.'

Konni eyed the lad. 'So you are a writer, Karl Johan?'

'Yes, I am a pen–fighter.'

'If—when—the *Nya Pressen* is suppressed I will print a new newspaper called *Fria Ord*. Send me your articles. We will need all you activists of the Kagal, shooting clubs, choirs and youth group networks to smuggle it in from Sweden.'

'Bobrikov calls Finland the Promised Land of associations.' Näs puffed on his pipe, nodding a cautious support. He was not yet ready for the active stance, but would later be enticed to the left. People from the nearby western villages—Hirvlax, Vexala and Storsved—were closest to Sweden and most receptive to radical ideas, which Munsala's Priest von Essen resisted. But then he had his own problems: many of his flock deserted the state Lutheran Church for the Baptists—whose first parish was at Monäs and the nearby hamlet of Monå. In 1897 von Essen reported as a crime that three people had been baptised before reaching the age of 21. The influential Anders Svedberg had criticised the clergy and supported economic and religious freedom. He sided with the Baptists who wanted to form their own individual parishes based on equality, democracy and independence.

'We must fight for independence,' Näs cried. 'Of all realms, social and political freedom. The church must separate from the state. I raised my voice in the Diet.' Indeed, he had separated Munsala school from the church, and won an enemy in von Essen. 'School was built for the children of the people,' Näs proclaimed, 'not for the priest, who should preach in the church that was built for him.'

Baptists and Munsala Socialists supported pacifism. And where better for that, with Monäs nearby, so close to Sweden that people joked of the 'Monäs Pass'? From here activists and pacifists fled across the winter ice highway, rowed or sailed in the thaw.

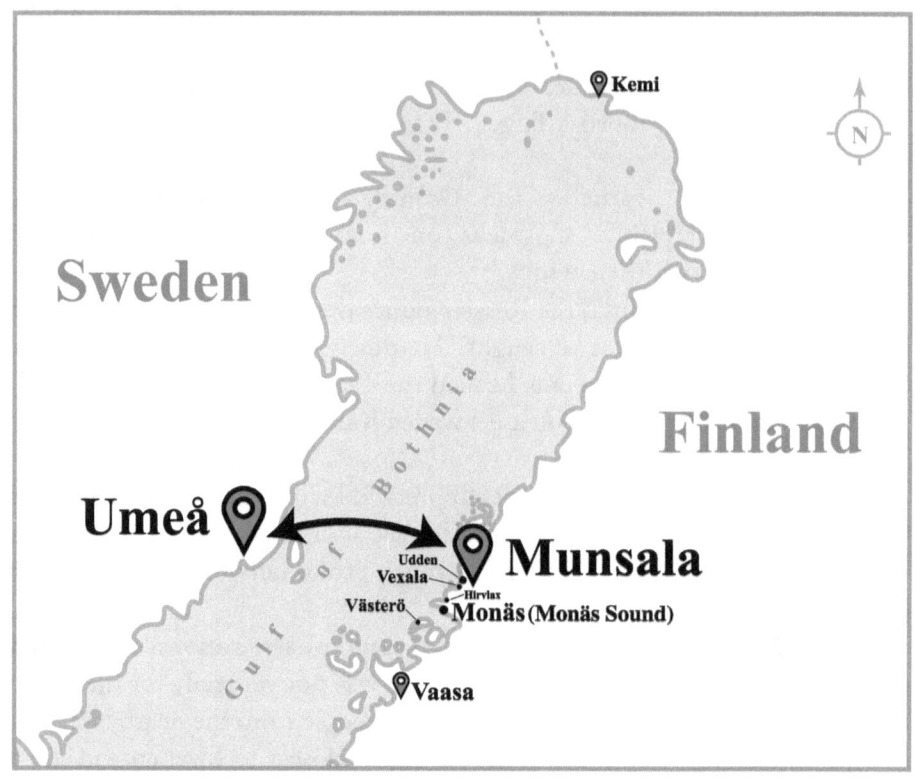

The Gulf of Bothnia escape route to Sweden, dubbed 'Monäs Pass'.

Karl Johan's father Anders fumed that his son associated with radicals and took unnecessary risks. But other attractions drew KJ into the fermenting circle. He had grown interested in this young girl named Kerstin.

Russians skulked around the area but they were wary of the District Prosecutor and his wife. Raids of their house were rare. High office gave protection that mere crofters lacked. Priest Von Essen also was alert for information. He pursed his lips over the 'loose talk' at the Udden manor house. Like many leaders of the Diet and Lutheran clergy he supported the Fennoman movement's push for Finnish language and culture. And in these risky times it was unwise to inflame the Russian oppressors.

Secret societies abounded. For KJ to be noted by the secret police he must have been in the thick of them. Events of the tumultuous early months of 1899 would propel his plans to escape.

The Great Address

If our hearts are not united,
If we work against each other,
We cannot fulfil our mission,
Then our land shall never flourish.
K. J. Back, *The Concentrated Wisdoms of Australia*

So long as Karl Johan returned home in time for the morning milking, his father held back his reprimands. But KJ was in caught up with other ideas, his head tainted by activists and his heart captured by that flighty girl, Kerstin. Mixing with men who risked all their lives.

Anders exploded when during that bitterly cold week of early March 1899, KJ disappeared on his skis for days on end. With a satchel on his back he collected signatures around the villages to add to the elaborate engraved petition called the Great Address.

'Son, this is dangerous!' Anders thundered. 'You could be sent to Siberia if you are caught. Or killed. Do you want to be whipped by Cossacks on horseback?'

'Pappa, even the police are out collecting names. The Finnish ones, not the *Ochranen* military. Half of the people of Jakobstad have signed, and all of those in Monå. Have you, yet? I'll hold the ink pot.'

Anders rubbed his furrowed brow, shrugged but signed his name.

'Because Jakob Näs comes from that area.'

'Pappa, how can you block your ears and eyes that the Tsar broke his solemn coronation vow? We citizens of Finland must express our anger that he has betrayed us.'

'Leave that to other people, or you will endanger all our lives.'

KJ sighed. The plan was for a delegation of 500 men to bear the heavy books containing the petitions by overnight express train to St Petersburg. There they would demand a meeting to present them to the Tsar. After ten heady days of collecting signatures, KJ ached to join them. Anders would refuse if he asked permission. Would he defy him, catch the train to Helsinki and travel with his colleagues?

'We all must play our part, Pappa. Today, I helped an old man to write his own name. He wanted to sign with a cross, but that would not be accepted. So I wrote his name and he traced it. Can you imagine how excited he felt, to share this protest?'

'One that is stoked by dangerous men like Konni Zilliacus and Leo Mechelin—'

'Herr Mechelin is a respected professor and chairman of the council in Helsinki. Fru Hällsten predicts he will lead the country one day. And Konni writes for the *Nya Pressen*.'

'Which Bobrikov will suppress, mark my words.'

'They drafted and wrote the petition, yes, using their skills with law and language. Words are powerful, and they carry more weight with all the people's signatures.'

KJ's eyes shone, excited to play his part on the large stage of history. Proud that he encouraged some of those half a million signatures, collected from a population of around two million people.

It was a hero's quest, thrusting out into the villages ski to ski with challenging thinkers like Eugen Schauman. Arvid Mörne, just a year older than KJ and already superintendent of a folk high school, qualified with a Master's degree in literature and history, read KJ's writings and encouraged him to similar paths.

'Pappa, you think of me as a young boy, but I can raise my slingshot of words against this Goliath who robs our freedom.'

'Your words endanger us.' Anders slammed the table. 'I forbid your useless scribbling!'

Did his words drive a stake through his son's creative talent?

Did KJ join the delegation to St Petersburg? We may never know. Was he a mere bit player on the stage of Finnish history?

My clues are that he was rumoured to have an illegal printing press—proscribed by the Board of Censors under Bobrikov's orders.

–KJ, Birgit said there was local gossip that you had to flee Finland from the police, not the Russian military, because you printed counterfeit money. Is that true?

–*How would she hear this, no people would be alive to tell such stories.*

–It's just hearsay. But you needed money to travel out of Finland.

–*You think me a criminal?*

–They were desperate times, and you were determined to migrate. Needed to. Where could you hide it? Up in the loft of the Munsala farmhouse?

–*Schoolmaster Svedberg encouraged my writing; he had access to printing equipment for the school. And the newspapers he published.*

–So it was true? You printed money? Or was it propaganda?

–*I never said that. Of course I wrote poetry, articles, dramas and acted those.*

My other clue is that Karl Johan wrote in a letter to his brother '*Thank you for your congratulations on my pen-fighting.*'

'Kerstin'

The rays of my imagination are still playing with the brilliancy of that loving
face that has now been in the grave for half a century.
K. J. Back, *The Royal Toast*

The village lads buzzed around Kerstin Matsdotter like flies to a honeycomb. For years KJ had whiled away Priest von Essen's long sermons by looking at her across the pews. But he hung back, thinking himself too ordinary to catch her eye.

All this changed the summer of his communion class. As he guided the cows to pasture, Kerstin appeared in his path carrying a heavy milk bucket. What could he do but carry the pail? When they reached the pasture at Tjiitiika, she made no move to continue across the hayfield to the Matsdotter farmhouse. She flopped under a spruce tree and fanned herself with birch leaves. Too inept to converse with such an angel, KJ pulled a book from his knapsack.

'What are you reading, KJ?'

As he explained Socrates' reasoning her eyes brightened all the more. 'I used to hear Herr Svedberg discuss such books when he visited Fru Hällsten at the Udden manor house on Sunday evenings. She's a relative of mine, I help her serve coffee when people hold discussions there. You are so clever. Why not join us there on Sunday?'

Next day Kerstin joined him in the pasture and held out a book. 'Would you help me read this? My Pappa thinks education is a waste of time for girls. He says with my work for Fru Hällsten there is not time enough for our own farmhouse as well. He forbids me to attend the Svedberg school anymore.'

KJ sighed. His sister Anna Sanna begged Anders to let her go to school but he refused. KJ had taught Anna Sanna to read until that black night in 1892 that turned her against all learning. She and Kerstin were the same age and, as children, they played dolls' tea parties.

Now, Kerstin laid her shawl under a spruce tree. She patted the space beside her and her luminous eyes invited him to sit with her. Karl Johan knocked over the bucket in his haste to join her. His hands shook as he righted it. Hot blood crept up his neck to inflame his cheeks.

KJ fixed his eyes to the page. 'Listen as I repeat the syllables and join them into words.' She leaned closer to give her full attention. Her hair brushed his face, fragrant of camomile and raspberry. Her breath was sweet with blueberries from the lane. KJ couldn't resist her.

Back at the farmhouse, Mamma noted his dishevelled clothes and pulled a stalk of hay from his hair. Her silence accused him of all the sins listed in the Bible. Anders sniffed the wind of transgression.

Each day Karl Johan looked for Kerstin's bright hair. How could he miss that? He preferred the fiery curls to the other milksop blondes. Did she hide from him, prefer another's company? But next week she joined him in the barn.

'You cannot imagine the talk I have heard, while in Vaasa! Fru Hällsten met with Lucina Hagman—she is president of the Feminist Union—and the Hellman sisters. They plan to form a women's society. It will be called the Martha Organisation, to enlighten and teach household crafts but also protect Finnish culture. And defend the rights of our country.'

'You meet such interesting people, Kerstin. I wish I could come with you.'

'Interesting? Hear this. Bobrikov was in Vaasa last week. He's touring the provinces to plot his next foul restrictions. I planned to hide a knife, climb into his carriage and stab him. Imagine how that would feel, to rid our country of that louse. But he left for Helsinki the next day.'

She brightened. 'Fru Hällsten will begin a Martha chapter here in Munsala and I shall help her.' Then she sighed. 'It has been such an exciting week but now I am tired. Let's rest in the barn …'

As I leafed through KJ's books and read his letters, I imagined the next part of his saga.

Occupation and conscription

They told of the bayonet and lead, the shrapnel and the dirk, the tramp, tramp, tramp through ice and snow, with bulging blisters on their feet.
K. J. Back, *The Royal Toast*

Men struggled home from the Crimea worn and broken in mind and body. KJ would not be sucked into the Tsar's dirty wars. The idea of conflict chilled his blood.

His friend Mats Backlund muttered tales of young men who cut off their own trigger fingers to avoid fighting. But KJ needed all his fingers. 'The pen is my sword,' he said.

Urgency increased with the appointment of Governor–General Bobrikov in Autumn 1898 and Karl Johan's birthday in October. By law, men from age twenty–one were balloted for military service. The Conscription Act of 1878 was torn up in favour of the 1899 February Manifesto that conscripted Finnish men for three years.

The family argued back and forth in whispers. One thing they agreed: KJ must emigrate and brother Wilhelm follow.

But where? Many Ostrobothnian folk had been lured to the gold rush in Alaska with promises of free land to settlers. Yankee recruiters gripped Finland with America Fever until spruiking was banned in 1880. Some homesick immigrants straggled back, poorer than they left. They had endured near–slavery conditions in the mines, their meagre wages squandered. They brought back unsettling suggestions that poor farmers should be equal to those whose rich earth brought abundant harvests.

KJ's father Anders Back visited the ports of Jakobstad and Vaasa, selling potatoes and rye for ships' provisions. On the quiet he quizzed sailors: 'Where are you bound?' Ships were searched and rumours spread, especially against Swedish Finns who were thought of as privileged upper–class colonists. Ears pricked, and bribes might tempt some to reveal any escape plans to the Governor.

Vaasa harbour was full of steamships bound for Canada. The captains were willing to keep their mouths shut for enough money. But KJ shook his head and huddled into his padded coat. 'Winters there are endless, murky grey and black like Finland. They'd freeze my soul and body just the same.' Instead, he dreamed of exotic sunny places, of the glow of tropical flowers and of lush fruits. He craved warmth.

Whiskery one–eyed sailor Erik Johansson nodded, wiping his strawberry bulb nose with his sleeve. 'Ah, then it's Australia you'll be wanting,' he suggested.

KJ frowned. 'Austria is all snow and mountains, almost as cold as here.'

Erik jabbed his pipe at the southern horizon. 'No, *Australia*. We're bound there next month, from Hanko port.' At this KJ recalled a book in the Svedberg School. It had contained a tantalising sentence: *Australia is a huge continent, mostly desert.*

The word 'desert' warmed KJ's soul like a stove–heated brick in a December bed. Australia sounded a good way from Russia and that suited him. Word of a gold rush enticed Samuel Wiklund to sail there a decade earlier. His wife and two children never saw him again. Mamma recalled that a relative, Anders Ohls, headed that direction years ago. She pulled from her drawer a letter dated 1895 that described a paradise:

> *On Sundays I go to the sea to fish as I live fifty steps from the beach. I look over the stormy blue ocean and think that sixteen thousand miles north is our poor old father's land. I feel free and happy in Australia with its warm sun.*

With fingers numb from frost, KJ scribbled his address, 'Durras Mountain' in his notebook. He must share this with Isak Sikström who also planned to flee. Mamma read that letter one last time then pushed it into his hands.

'You need it, to find Anders in that large country.'

Anders took a cart load of potatoes to port. 'Pappa, promise you'll buy me an English dictionary,' KJ said. Anders sought out the sailor. 'Erik, where is fertile land in Australia?' He passed a bag of *markka*. Bring maps and rainfall charts and I will have more of these.'

Seven months later when *Astrea* docked, he slipped Erik a bottle of schnapps in a dark corner of a coffee house. Anders studied the maps and charts. He said, 'Karl Johan, head to the most easterly point; there must be ample rain there.'

The Tsar's February Manifesto asserted the right of the imperial government to overrule local legislative bodies. The Finnish army was absorbed into the Russian.

Mutterings of 'it will be conscription next,' were heard across the countryside. They were correct.

In the next weeks, Anders' blessings at mealtimes turned into long prayers entreating God to bring his sons to freedom. He read aloud from *Genesis* how God told Abram:

> *Leave your country, your people and your father's household and go to the land I will show you... and I will bless you.*

The Ballot, 1899

It is no wonder that so many lose God in the church, when the church is so big and
God is so little.
K. J. Back, *The Royal Toast*

KJ was indeed balloted for conscription on 27.4.1899.

Munsala Church

The church was the hub of information so it fell to the parish priests
in each district to read the list of names drawn in the ballot. K-G Olin's
book *Grafton-affären* tells how on several occasions protest singing drowned
the priest's voice. In over a hundred instances the selection process was
sabotaged. Sometimes the draft documents disappeared. People refused to
elect representatives to the draft commissions, or boycotted meetings so

quorums failed. The Jakobstad priest Johannes Arvonen ignored the directive from the Kagalen when he read the manifesto of military service in the church. A public meeting demanded his resignation.

Let us suppose that Munsala was no different. And that a later, similar, event in Jakobstad church occurred here.

Take a pew inside its massive stone church, where Gustav von Essen is about to read out the list of men conscripted for three years into the Russian army. There sits KJ, hunched inside its white walls, holding his breath, ears pricked for his name. Little wonder he developed an allergy to the church.

~

All those years they sat, backsides chilled on the pew, like prisoners within metre–thick walls as the priest droned through sermons. They wriggled their haunches to ease the numbness that crept through their joints. That day ice froze into KJ's bones as von Essen proceeded into the church bearing a list of names of the men called up in Ballot Number M6.

The night before the previous list was to be read, the priest had forgotten to lock the vestry door so the young men found the paper and burned it. That did not delay the news for long.

Karl Johan held his breath as the priest wound his torturous way through a dreary sermon about the evils of liquor. His eyes traced the folds of von Essen's wrinkles as if he knew this to be the last time. Gustav von Essen placed his *pince–nez* on his bony nose and peered at the paper. Karl Johan's limbs shook like autumn leaves flung to the ground by arctic winds. The priest's pucker of a mouth churned to find saliva enough for each name. His eyes glinted with moisture as he wheezed, 'Karl Johan Back'.

Karl Johan fell back onto the pew, stunned by the force of despair. For all he had expected this thunder to crash into his life, he felt limp as seaweed.

But then *sisu* prevailed. Even on holy ground he would fight this injustice. Martin Luther would not accept an unjust hierarchy. He rebelled, just as they did. Jumping to his feet with others in the congregation, KJ bellowed Luther's battle hymn, *Vår Gud är ossen väldig borg*—'A Mighty Fortress Is Our God.' That hymn told that 'God hath willed His truth to triumph through us.' King Gustavus Adolphus of Sweden had this song played as his armies went into battle in the Thirty Years' War. It was the anthem of the Swedish socialist movement.

Did Karl Johan really believe God would protect him from the might of the Tsar? That overfed distant dictator who sent his minions to control the Finns? The Governor–General would set his Cossack oafs onto them, and would squash civil disobedience like a flick of a bony finger to kill an ant. However much KJ and his friends sang hymns to entreat God, he was as much an absentee landlord as the Tsar in his opulent palaces. Even if they crept into the parish office on a Saturday night to burn that list, the Russians would renew their power over them.

It was a forlorn hope. Karl Johan knew that there were slim chances a *Deus ex machina* would swoop down and rescue him.

He must fashion his own freedom. Even though his father berated him in the vestry.

'I am a pacifist, Pappa. I shall never fight their unjust wars. The Bible says: "*Obey God before earthly lords.*" And Martin Luther wrote "*Be a sinner and sin boldly*" to a friend.'

Anders shook his head. 'You forget the next line: "...*but believe and rejoice in Christ even more boldly. For he is victorious over sin, death, and the world.*" And the paragraph before, in that same letter said, "*Let it happen, let the will of the Lord be done. Amen!*" You must not resist God's will in your life.'

'So you would let the Russians run rough shod over your life? I cannot. My conscience is clear. I am a pen–fighter; this gift God gave me. I must exercise that against the Russian invaders. Would you have me bury my talent in the ground?'

'Useless scribbling! I forbid it.' KJ flinched.

Ulf Bexar and Mats Backlund circled Karl Johan. They scuttled him out the vestry door and down the lane through the forest to Udden, the manor house by the sea. Another activist for Betty Hällsten to hide from the Russian military.

But even this relatively safe house was sometimes raided. Perhaps he also stayed with Herr Näs, who is credited with singing at a youth group party a variation on *La Marseillaise*. Is it a stretch of imagination that KJ helped him change the words to '*Our Finnish soil shall drink the Russians' blood*'?

When the Russians had bigger fish to hook, KJ ventured home to hide in the attic as young Edvard kept watch around the house.

Octopus tentacles of fear constricted his chest.

The Call–up

While hearty despots swing their rod
And bid defiance to their God,
A simple hermit in a den
May rule the nation with his pen.
K. J. Back, *The Concentrated Wisdoms of Australia*

Next day, Priest von Essen cornered Anders in the vestry.

'Anders Kyrkback, rein in that firebrand son of yours. Or your position here is untenable. He abuses his authority as chair of *Ungdomsförening* to agitate against the ruling powers—'

'They are not our rightful rulers, they were not appointed by God,' Anders could not resist saying.

The priest's eyes narrowed as he poked a bony finger into his chest. 'It is clear where your son learns his resistance to authority. You are responsible for him. False steps will be punished on you both, Kyrkback. There are others might value this position of churchwarden. Erik Viklund is a worthy man who has expressed willingness to serve.'

Anders held back a sniff. Could von Essen forget Anders' faithful service to the church, the many nights as well as Sundays when its business kept him from his family? So Sanna reminded him often enough.

In the weeks that followed gossips noted that the priest met with the Russian military at their barracks south of the village. The Cossacks' usual route was the high road into Nykarleby. Now they found reason to ride past the Back farmhouse.

KJ's fingers shook as he tore the wax off papers from the Governor–General and deciphered the Russian words. It ordered Karl Johan Back to report for military duty in Vaasa next month. Whispered plans turned to action.

That last night, Anders beckoned KJ into the barn. He added a wad of *markka* to the bag of silver stashed under the floorboards. 'I wish there were more, son.' He had sold the southern hay field to afford this passage. KJ's birch bark knapsack was already hidden in the barn at Tjiitiika, packed with a few cherished books and a change of shirt and socks, some hard bread and salted herring.

Farewells were rushed and secret. Wilhelm's sharp eyes followed KJ's every step; sisters Sofia and Anna Sanna clung as never before. His heart ached to farewell four–year old Edvard. KJ poured his love into the lad since the other children died. He cried and begged for more stories. KJ sighed, knowing tomorrow there would be none.

His throat tightened to farewell Mamma who clutched him close enough to break his ribs. She knew how to calm her son when regret and grief hung shrouds over his mind. This feisty woman chased thieving gypsies from the house waving a hot frypan but she was sensitive and understood the darkness in his spirit.

Anders pumped at his son's hand for many long minutes while conflicting expressions flickered across his face. His Adam's apple wobbled and he added an awkward hug. '*Lycka till*, son. Good luck. God bless you and guide your path safe to freedom in the Promised Land.'

Then KJ slipped away into cover of dark fir trees. His heart thumped like the church bell tolling. KJ turned back for a last glimpse of faces at the window. He grasped memories close like fingers into mittens, as the wind blew away this last sight of kin. A tightness formed in his throat: *I'll never see them again. Not in Finland. Maybe in heaven, if I can believe Priest von Essen. But his words make little sense to me.*

Too long he tarried, looking back to imprint family features on his mind. So he cursed when Kerstin Matsdotter accosted him near Tjiitiika barn. Her eyes sharpened bright. As she clutched his sleeve a rush of blood ran up his neck to flare in his face.

'Back,' Kerstin jabbed a finger at his chest, 'shall you go?' She cast a searing look at the birch–bark food bag. 'Away?'

KJ pointed towards Tjiitiika. 'I go to repair the roof on the barn.' He pushed her away. 'Today I have no time for sweet–talk or dallying.' *Or ever*, he thought.

Kerstin flinched that he spoke so coldly. Indeed the words sounded cruel after their last meeting. 'Take me with you, KJ,' she begged, clutching at him. But he thrust her away again.

'No, Kerstin, you must stay. How will the women's Kagal Movement and the Martha Association manage without you? You are now a leader.'

Kerstin shrugged. 'They will enlist other patriots.' She sniffled.

'Don't cry—!' You, of all people?

'But you must stay, I need you with me.'

'You know it is too dangerous to stay.'

'Then I will follow you. In Helsinki I heard Matti Kurikka speak at a rally. He intends to lead a party to Australia to form a utopian commune.'

'It is close to daylight, I must go.' Karl Johan pushed her arm away, gave a quick embrace then grasped his ski poles.

As he hastened away she called after him. Her words were scattered by the wind. 'KJ... cannot... raise... chil...d alone...'

Kerstin's grilling cost him precious minutes. Each stride jolted his knapsack into his back. One word pummelled his mind—'barn, barn'. A question tantalised him long after, followed him across the world. Kerstin's despairing words thrown at his back: did they speak of a *barn*—child—she would bear?

Crossing the Gulf

Remember every move you make,
My thoughts will follow in your wake,
My heart is wrapped in thine.
K. J. Back, *The Concentrated Wisdoms of Australia*

At the Tjiitiika barn KJ stamped his feet against the cold, waiting for Mats Backlund until he straggled in. His eyes were bleak and his face long as a Finnish winter. Mats fretted like a wolf tearing at bones over how his woman clung and begged him to stay.

KJ gave him no time to linger over excuses. He hustled them off towards Monäs. There they checked for snooping eyes as they faced the white expanse of the gulf ahead. KJ scanned the compass, his gaze darting up and down the coast. Military police manned this stretch.

They grasped the ski poles, tested the ice for firmness and kicked off into the stride–and–glide rhythm. Since childhood, this thrust–and–swish rhythm had lifted KJ from many a dark mood.

But Mats was beyond calming. He lagged, moaning of wolves and potential dangers. 'What if we strike weak ice? I can't see clear in this half–light!'

KJ pushed aside his scarf and roared. 'If you kept your trap shut you'd make faster pace.' The words huffed billows in his face.

This quieted Mats for a minute. They turned their faces towards Sweden. But after a dozen strides, Mats threw down his pole. He cracked just like the ice he dreaded. 'No, I cannot leave. Ida is pregnant. I can't let her rear a child alone.'

So that was the crux of it. 'She can follow you to Australia. There are opportunities for a family.' KJ shared his qualms, but resisted divulging Kerstin's last uncertain words.

'All that way, across the wide world, a woman and child alone?'

'If you stay they'll take you away to Siberia. Few return from there.'

Mats picked up his pole for a listless poke and stride. He stalled again, squinted to the dim lights on the shore. 'Even if I fight for the Tsar, at least I suffer beside brothers and friends. If I stay alive, I can return to my wife and child.'

If. 'Move, or patrols *will* catch us! We can't dally close to shore.'

'Even if I survive this escape and the journey to Australia, how could I ever return? Here—' Mats fumbled in his knapsack, pushed his passport into KJ's gloved hand. 'This is more use to you. I'll risk my chances here.' His long bear hug near–suffocated KJ. He muttered, '*Lycka till,*' and dissolved into the enveloping dark.

A wave of fear swept over KJ, fear of detection while he hesitated, while ice numbed his feet. Fear that all their plans were for naught. He gasped a breath of icy daggers. Desolation swamped him.

The decrescendo rhythm of Mats' striking poles faded into lonely emptiness. KJ was tempted to follow him home. God, how he was tempted!

He stood in a nether world thinking evil spirits grasped his ankles to freeze into a chill eternity. Alone in a nothing of whiteness his toes burned, his bowels and joints loosened. A magnet of longing pulled him back towards home.

But there was no place for him in Finland. He set course for the great Southland. Time blurred until he struggled onto a Swedish wharf and collapsed to rest before heading south. He threw off his sweaty jacket and shut his eyes against feathering snowflakes.

Mamma's anxious eyes peered into his mind. KJ longed to send a message home that this most dangerous stage was accomplished. It was too risky. He hugged his jacket and turned his back on Finland. Best to forget the fragile lace of hoarfrost and dazzling ice; the snow fights with brothers; the flare of young love.

Secrets were left that he was glad to bury. Some sprouted, grew shoots that he would never see. Wilhelm brought Kerstin's letter when he and Anders arrived in January 1903. KJ ached to return, to find out if her news were fabrication. But never could he span the mountains of waves back to the land of the Northern Lights and the midnight sun. He must seek new light.

Sanna

What mother knows to what future she rocks her child?
K. J. Back, *Concentrated Wisdoms of Australia*

Directly across the Gulf of Bothnia, KJ's mother tossed through long nights. Sanna was no stranger to pain; many children, still tiny, died. Even such razor–sharp agonies could not prepare her to lose her grown son Karl Johan as he crept off into the forest in 1899. She tossed under the covers. Was he chained in some prison awaiting court martial, even a firing squad? Or worse? Each night her mind was lured down such valleys.

Clutching her kerchief, Sanna threw aside the bridal patchwork quilt she'd woven during long nights when she awaited her first babe. Nearly three decades later, she ached just as sharp for the deaths of that child and the next—both called Karl Johan. Their third son was now lost to her.

She huddled in the living–room rocking chair. The candle wavered over their only photograph of him, taken at the time of his confirmation. Already she struggled to recall his grown features; could she retrieve them as years stretched on and faculties waned?

Sanna relived KJ's last days at home, his hugs that squeezed the breath from her lungs. So much she longed to tell him, but dared not! Who knew what ears sharpened as nosy folk passed outside the kitchen window?

Now, she stumbled to the desk, dipped a nib in the inkwell:

> *Remember to keep your feet dry. If only I knew which herbs grow in your new land to make teas that cool fevers. Your uncle's letters gave little information. Please send a photograph as soon as you are settled. I fear I will lose memory of your features in my old age.*

Sanna realised there was no address to post a letter. She threw down the pen into an inkblot and cried. Moonlight filtered through the window and silhouetted the apple and cherry trees her son planted. Through her tears she again saw him pause to stroke their trunks. His satchel bulged with apples from the barn. He looked towards her and lifted an eyebrow in what she alone saw as a parting signal.

What could she do? Run and accompany him on the path across the field and into the forest? That would only draw attention to his going. Would it help if she could rage aloud as when her babies were torn from her, stiff and cold? Did that ease her grief or longing for the heartbeat that synchronised with her own? No.

To farewell a grown son to the seas was worse than emptiness of arms and cradle. She ran to the privy and sobbed, stuffing her shawl in her mouth to block the sounds from passers–by in the lane.

Reminders of KJ were everywhere. As she walked past the barn at Tjiitiika she wondered whether he hid his knapsack under this sack of grain or that on his last twilight. Beside the Poor Man statue *Fattigubba*, his voice still rang in defence of the poor. As she carried a bucket of water from Klockars' well, she heard him say, 'Mamma, let me carry this weight for you while you admire the colours of that moss.' She wished for another chance to walk together, taking the cows to pasture in Gräsön. Now she would welcome his prattling of Socrates or Döbeln or Runeberg. Instead of chiding him about wasting time learning these things—'I barely understand their meaning'—she would ask him to explain.

Everywhere, she encountered such memories. Weeks turned to months. Lead hardened around her heart.

Banging woke the family late one night. Anders threw on his heavy coat and opened the door. Officers loomed in their fancy Tsarist uniforms of grey felt, gilded epaulets and red–emblazoned shoulder–boards. Sanna flung a shawl around her trembling shoulders. She tiptoed behind the door, peered through the crack.

What if they arrest Anders and charge him with complicity?

'Where do you hide your son, Anders Karlsson?' they demanded.

'He is not here. Er, he is helping an uncle on his farm,' Anders answered.

'When will he return?'

'When the fences are built.' Sanna shivered at Anders' bold tone.

'Immediately when he returns, he must report for duty in Vaasa. Otherwise…'

As the officers passed the larder, one lifted a leg of ham from its hook. He heaved it over his shoulder. Anders met Sanna's wide eyes and shook his head.

'Thank God they did not push their way up to the loft.' Sanna huddled into her shawl. 'Tomorrow you must take the printing press to Udden. Or we will all be sent to Siberia.'

~

The strictures worsened. Regulations posted in the church informed the villagers that it was illegal for young men to travel after they reached the age of sixteen. Wilhelm's plans escalated.

'But Anders, he is so young!' Sanna cried.

'Young, yes, but he is a sensible lad and learns fast.'

'How do we smuggle out another son when the Russians watch us like hawks?'

'If he leaves before age sixteen, with a valid passport, they cannot stop him.'

'So I *can* travel legally, Pappa? Not ski over Monäs Pass? That frightens me!'

'You must have a paper from the parish office that states your official age.'

Anders tugged at his ear, a habit that showed troubled thoughts. Wilhelm could stay another year if his father used his position as churchwarden to falsify his son's age.

'When he is settled we will all emigrate, before Edvard faces such dangers.'

'At my age?' Sanna waved her arthritic and chilblain swollen hands. Shrill laughter covered terror. Must she face such uprooting to keep her family together?

'Yes, Mamma,' Wilhelm cried. 'You and the girls and Pappa must join us in the Promised Land. You want to see Karl Johan again, surely?'

Deep to her marrow she longed for that! But Sanna knew, as only a mother can know such things, that her eyes would dim before they lit on Karl Johan again.

'But these are Finnish pine trees,' Gretchen, Anders and Sofia Storvist pronounced.

Myth Dispelled

Parting from your best brother who is setting out for the North when you are leaving for the South, well knowing that, as you have different distinctions, it is utterly impossible to travel the same road. Always remember that he has as much right to his ideas as you have to yours. Let your last word be of a friendly nature, and give him to understand that you are parting on principle, and that if he enters into any walk in life you will always be prepared to give him your support provided that his work is consistent with your ideas.

K. J. Back, *The Concentrated Wisdoms of Australia*

When Gretchen, her husband Anders an daughter Sofia flew to Australia, I picked them up at the airport in Brisbane. We drove south past the Gold Coast en route to Byron Bay. After checking into our beachside motel at Cabarita, we headed for the surf. They shrieked at the huge waves and salt, so unlike the Gulf of Bothnia.

Next day, we set out on my guided tour of the family heritage sites. Byron Bay lighthouse at sunset, Brunswick Heads and the red brick house in which we enjoyed many family holidays. Mullumbimby, then Billinudgel to visit the Holm family. Granddad's nephew Wally was then in his late nineties—but bright as a lad. He showed photographs crammed on his dresser and told his stories. Wally directed us to Mooball, where my grandparents married and first lived together. "You can't miss it, look for the big trees. Those seeds came out in your Granddad's pocket.'

'There are the Finnish trees Granddad planted,' I pointed up the hill.

Gretchen shook her head. 'They don't look Finnish at all.'

Wally, savvy as a youth, had misremembered? This was a worry, for what else could I believe? What other supposed truths of family lore were mythology?

Wally's story was redeemed when we drove up the twisty road to Wilson's Creek, where Granddad and KJ built a sawmill on their first land. A local historian had sent me maps so I knew that KJ owned property just behind there, after Pioneer Bridge. At a t–junction café looking out over a huge bluff I could point and say, 'Over there, probably up that ridge, was the saw–mill and land owned by KJ, the mountain he called Gibraltar.'

'Those trees are Finnish.' Gretchen pointed behind the café. Bless you, Wally, you were right!

They were heady days with my Finnish relatives, seeing the Mullumbimby and Wilson's Creek area through European eyes ('like Norway'), hearing squeals of surprise at dumper waves as we swam in the ocean. Sitting on the sand under a tree at Noosa beach as Sofia learned to surf: with our eyes seawards, we missed the brush turkey's foray into our picnic basket. Drinking aperitifs on the Noosa River at sunset, to a cacophony of birds settling for the night. Updating on family of many branches, while sensing unexpressed hurts that linger, rooted from—where?

Yet, Wally, our oldest living relative, born in Finland, told stories that Gretchen corrected; the trees, that six lads sailed with Granddad. Yet shipping records showed only two. And was Granddad 15 or 16 when he emigrated? How easily the stories could be mired in myths. How could I trust any of the information?

Gretchen told of the folders of letters that her grandfather Edvard carefully preserved. They must reveal the real stories.

I determined to return to Finland and seek the truths stored in its mists.

Over decades and many visits to Finland I fossicked for the story of KJ crossing on the ice. There I reached an impasse. No, Gretchen and Rolf insisted, that's not the story we have from Edvard; KJ took a train south to escape Finland.

'A train?' I was dashed. How prosaic. Even a steam train doesn't muster the same drama or evocative atmosphere. 'But Wally said ... and Granddad said ... and a book written by Olavi Koivukangas supposes in a footnote, that he escaped via the "Monäs Pass". Surely the leading expert in Finnish migration, then director of the Institute, writing the definitive book, *he* can't be wrong?'[1]

Gretchen shook her head and wrote the station, 'Kovjoki' in my notes. Then she showed me the family Bible. There, black handwriting states KJ left on 26 May for Australia. So the story of crossing the Gulf of Bothnia on skis was a myth. But still I held to it. Perhaps KJ sailed or rowed across?

My doubts festered. If this crucial story was wrong, how much else was? Did the family embroider the truth to such an extent that I couldn't trust any of our family lore?

I glared at that photograph of KJ resplendent in his frock coat, an orchid

---

1 Koivukangas, Olavi, *Sea, Gold and Sugarcane: Finns in Australia 1951-1947*, Turku, Institute of Migration, 1986, p.189.

in his buttonhole, taken those few years after he fled Finland.

Bother it, KJ, why did you let me continue with the idea of you crossing the Gulf of Bothnia on skis in winter? Somehow the family latched onto that story, but was it confused with your brother–in–law Erik Johan Nyholm? I truly wanted to find the truth, as far as I could, from a hundred years' distance—

—What is truth?

—Surely this note in the Bible is correct, clear in black ink, that you fled in summer, not winter; under the midnight sun not Northern Lights. So much for ice, for struggling against a blizzard!

—You did prefer that version, so why spoil a good story for you?

—You held out on me, led me on. The truth was there all along—

—There is more could reveal.

—You could make it easier for me. I feel conned that I had you going the wrong way. We'll rewind you and send you back across the Gulf but this time on a row boat, your hands raw and bloodied, your tongue parched, your face and hands fire–red from the burning of the sun all day as you haul weary arms across—

—No, never, I cannot return to Finland, the idea makes my stomach retch and heave worse even than the rolling of waves in the Pacific Ocean.

He pushes me away, opens a newspaper and hides behind it.

—But you don't have to cross the ocean. Just across the Gulf of Bothnia.

—You have no idea, you silly ignorant woman, how my legs shake at the thought of going back where I was hunted and vilified and threatened. Do you try to boss me, like Sofia and Wilhelm? Why should I allow that? I live now in a free country.

—Yes, of course. But couldn't we together revisit Finland in 1899? Come on, snälla du, KJ, put on your knapsack and let's look for that fishing boat by the shore at Monäs. As you had your seaman's licence, it should be an inconspicuous journey.

—Why drag up history? I left it behind in Finland when I gladly shed my old skin.

–Was your friend with you? Did he start off together with you, but turned back?

–No, I cannot face the farewells, arms clutching at me, so close I feel their heartbeats against my chest. I cannot feel the terror of soldiers wrenching me from under tarpaulins, of bayonets prodding my shirt, tearing the woven wool so chill air rushes through. I cannot look into soldiers' mean eyes, see them leering triumph at my discomfort. Or the white faces of friends and family who watch aghast as I am wrenched away.

Sorry, I pushed too hard. As I walked from the farmhouse to the church and sat shaded by KJ's spruce trees I imagined his last days before leaving home …

Leaving Home

Be still, my soul: Thy God doth undertake
To guide the future as he has the past.
Thy hope, thy confidence let nothing shake;
All now mysterious shall be bright at last.
Be still, my soul: The waves and winds still know
His voice who ruled them while he dwelt below.
Katharina von Schlegel

The time has come. Tonight I must flee Munsala. How can I store mind enough pictures to carry across the world? Mats and I chew snuff, propped against the cemetery wall under my spruce trees. It cheers me that these and the cherries in the orchard leave some mark of KJ Back in my country. My *vård träd* trees will grow with the family even though I cannot.

I bide my time for telling Mats the plans for tomorrow. We both need to preserve the peace of the afternoon before returning home to the snivelling of family.

'Hush, hold your news,' Mats mutters, spitting out his snuff dregs. We wait while a funeral procession weaves down the hill from the church. How many of my relatives were carried in a box down that path towards this same sheltered spot? How many more will follow—but my muscles will not lift their coffins.

'Those sharp-nosed biddies will head in our direction on their way to drink coffee.' Mats springs to his feet. 'Come, let's take a last swim together at Udden and throw in a line for some *sik*.' We sprint along the lanes. Our toes squish through moss, crushing yellow wildflowers. Raspberry canes scratch our legs. As we sit to catch breath on the wooden set on the jetty Mats winds me with the words:

'This sea will be tame to you when you are swimming in the Pacific Ocean.'

'What do you mean, to me? We will ride those waves together, Mats.'

'No, KJ, that's what I have to tell you. Here,' Mats handed me his passport, 'you will make better use for this than I can.'

'Mats, you need your own pass.'

'You use it. I must stay and support my wife, Ida. I will be a father by year's end.'

That pulls me up short. It was just a few months ago that we threw rice over them as fiddler Wilhelm Munsin led them from Munsala church, dressed in their white wedding finery. A child. How could I argue against that?

'Ida and the babe can follow and join us in Australia! You must come with me!' A choking of panic rushes helter-skelter through my veins. Always I envisaged us two lads rollicking over roistering seas, tackling the world together. That thought strengthened me in my farewells.

'No, I must stay with my family. And who else could chair the *Ungdomsförening* with the same spirit as you have done? I will say I lost this pass and apply for another. That may stave off the call-up while they search the parish records to check my age.'

'What an old married man that you have become, weighed down with your cares! Promise you will follow, Mats, bring your family, won't you? I will look out for fertile land near my farm, we can share tools and horses and bulls. I'll send money for your passage when I'm settled.'

He mutters, 'After the Russians are sent packing from Finland, perhaps.' His eyes avoid mine as he looks out at the jigsaw chunks of rocks that guard the sea. Those reeds that line Finland's lakes and seashores, would I ever see such again, did they grow on Australia's shores?

He diverts me: 'It's so hot. What are we waiting for? Last one into the water is a migrating goose!'

We throw our clothes in a heap beside the rushes that line the shore, splash water and race each other across the bay. So long we swim that the cows trumpet to remind us of the time. Of late, Father has been softer in his manner but he forgets and roars: 'Where have you been, wasting time while five cows cry out for milking?'

He remembers that next day there will be no milking by Karl Johan Back. He lays a hand on my shoulder, an awkward pat as clumsy apology. 'Never mind for today, son. Anna Sanna can finish for you,' he mutters.

~

Puffing like the steam train whose pistons already churn I climb the steps, the last aboard. The train lurches away. I collapse onto a hard wood bench.

The sun's constant surveillance sears into my eyes. Even when I close them, I can feel its shafts and infernal arrows of gold and red. My carriage clatters over the rails and my eyes shudder open. Sparks of pain run up each knob of my spine to hammer blows into my forehead.

With each lake and river that we pass—Finland is a nation of water— my eyes squint against the power of sun, as its magic turns cobalt blues into rippling gold. Day and night blur an endless band of light across my eyes. There is little chance of sleep in normal Finnish midsummer. This one is worse.

The midnight sun brands this last picture of my homeland into my mind. Like a shadow show at a village fair, the outlines of fir and spruce, of houses and barns dangle before my eyes. Even when I shut them tight against the glaring ball of flame they bounce into my mind. Light burns through my eyelids in unforgiving hallucinations of hellfire and brimstone that Priest von Essen leashed onto me. However tight I screw my vision shut, they stare me down. My brow furrows into plough trails from squinting.

Snorting and jolting like a primeval beast, the train bears me south. It spits dust and grit. Steam, hot as Hades, stings my eyes, thickens my tongue. My lids drift down, seeking respite for a body and mind exhausted long ago. But I wrench them open from snatches of sleep. Russian police might board the train and pry into my knapsack. I clamp my mouth shut for fear of muttering indiscreet words.

A jumble of raw feelings courses through me; relief to be on my way and yet, with it, a chill. I alone must find directions while cast adrift on an uncertain stormy voyage. For years I longed to be my own man, free from my father's directions and interventions. Now he can no longer control me, yet my jubilation is muted. But it is a relief to escape the guilt that skulked behind my parents' love, like a malevolent two-faced troll.

The train stops at Tampere. After all the heaving and shuddering movement, my feet slip and dance oddly. I wander aimlessly by the lake whose ruffled and shining water mirrors my moods. My spirits revive to breathe crisp air, free from grit, coal dust and soot. I light a pipe and lean against a birch tree to reflect on that unsettling sense of being rootless.

In a traveller's hostel in Hanko, three-tiered bunks line the walls. I keep to myself when fellow passengers ask my business. During my fitful dozing, a kaleidoscope shuffles faces before my eyes. It jumbles the loved ones I left behind, the parents who expected me to be three sons all rolled into one. And the woman I might never see again. My body warms to think of her.

Women cook potatoes on a brazier outside. In smoke ridden

nightmares the priest's voice says 'You will burn in hell, Karl Johan.'

Fire. I scream aloud to remember little Johanna; her flesh scorched bright red, her pitiful eyes pleading to stop the pain.

'Shut your trap, you wake us with your noise.' A grumpy voice rouses me from the next bunk.

~

In the dawn light, I blink. Where am I? Hanko. I pull on my trousers and boots and wander along the waterfront. My last steps on hard granite Finnish rocks.

The weather matches my mood as our ship sails; rain lashes the decks so my final glimpse of Finland's granite cliffs is hazy. The SS *Arcturus* ploughs through sullen waves.

The bar opens and soon passengers become too drunk to see or walk straight, let alone dance to the accordion. But I cannot drop my guard. I pull my jacket closer and huddle under shelter of a bulwark on deck. I feel very alone.

One clear picture fades all too fast; of Kerstin's face washed with tears. How she cleaved to me as I flung away her arm.

Karl Johan to England – 1899

Luck is like an ocean wave,
Sweeping in so full and fat,
Mostly taking all it gave,
Often more than that.
K. J. Back, *The Royal Toast*

'Head for the most easterly point,' instructed my great–grandfather, Anders Back, as Karl Johan fled. 'There must be rainfall.' This has been a constant theme in family lore. And so, after a hazardous voyage, his eldest son settled in the Byron Bay hinterland in 1899. Anders brought Wilhelm—my grandfather—to join him in January 1903.

For my kin the Byron Bay area is a significant place, rich with history.

Family patterns circle around Byron Bay like the arc of the lighthouse that shines its nightly reassurance onto the ridges where the brothers settled: Bangalow, Coorabell, Wilson's Creek, Goonengerry, Mullumbimby. Thirty kilometres north is the small hamlet of Mooball where my grandfather married Christina in 1908.

Unlike KJ, Granddad's passage to Australia is documented on the *SS Ophir*, arriving 17th January 1903. His father Anders brought him out with two friends.

But KJ? My scant information is that he travelled through Suez. How could I find shipping records for someone who sailed under a false passport? Genealogists pay fees to search names, dates and ships; I could only wonder over Swedish names on shipping records and passenger lists from the Institute of Migration. On KJ's application for naturalisation he wrote that he arrived on the *Australis* in July 1899 but the ages and names don't match. You hid your tracks well, KJ.

In the transition from sail to steam, what kind of ship was it? Having lived his life by the sea, was Karl Johan employed as crew? Did he jump ship in Sydney and so hide from the shipping company as well as from the Russians?

One of my few concrete facts was that he gained his seaman's ticket in 1898.

A book of shipboard diaries from this era fed my imagination about the conditions he may have faced. I pictured him, twenty–one years of age, relieved to have escaped Finland, yet on edge with fear. He spoke only Swedish and some Finnish but he constantly had his nose in an English dictionary. I imagined his word list expanding each day, his basic phrases proliferating. Jottings in his journal might have read like this:

Rough. Mycket/much vind. Många/many sjuk/sick. I sailor–man. But here sick.

I discovered that, in 1951, KJ wrote a will entrusting his executors to publish his latest book, the story of his life. 'I have some very important writing ready for publication,' he wrote, 'and if life and health permits it, I hope to have it copyrighted.' My efforts to locate this manuscript were unsuccessful. In the meantime, I reconstructed an account, drawing on letters he wrote.

~

After my escape from Finland I collapse in a *sorg*, exhausted in body and mind. I remember little of the ship bound for Hull until customs officials ask to see my passport. My fingers shake and I hold my breath so tight my ribs hurt for days after. After they wave me through, nobody else is concerned with my papers. A bus takes me to the train where I huddle in a corner.

The journey to London is a blur of cathedral spires and thatched cottages. As I doze Russians chase me in dreams around the cropped hedges. After two hours we halt. I weave through London's maze of buildings, streets and lanes crowded with peoples and carriages and new-fangled automobiles and omnibuses. Directed to the Scandinavian Seamen's Mission hostel at Rotherhithe, I fling my weary bones on a bunk. Much later I rouse to a stomach gnawed with hunger and seek a breakfast of rye bread, cheese and buttermilk, washed down with coffee.

Fortified, I set out to explore on foot that ant's nest of a city, teeming with people rushing about their affairs. I backtrack the narrow lanes in case spies follow me and become lost. First I must stand before the Houses of Parliament where, for British citizens, democracy is enforced—*enforced!*—by law of the Magna Carta.

Imagine; a law ensured their freedom! How I envy those uncaring faces that hurry past without a glance. They have no idea of their fortune while dictatorship and repression blights us in Finland.

I am tempted to stay here but I need the safety of distance.

A bookshop entices me; I must purchase English language books to assist my studies of that tongue. Some hours later I stagger out heavier in weight and lighter of purse. Long into that night I thumb through the books, lexicon in one hand. Many words—'man' for instance—are the same and some easily guessed, like 'house' for 'hus'. With both body and brain exercised, my sleep is less fitful.

Over breakfast, busybodies try to learn my plans. Russian spies infiltrate such hostels so I hide my head in my coffee cup—until the old sailor Bengt with skin hard as leather mentions Australia: 'It's folly to sail there in summer for sunstroke kills many.'

I block such prospects from my mind, for what life do I have without crossing this Rubicon? I ask about ships to Australia and the cost of a fare.

Fifteen guineas for a steerage passage! After paying for lodging, food and my cherished books, my marks exchanged for sterling fall short by ten guineas. Noting my bleak face, Bengt points to a notice that seeks crew to sail to Australia next month.

'I intend to sign up,' he says. 'Come with me.'

Captain Anders Olsen, being Danish, understands my Swedish, since our languages are so similar. Blue eyes pierce through my desperation.

'What sailing experience do you have, Mats?' (For I was using his name and passport.)

'I earned my seaman's ticket a year ago in Jakobstad, for trade to Sweden.'

'The Gulf of Bothnia is child's play compared to the Cape of Good Hope.'

'But I have Viking blood in my veins, sir,' I say. He smiles at that, taking my papers. When his face creases into a frown I realise my mistake.

'Also, you appear to have two names,' he says. 'One of these documents is false. Or else this is stolen and you are no real seaman?'

'Indeed I am, sir! My friend stayed home, I have his pass.'

'So you escaped Tsarist conscription?'

I can only nod, for a lump chokes my breath.

'Hide the ticket, Mats. I will sign you on for a year, for your face is intelligent.'

'Thank you sir'—my voice comes out uneven—'though this passage is enough.'

'I cannot be forever hiring and breaking-in crew. You want this work or not?'

'Yes, sir,' I say. 'Thank you, sir.'

∽

The massive ship that awaits me at Tilbury should give safe passage across the oceans. Yet it is cramped full with hundreds of bodies. A sailor leads me through a labyrinth of alleyways, shows me my bunk and hanging canvas bag to store my belongings. He gives me an enamel plate, knife, fork and pannikin.

Amidst much noise and confusion, I report for duty. The mate sets me to crank up the gangway after a bell clangs to signal that visitors should go ashore. There is a clamour of whistles blowing and weeping. Foghorns give mournful sympathy. We untie the vessel's fastenings as spectators cheer and throw their hats in the air. Champagne corks pop and orchestra music filters down from the fancy first class saloon. Many passengers wipe tears from their eyes to leave Old Blighty. For me a thundercloud lifts. I laugh aloud to see the stretch of water increase between myself and tyranny.

The Voyage

Many men, heedless of the present, allow a bright future to float away to a gloomy past.
K. J. Back, *The Royal Toast*

Gripping the rail, I watch tugboats steer us safe passage. As the English coast fades, the knots in my stomach ease. With relish I wolf down a hearty dinner of beef and potato stew. I soon regret such enthusiasm when the weather turns foul and we ride waves as big as houses.

I am a sailor of some experience, with a seaman's ticket to prove it, but the captain was right: nothing of the Gulf of Bothnia's flat seas could prepare me for the turbulence past the English Channel. While I dangle high up in the ropes our ship gives a sudden lurch. I wrench my wrist trying to gain a hold. The mate rues sending me aloft to reef the sails for my repast is expelled onto the deck over his feet. Cursing my ashen face he calls me a 'good for nothing' but allows me return to my bunk.

All through the night and next day I huddle close to the heads. Later I attempt some barley and potato broth but my throat is so stiff with retching that each swallow is agony.

What fate propels me to leave familiar shores, to throw myself into these great seas? We cram into the hold with sweaty bodies close like sardines in brine, bumping along with the raging seas. I am lost in a nightmare cacophony of folk talking gibberish languages.

We pass the Bay of Biscay but see little of it for driving rain. Queasiness steals all my appetite. Constant storms lash our ship, send mountains of water smashing at us. The decks and galleys are perilous with slippery water. A wall of sea washes over the side. Seamus Reagan is sucked away with it, for all his clutching at ropes.

The contrary wind whips up a surge so strong that it breaks the tarpaulin and swamps the hatches. The ship rolls so badly that tins and buckets fling from one end to the other. We cannot pull down the tables for eating, but few have the stomach for food, even if we should find the path from plate to mouth.

All through the night, our ship lurches. We lean at such odd angles that there is no knowing up from down. The rolling waves send misery into my guts.

'I will never go back to Finland,' I swear, 'I don't like to go over so wide water that I don't see the land.'

It comes to me that I needed to replace the guts I have lost. I lack *sisu*, that most Finnish strength of resolve. So whenever my eyes can focus on a swaying page, I apply myself to my books and writing as my best form of solace.

My intention is to write a journal of my experiences in this great wider world, but there is little opportunity. My off-duty time allows only a few scribbled notes between puking into a bucket.

After four long days and longer nights the gale sinks into a fair wind and the leaping of the ship eases. I regain my sea legs and can breathe air untainted by vomit. I pull out my notebook and pencil stub to write my journal on the trestle table where we eat.

The unruly Danish boys peer over my shoulder. They try to decipher my writing and read it out aloud for the merriment of all. Their guffaws increase as it becomes apparent Munsala dialect has particular phrasing not common to Danish.

Noting my study of the English dictionary, the captain orders the mate to change my roster so I can attend schooling classes on the deck in my free time. These are intended to occupy the children aboard, but the schoolteacher, Henry Wilcox, helps adults in learning English—for a motley mix of nationalities are amongst us. Even with my rudimentary grasp of the language, I progress faster than some Danes whose ignorance is displayed when they hold their books upside down.

The classes are a joy, even though our teacher has only a few slates and English Grammars, books about geography and history and some about the colonies. I master all pages that spell information about Australia, and of fortunes made on the goldfields.

Silence feels strange when the winds drop, so still that we are becalmed. Yet I so fear climbing the rigging that I confuse the knots.

Strange phosphorescence engulfs us at night after the lowering clouds clear. The sky shines with the silvery way of stars, millions of light pricks. This is the path of the birds in Finnish mythology. We sing and dance to the accordion and fiddle and tin whistle, washed along with rum. I attempt to play a polka on the mouth organ I bought in London. I write and produce a satirical song for singing with my Swedish and Danish compatriots. The humour escapes most. Listeners show little understanding of my poems but when I sing them they laugh at my off-key voice.

The sun shines with sharp-edged brilliance as we pass that massive rock called Gibraltar. We try to capture birds or flying fish to supplement our rations of salt pork, beef and cabbage. Nils Christensen snares an albatross that measures nine feet from wing to wing. Others help him pluck away its feathers but I cannot eat this fresh meat. Finnish myths tell of death for those who do so. But I cheer crewmates by acting out my song about birds that migrate from one end of the world to the other, just as we do. They ask for more stories after that.

Fine weather gives us pleasant days and glimpses of new lands. We anchor at Naples. Small boats bring vendors all gabbling at once to entice us to part with our money for fruit and trinkets. We pass between the rocks of Scylla and Charybdis. Old salts tell tales of sirens luring travellers with their singing, where they fell to perish in a deep chasm. After Calabria we sail through the Straits of Messina, flanked by the volcano Stromboli and, on the other bank, its partner Etna.

After lively times in port, there are idyllic days back at sea; I occupy my off-duty time reading my dictionary and the few cherished books I stashed into my knapsack before I left. I chose Socrates for he would keep my mind busy and Homer's Odyssey—for am I not embarked on such? Pappa had pressed a prayer book onto me. So disturbed am I when several bodies are plunged into the deep, I spend some time formulating all the questions I'll put to God, if I should ever meet him.

Suez Canal

The Suez Canal is an organised piracy that has never had its equal anywhere in the world in the last 500 years. Nor is this piracy free from bloodshed and human sacrifice. The Suez Canal is over capitalised and a burden to the world's commerce. It should be taken over by the Curator of International Currency and made free entry for all nations.
K. J. Back, *A Solution of the World's Financial Problems*

KJ expanded his horizons in 1899 and triggered ideas that he would articulate thirty years later. But then he could share them only with his fellow Scandinavians while he struggled to learn more English. I imagined him pulling out his notebook and stub of pencil to scribble new words as he learned them:

Suez Canal. Öppna/opened 1869. 90% desert. Sinai Desert. Moses. Långsam. Dum ~~idé~~ idea. ~~Bättre~~ better idea. Euphrates Canal through Persian Gulf.

KJ's innovative concepts crystallised in 1932 when he published *A Solution of the World's Financial Problems*. I located this in Sydney's Mitchell Library:

> *Under the credit system of finance a ship's canal will be dug from the Mediterranean through Syria to the Euphrates River, permitting the world's tonnage to pass through that way to the Persian Gulf.*

But this is getting ahead of KJ's voyage; let us proceed with his account:

～

Our ship takes its turn to crawl along the Suez Canal at about eight kilometres an hour through the locks. Alongside we see caravans of pilgrims heading towards Mecca. Many ships carry folk from nations far and wide. A jackal prowls on the canal banks hoping to find a carcass. Ottomans and others fight against the British who've taken control. The pirates attack boats that cannot afford to pay daylight robbery charges and many are killed—a criminal waste of life, boats and cargo.

Thieves and robbers have multiplied since the time of Moses. Much later, when my English is fluent, I form my scribbled notes into my book:

> *Numbers of sailing vessels, that could not afford to pay a steamer to pull them through the canal and then pay the canal dues on top of that, have had to face the heart-breaking voyage along the coast of Africa, where they are wrecked in the attempt. The ancient pirate stabs the crew, robs the ship of its cargo, and then burns the ship.*

This 'highway to India' canal is clever engineering by de Lesseps to connect the Mediterranean and Red Seas. He has overcome all obstacles like blocking of mud at Port Said and sand from the deserts. Pharaoh Sesostris attempted similar in 1897 BC but Aristotle wrote that the sea was higher than the land. In 1869 AD, after ten years' labour it now allows us passage over a hundred and fifty kilometres on water.

We head for Egypt. Fancy travelling so near to the Sinai Desert! We sail past places we read of in the Bible, where Moses wrote his commandments on slabs of stone but smashed them in his rage. I think of Pappa.

Captain Olsen points out the spot where Moses led the Hebrews across the Red Sea without so much as wetting their boots. He tells that, when the tides reach low ebb, it is possible to cross on land that was otherwise covered with water. (Our priest at home would scoff at that.)

Sirocco winds blow desert dust and grit into my eyes; it creeps into lips, nose and ears and fills my lungs to choking.

The jabber of different languages in the alehouses is like the Tower of Babel. I try to talk with American and Canadian sailors, using phrases from my vocabulary list. Their words sound different from what Mr Wilcox uses. They laugh at my accent, saying 'W-w, with your mouth forward. Not v, *w*.'

We ride donkeys to the Arab quarter, see lavish and vividly dressed women, hear strange music and travel in rickshaws feeling grand as the Tsar. In that climate as steamy as a sweating sauna we hold our noses. Rotting garbage in street gutters breeds plague. Their cooking is so full of garlic, spices and curry, it makes us cough. Our noses and eyes stream water. We bolt for the stinking hole in the ground that passes for a privy.

In Finland, all are rosy faced, scrubbed clean with birch twigs in the sauna. The dive into icy lakes fair shrivels our balls. Mamma scours our kitchen and scullery against germs. How she would shake her head at these heathenish places and dirty peoples.

Egypt, once the 'cradle of the world' is filthy and uncivilised; 'fellahs' are treated like beasts of burden, forced to transport heavy loads on their backs and even their heads while running on unpaved streets towards the market place—under a sun fierce enough to melt rocks.

I peep through the door of a school where urchins sit cross-legged on the ground, skins black as sin. They pay little attention to the teacher; none have books and the cane is kept busy. I bless Herr Svedberg's wise teaching, on those few days Pappa allowed me freedom from chores.

As our ship prepares to sail, hawkers in canoes pester us to buy tobacco, fruit, oysters and fish. Black men teem around, stark naked, begging coins from the passengers. When we throw a farthing into the water they plunge after it, brandishing it before stuffing it for safekeeping into their mouths.

Travelling the world, hearing new languages, eating strange food, all is an adventure.

Until my experiences in Suez fair frighten the heart out of my chest.

The Quarry

Every sea has its waves, and every ocean its breakers. The one who expects to sail where there are no dangers or difficulties will be sadly disappointed.
K. J. Back, *The Concentrated Wisdoms of Australia*

In nightmares I still see the jackals prowling the Sinai bank of the Suez Canal. Their hyena eyes snap in the glow of electric lanterns. I struggle through sand hills, lost in their shifting mazes. I shrivel in heat like a sauna. Buzzards tear at carrion and swoop on live locusts in flight.

The first warning of danger ahead is the prickling down my spine; two-legged wolves have picked up my scent but I have yet to recognise their approach.

Sirocco dust stings my eyes, blurs a last glimpse of the Mediterranean Sea. But it's futile to look back. Europe has no place for Karl Johan Back. Nor can I see my way forward. Could I disappear amongst caravans of Bedouins or pilgrims headed for Mecca?

After Port Said ships take the turn into the womb of the canal. They pass through the Bitter Lakes to rebirth in the Red Sea. Sailors point to the mountain where Moses wrote the Ten Commandments. And the wilderness where the Israelites wandered in circles for years—just as I stumble on my path between hemispheres.

Before we dock in Suez, Captain Olsen warns, 'Watch your back, Mats.' He speaks true: Russian military police push aboard even as the ropes are tied. Their accents alert me. I know enough Russian since the Tsar's orders tried to silence our native tongue.

They accost my mate Bengt, hearing his Swedish accents.

'We seek Karl Johan Back. Is he aboard?'

Bengt shakes his head. I slink behind a lifeboat. Sweat soaks my shirt.

'We know that this ship carries illegals. We must inform your captain.'

Leather boots clomp past me. So close they walk that I recoil from the

93

putrid cabbage and onion on their breaths. I mutter all the prayers I can remember and invent more.

'By the authority of Tsar Nicholas II, we will inspect all passports.'

Mats' passport has got me this far but I quiver to face these louts.

'You have no rights on my ship in international waters,' Captain Olsen thunders. 'My sailors will remove you, if you don't go easy.'

So the Tsar's tentacles reach even to this outpost in the desert. How did they discover my ship? Did someone telegraph its arrival? Through those jangling wires stretched between wooden posts? Even here, Russians stalk me. They follow like a *haminja* familial spirit. These vultures will track me even to Australia.

'Bengt, they must not catch me. Or I will jump in the sea and take my chances with the Arabs.' I run aft and slide into the water, thrash to shore. Then collapse under a palm tree, gasping. Shivers rack my body, even in fierce sun.

Russians still patrol. When my heart slows, I slink into a tavern and accuse a Yankee sailor of taking my pot of rum. This ferments a fine rabble in which to hide. I am something of an actor. Some liquor does ease my distress but I keep my wits clear. While the police sort out the fight, I slink away.

At dusk the captain sends Bengt in a rowboat for me to slip back on board ship. I crawl into my bunk, pulling the blanket tight until a mournful hoot announces the ship sails. From my pocket I pull the letter written home, tear the paper into small pieces and strike a Vesta match on my boot. The ashes flutter down, light as butterflies, absorb into sea and sink.

My gut wrenches as if a knife cut my umbilical cord. It severs me from family. They cannot aid my flight. Karl Johan must find his own path along the great whale road.

Suez fades on the horizon. I stagger as if the seas have churned into a wild tumult. But it is simply distress. My heart aches to put my feet firmly on the ground of my own land. I yearn for earth in which to sink roots. To plant seeds, to nurture shoots that will grow to harvest and nourish my depleted body.

The path of the birds wends across the Milky Way to the warm edges of the world. How I crave heat. Ice weighs my spirit. Where will it find a nest? In my sweaty hand, I clutch the soul-bird carved from birch while hiding in barns before I fled. This *Sielulintu* comforts, has kept me company all this way from home. Reality chills my fever. I have no home.

I will never cross the sea back to Finland.

To The Southland

I have wandered from my country,
And my ancient home abandoned.
Kalevala

Only when Bengt tells me that our ship is far from land can I release the breath I have held so tightly. The coastline fades. I clutch at the rail. There I nearly lost my freedom. I slink back to my bunk to shiver in a delirium of fear.

Again the captain speaks up for me. 'Leave him be,' he tells the midshipman who complains of my laziness. When we dock at Aden, I skulk below deck.

Nightmares tangle me in frenzy, both day and night. As the seas again surge high as houses, my stomach knots all the tighter with dread of capture. The scorching sun sends hallucinations and sweats of terror.

Sometimes I wonder if I only dream of death, but wake to find it all too real. Jens Jensen suffers sunstroke and falls to the deck. The doctor applies ice to his forehead but he dies within the hour, and is thrown into the sea before the body can decompose.

The heat is oppressive. Fierce winds and strong currents lash our ship across the Indian Ocean. Inertia drains all my will for learning or writing. We take aboard fresh food in Ceylon. Again, I hide in my bunk but ask Bengt to buy tobacco, bananas and coconuts from natives who flock to our ship. Earlier I dreamed of crossing the Equator. Now I have no interest in Neptune and the shenanigans.

One day, as I pour the slops over the side, a bird perches on the rail. My mates crowd around and thump each other on the back. Land is near! That bird lifted us from our doldrums. I pull out the journal I have neglected.

After months aboard our spirits bubble as we vie to be the first to sight Australia. Before we enter Fremantle harbour, the Health Officers sail up in a pilot boat. They moor alongside and call to the captain, 'Have you had deaths aboard? Cholera?'

A quarantine doctor boards to check all crew and passengers. We are allowed to visit the port for some hours. I hold my breath as a customs official looks at Mats' passport. He stamps it and nods. I have reached my new country.

I walk unsteady, after the rolling of the ship. Winds of hope lift my feet. I sing aloud 'I am free! I am walking at the end of the world!' Blue-green waves tempt me in to splash.

Sun stabs into my eyes. Dull green leaves are drab like spruce. I sniff a strange smell— tangy? Birds screech and cackle. I pull at my collar in futile efforts to relieve the itching, and scratch at the prickling sweat soaking through my woollen shirt.

Mr Wilcox laughs. 'You find this hot? It will become worse soon.'

I feast on exotic fruit—soft peaches dripping with juice as well as passionfruit. Pineapples too with their prickly tough skins; so sweet once wrestled open with my *puukko*.

When I ask the pilot what soils and rainfall are needed to grow such fruit he looks blankly at me. Bengt who speaks better English says that they thrive unattended with so much sun. When I have my own land I will grow every fruit possible in this land.

Our ship heads east for Cape Otway and a brief halt at Melbourne port, before our last leg to Sydney. Our vessel skitters through a dazzling harbour towards The Rocks. It has borne me across the whole world to paradise, far from Finland's darkness and oppression. There, frozen earth preserves the memories, the bleak darkness of guilt and sorrow. Here, a new Eden beckons me.

We dock at a wharf, and all hustle down the gangplank, to greetings and calls of hawkers selling fruit. I am torn between relief to have arrived safe and knowing I must jump ship. Never can I face those seas again. Does Captain Olsen read my mind? His direct gaze bores into me but he says naught. As I pack my knapsack with my belongings and books, I long to shake his hand and thank him for protecting me at Suez. He was better than a father to me. I dare not. No risks may threaten my freedom.

On shore, I first need advice to find transport to the territory where Father's maps show rich earth and much rain. I am well primed by my language book and have practised the words to say. I accost a friendly face, hand outstretched. 'I am stranger here,' I say, rolling each syllable off my tongue, just like the book instructs. He shake his head, shrug and walk away. Was the book wrong? Had the teacher taught me false sounds?

'Where is ship to Byron Bay?' I ask other men. They laugh.

'No sheep here, mate, they're all inland on properties.'

'No, ship, ship,' I persist. 'Boat.'

I point to the harbour where steamships are docked.

'Ah, ship,' they laugh. 'You want to sail the seas?'

'No. Not Europe. Here, Byron Bay. Much rain. Rich earth?' I point north.

They elbow me, jeering. 'You best go back where you came from, mate.'

'Land, I seek land. And work.'

'It's a big country,' they shrug. 'Tough times but plenty of land if you got money.'

My stomach sinks that my attempts to learn the language have failed; I am alone in this big country where the local people do not understand me and I can barely guess their meanings. I sit on the grass of my new country and stare at the water.

Free, yes. But so alone.

Then in the tree above me a bird cackles. The jackass. I have left behind the gloomy swan of Tuonela for a country where even the birds laugh.

Sydney, 1899

Land of our future and our past!
Let not thy poverty thee quell,
Be free, rejoice, live well!
Johan Ludvig Runeberg, *Our Land*

'Mats, what's the problem?' Mr Wilcox speaks slowly, not tight through his nose.

I cannot admit that my English efforts failed so I say, 'I need work and ship to Byron Bay.'

He takes my arm. 'First we'll find you lodgings at the Scandinavian Missionary Sailor Home. And I read in today's newspaper that there are harvesting jobs in Scone.'

'Scone?' I ask, leafing through my lexicon; I find only something to eat.

The people at the Sailor Home offer me a bed and food for a shilling and tell me information for steamers. Part of their service is to greet new ship arrivals and take them to the correct steamer. Soon, I will write to Wilhelm and direct him to contact such homes. He is nine years younger than me, a bright lad but I worry to think of him alone in London and Sydney.

> *You would be taken to the steamboat and not have to worry until you get to Sydney where all the nitwits headed for Queensland are herded like sheep to the other boat. I would meet you. Let me know, and I will take care of it.*

Next morning the sun blisters my fair skin, even at early morning, as I walk towards the harbour and sea breezes. Bondi Beach is like Midsummer Day back home. Women and children wear white smocks and many roll their stockings down, even lift their dresses up to show their bloomers.

I hitch up my trousers and paddle barefoot in waves that leap and rush at me. A bigger one surprises me; it knocks me sideways, spills my hat off my head. I spit out water tangy with salt. The sea is restless, a constant churn of froth, unlike the flat waters in Finland.

The sun burns like a sauna so I return to the hostel, pulling my hat low over my forehead in case any sailors recognise me. Sweat runs into my eyes. Aboard that ship are Bengt and Captain Olsen. My heart aches to farewell them. But I must not.

Men line up hoping for work on the wharves. They grumble about their worries and hope that 'the Union' will rescue them before their children starve. Many live in ramshackle lean-to shacks; this country is pinched by Depression.

I feel my purse, knowing my funds are nearly finished. But Uncle Anders wrote to Mamma that he found work. I pull the tattered letter from my pocket and again read his words from Durras Mountain on 25th July 1895.

> *My precious sister, it's been quite some time since I got your much-awaited letter but I haven't been able to answer it since I've had a lot of work. I recently finished two contract jobs that earned me £82 and now begin with another contract. So even if the times are bad I am well and can't complain.*
>
> *Sanna, there is no country on earth more incredible and I am happier and more satisfied than before. Every day makes me a little richer. I am glad that I am free. I have letters to write to Anders Svedberg but I don't have time as I must milk seven cows before sunset.*
>
> *I wish you well and everybody back at home.*

So he had not heard of Svedberg's death. And why did uncle Anders Ohls sign himself 'Mr Andrew Jacobson'? His father was Nils Andersson Ohls. But it comforts that a relative has lived here many years and knows how to survive in this vast country.

My belly rumbles, reminding me I need an income. I must seek this place called Scone. But first I want to see something of Sydney. A wide street leads to Centennial Park and the Domain. Here men stand on their soapbox and shout tirades about poverty and needing work. They call on these unions. It amazes me that people can rage against the government in public without being arrested. So I also stand on the soapbox and speak my poems about freedom but they laugh at my Swedish.

'What is this dago talk?' a man jeers at me. 'Must be straight off the boat.'

Their mocking frightens me. They might tell the government to imprison me or send me home. I spend a precious coin to hurry away on an electric tram then hide several blocks distant in St Mary's cathedral. A pompous sacristan reminds me of Priest Gustav von Essen. His brows beetle low to chastise me for my failings. My stomach churns to think of that catastrophe in Munsala church. I must leave before I collapse. Knocking against knees I scramble from the pew so hastily that a beak-nosed woman in crinoline skirts tuts at my bad manners. My heart pounds so loudly she must hear it above the organ; I nearly pass out onto her leather boots.

I stay upright long enough to reach a bench in the cemetery and force long, slow breaths through my lungs. The headstones divert me to write a poem similar to Gray's *Elegy*. This fancy so engrosses me that I forget travel.

Sunset streaks the clouds red and orange and night is swift to fall, without so much as twilight. I rouse myself to return to the Sailors Home, hoping my bed is still available. All night I toss, pondering whether to go to Scone where workers are needed, or look for my uncle at Durras Mountain. A relative's advice would comfort me.

Next day at the booth for steamer tickets I hold out money. 'Durras Mountain?'

'Milton,' he says. 'Or Bateman's Bay.' I feel stupid to not understand the coins but relieved that he returns some change to me.

At Seven Mile Beach, the sand is golden so I lie all day as sun pours into my body. My skin tightens, turns red and aches. Through my dozing strange birds cackle and warble. Flashes of blue and green and gold wing through trees. At sunset the birds congregate in the trees to chatter about their day.

Next day, I walk to Durras Mountain but do not see anything of Anders Ohls or Andrew Jacobson. A plumber named Bill Collins offers me work. For my first task in this new land he sets me to fashion a funnel with tin-snips and a soldering iron. I apply all my ingenuity to the task. Bill wants me to stay and work for him. But after some weeks I decide to go to Scone. I know how to harvest from home. Besides, hiding is easier inland.

There I earn six shillings a day for six weeks. But it plagues my mind that perhaps Anders was in Durras; did I look for him in a wrong place? Or did I leave too hastily and miss him? I decide to return and fortune smiles on me. I meet him on the boat as I travel. It transpired he had been in Milton and was journeying back to the Richmond River.

He told me to follow him and both of us will have jobs with the same person. He will now be boss for a lot of black people and has thirty shillings per week and I will get a little less money.

'We Finns know timber,' Anders says to me, 'and cedar trees fetch a high price. They call them red gold. Contractors respect our work.'

'But these natives, are they fierce?'

'They give me no grief for I treat them well. But take care in the forest; some revenge the timber cutters for they take cedar where birds and animals lived.'

Anders is a good man; I can rely on him. After the harvest is finished in Scone, I sail to Byron Bay. Wide sandy beaches are a true paradise. My brightest dreams have been surpassed. Sun pours kindness into my joints but I now know it also burns exposed skin. So I sit under a palm tree, take my stub of pencil and write home:

The country is beautiful and the price is not much for such fertile land. The climate is idyllic because the winter is very short and seldom too cold.

I have arrived at the easterly point of Australia, as Pappa directed. Indeed the grass is green and lush; the soils are rich from being the rim of a volcano.

Again hunger reminds me I must find work.

'I seek Andrew Jacobson, in timber logging camp. Do you know him?'

'See that mountain range, mate? Take that track up the range to Coorabell.' I scramble upward but find an easier path further north.

'Hey, mate, don't go that way, yer'll get yourself killed.' This man sounds fierce but his mouth flashes teeth in ochre skin.

I respond that this is an easier path, that the other bush is prickly.

'Easy way to get killed, walking along the shoot—'

'Guns? Soldiers?' *Are Russians here? When do they leave me alone?*

'Come over under these trees. Quick!' He looks at my trembling hands.

He pulls me under the big eucalyptus trees as I hear a shout of 'Shoot!' A huge tree trunk hurtles down the hill. I jump further into the scrub. 'Ah,' I say, 'like in Finland we push logs along in rivers, here you throw them down mountains.'

'Yeah, quickest way, cheaper'n bullockies. Get in the way o' that and yer a goner.'

'Goner? The animal that creeps along the ground, takes my bread?'

'Nah, that's a goanna. Goner means capito, finito, dead.' He points. 'That's called a "shoot", I guess 'cos the logs shoot down fast as a bullet.'

'You saved my life. Thank you. My name Karl Johan.' I shake his hand.

'Bill. We don't hold with foreign names here. Best we call you Jacky.'

When Anders returns a week later, he finds me already at work with his team, felling and dragging logs by bullock drays with a boss called Harry O'Meara.

With food in my belly and work, I feel hope—until my first misfortune.

Mother Sanna, 1900

More will be thy mother's trouble: great the anguish of thy parents.
Kalevala

When summer faded a post card arrived in Munsala. It was signed from Erik Johan Nyholm, but this card showed a view of pyramids. Sanna knew Susanna Nyholm's son still worked in the Californian redwood forests, though he would come home soon. Karl Johan did not dare to sign his name because spies looked through the post. Yet it sent greetings to 'family' and a cryptic note that the Tsarist military regime sprouted ears and eyes far from Finland. Amidst that riddle was scant reassurance.

Midwinter: After dreading the worst, Sanna's spirits lifted for a time when several letters arrived reporting KJ's safety. But she couldn't look into his eyes to know when dark clouds of melancholia overtook him. She began to compose a letter even though he had not yet given an address:

Remember, son, just before you left, we sat on the bench together and you nestled into the curve of my shoulder for a few moments? You needed my warmth one last time, though a young man facing the world on his own feet, alone, could not admit to it. In church I cannot focus on Priest von Essen's sermon for seeing your face white and strained as he read from that list of names.

Once I laughed out loud as I entered the church, so villagers nudged and gave me startled looks. (They mutter behind their hands that I am become soft in the head, that anxiety and loss tore all sense from me.) I remembered how you asked Anders at that same place, 'Does the priest think he is the fourth part of the divinity?' And how your father flung a hand over your mouth. I understood your feeling powerless against the tide of events that would sweep you into war so repugnant to you. For, my gentle son, you would brush aside the mosquitoes that irritate us through summer, rather than swat them dead with birch twigs as we do.

When we attended the wedding between Katharina and Nils Anders I found myself smiling to remember. Your voice whispered too loudly at Anna Lena's nuptials, 'Why do women wear those big bridal crowns at their weddings? Is it to slow them from running away if they have second thoughts?'

Karl Johan, I can speak this aloud but not write it: I fear for you in your times of sorg. You are my eldest son but by no means the strongest. Fate asks you to forge a path alone, with no support from family. We sent you off with all the markka we could gather together. It was little enough to forge your future.

Spring, 1901: How wonderful to have an address to write to her son and tell news of home. How they prepared for the marriage of sister Anna Sanna to Erik Johan Holm, not long returned from America. There he worked hard to pay off his widowed mother's farm and debts. He saved money to build a farmhouse at Damskata, only a few kilometres away. They would live with her parents at first—another man around the farmhouse. A good man, Erik Johan, twelve years older than Anna Sanna but she was mature. He received a paper signed by the governor of Vaasa region saying he was not called for war service.

Concerns for younger sister Sofia and her fickle fiancée dampened their joy. And Sanna dwelt on the son lost to the other side of the world. Forever. Karl Johan's words were all too clear:

I remember Finland every day but I don't want to go there any more.

KJ extolled the climate and tried to persuade his parents to migrate, that *you never need to suffer from cold or from very hot, because the big ocean breezes always give fresh winds.* That food grew without effort or money. He made it sound like utopia.

Pumpkins grow so easy that there is no labour. I don't know any other

103

plant that gives so much to eat for so little effort. Seeds don't cost anything; after five months fruit falls on the ground and you only have to pick them up. They are so big you can only fit one or two in a sack and then they are so heavy you can't carry them.

Sanna's creaking joints warned she was too old for such change. Edvard showed others the letter he wrote to enlist support—news was passed from hand to hand:

As regards our father and mother it will be a lot of hardships to face but on the other hand if they once reach here I think they ought to live ten years longer here than they would in Finland and for that alone it is worth risking. The death rate is here very small; we never have to widen out any churchyards, all the cemeteries are too large and that in spite of the fact that we never disturb an old grave.

What an argument!

Sanna knew Finland would be her last resting place. Not in strange soil.

Her prayers for this son's freedom were answered. But was Karl Johan content?

Northern New South Wales

But the wind is friendly to me and the sun shines upon me
In this unaccustomed country.
Kalevala

Karl Johan's letters were penned in his black handwriting—I remember the old push pens, with fine nibs that were dipped into ink. It's a confident and clear script, with florid capitals. They helped me to piece together the story of KJ's early years as a settler—and created a jigsaw puzzle in which I could only guess at causes of rifts and bitterness that festered even with the great expanse of oceans between.

Some letters were undated so I had to guess the chronology. Themes emerged and were reiterated: the need for finance to afford his own land, and his loneliness in a strange new land, much as he revelled in his freedom. 'Sell up and come to Australia, you will have a better life here.'

–KJ, you said in your letter of 1899—

–I wrote they must burn my letters!

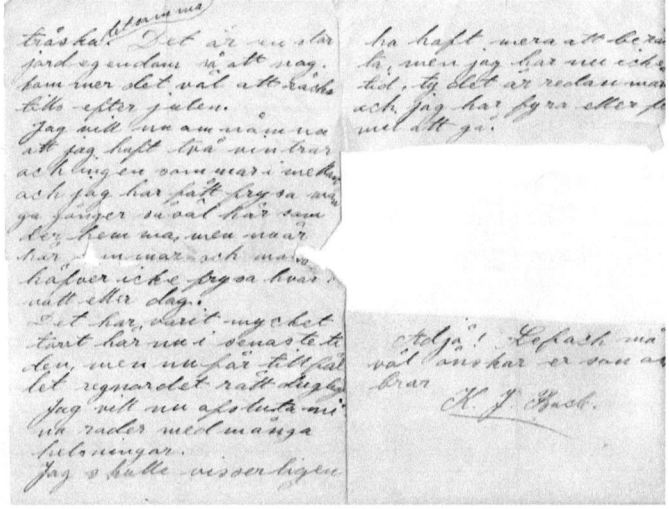

—They compromised. Some letters have holes torn so they did destroy sensitive information. How could any mother burn letters from a distant son?

—Even so, the envelope or stamps could have been used to trace me.

—KJ, calm down, there's no risk of the Russians finding you now.

—Police waited in Suez; they could find me in Australia, send me back.

—Relax; they can't get you now, wherever you are. Heaven? I gather you had little time for the church.

—Wilhelm and my father made enough prayers to cover the whole family. Who needs a God when they were busy pulling strings on all the family, like puppets?

—So you think Wilhelm played God?

—Or a dictator. He and Pappa and sister Sofia were the domineering ones. And Will wrote enough letters; who needs to read mine?

—KJ, it's a gift that your letters survived, in spite of your qualms. They paint a fascinating picture of your life. Sometimes a harsh note creeps in. Was it the stress of finance? Loneliness? Frustration of your struggles? I love your black humour:

> *From reading your letter I got the impression that you seem to think I've been dead. I'm sorry to disappoint you but I am alive and well. If I was to die I am sure you would get a telegram telling you the sad news immediately. The reason why I haven't written is that I don't want everybody at home to know how I'm doing or how I am living.*

> *When it comes to food it's not very good; I like what we had at home much better. I am not starving or anything, I eat what's cheapest and change my eating habits according to prices. I haven't eaten potatoes in many weeks; the prices are expensive. I live mostly on tea and bread. I've decided not to work for anyone else but myself.*

—You must have missed potatoes, that daily staple in cold Finnish climates. KJ, were you in hospital? You write:

> *I have not been sick since I came here and this may be the healthiest country. When I was at the hospital I saw what kind of injuries people had, a broken leg and a broken arm and a black man with a cold.*

—You had not long arrived in the country, was there an accident? Something went wrong, didn't it? KJ, what happened?

There is silence and I fear we have lost contact. Then KJ reflects:

For twelve weeks I toiled with diligence in the haven of the forest. Then my accident set me back. Yes, it suited me fine to be buried in a strange tangle of trees growing together so densely. Even the most persistent Russian would be hard pressed to find me.

In that time I didn't see the government's mint, or police or officials. I had put my earnings into leasing land but I lacked the funds to build a shack or buy tools to clear the thick timber.

I worked in a team for Harry O'Meara, sawing at cedar trees, twenty-five metres or more in height. We hacked through two-metre girths, our nostrils full of the tangy scent. Foresters of past decades had taken most of these trees; we easily spotted those remaining as their pink tipped leaves poked high above the canopy. Their bark crinkled in tassels and they grew long sprays of small white flowers.

Our lives were coloured green and red brown, from the sawdust and the rich earth. Under the thick canopy, the sun barely filtered through to burn my northern skin. As I wrote home:

> The heat is not so painful here at nights and afternoons, that's the best you can ever wish. And if it's too warm at midday, then it will be freshened rather much by the sea breezes; the sea is so nearby that you can see it.

Apart from the men in our team we saw only wildlife, strange hopping wallabies and possums that frisked along boughs and pointed their inquisitive noses at us. They would tell no tales. Life felt surreal amongst a web of vines that creep up and around trees, growing so strong they strangle their host. My dreams were haunted by keening koala bears whose mothers had been killed by crashing logs.

When blustery winds tossed and shredded the ancient trees, it was dangerous for any timber cutters aloft. At nights the whooshing of branches mingled with the howls of dingoes.

My fears kept me sleepless despite exhaustion. I'd climb through the tangle of bush and steep gullies to the ridge that dropped sharp to the plain. I'd look up to the stars, how bright they shimmered, different to those of the northern skies.

Anders—Andrew, now—informed me of their names. 'See, up there are the Pointers to the Southern Cross,' he said.

I couldn't see much cross at first. But this high dome, peaceful yet alive with shooting stars, calmed me.

The Australian Forest

Adversity is like a mighty storm, which breaks off all the deformed and unworthy limbs of the tree of friendship and brotherhood.
K. J. Back, *The Concentrated Wisdoms of Australia*

We were a strange band of men; the most that could be seen of any of us was a sawdust-peppered bushy beard with just our eyes to reveal who was who. We lived a rough life, sleeping in bark huts in a roll of blanket called a swag.

Our food was tough bread called 'damper' with jam. Sometimes we trapped animals and cooked them over a fire. I proved a capable fisherman. Birds gave us meat but I hated to kill them.

At nights, we'd drink billy tea and rum around the campfire with the old-timers, men whose white beards revealed their ages to be ninety or more years. They were hardy, though. Tough enough to live out long twilight years.

They told of the times when sawmilling was at its peak. My English language ripened with swear words through listening to Old Jimmy's tales of ghosts around Murdering Reach. How he rallied his mates to avenge the murder of Hopping Ike who disappeared there. He told of the hey-day of milling forty years ago, of accidents and fights. Stories of Old Brine, caught hiding in an Irish bog, convicted and given to a squatter for drudgery, so he'd run away to join the sawyers. Old Red Jack the Hopper had lost a leg but that did not stop him fighting when the drink got him. I gave him some distance.

The natives ate strange grubs and seeds. One day a strange scowling black-faced native accosted me. I pulled out my tobacco and offered him some 'baccy'. He took it gladly enough but his sharp eyes watched me sit on a log to fill my pipe. I jabbed a finger at my chest and said, 'Karl Johan,' but he made no reply. I was not surprised: most of my workmates found my name had one too many syllables. 'Jacky,' I said with another jab. I pointed the question towards him.

'Jacky,' he said. We both laughed and I said 'Jacky too?' as I held up two fingers. He again pointed to himself: 'Widjabul.' I took that to mean his native name or his dialect. He added 'Bundjalung.' This word I had heard as being the tribe of the area.

Then a jackass laughed in a tree nearby. He held up three fingers and said 'Jacky Three?' His white teeth flashed at his joke. So began my friendship with Jacky Too.

With sign gestures, I learned that his tribe had hunted and fished in the streams of the area for a long time. They grew grasses of foxtail on flat clearings and native kangaroo grass on ridges. Between 'walkabout' they maintained such grasses at Devil's Lookout, Goonengerry, Mullumbimby and Myocum, and burned off each year to prepare for the Spring growth. This Bora Grounds were sacred to them and they held ceremonial rites there. They felt angry that timber getters and bullockies intruded[2].

Seeking to appease him, I gave him a penknife and bully beef—he wrinkled his nose at that. In return he pulled plants and roots and offered them for me to taste. Such knowledge became useful for me when my finances were tight. Jacky Too taught me his language, which was no harder than English. We both spoke 'pigeon' English.

I asked, 'This place called Coorabell. What does it mean?'

Jacky Too stood on one leg, a foot on his knee. 'Home of the winds.' He made a whooshing noise.

I nodded. True, the winds did howl through the trees day and night, they twisted the boughs to lean and tangle into strange shapes. Though lonely, I felt newborn in this place. The air is fresh and clean, charged with energy and a potent life force.

Jacky Too trusted me for I gave him respect. He showed me sites that few white men knew; rock shelters and caves, ceremonial places and ochre paintings on cliff walls.

'Mind yourself when the rains come, Jacky,' Old Jimmy and Dan Withers warned. 'It's dangerous work following the logs down to the mouth of the river.' Though bullock teams carted logs out on rough tracks, it was quicker to shunt them down Wilson's Creek. We mounted logs by the creek bank and waited for a storm to turn the trickle into a current that would wash them to the port.

---

2 Brett J. Stubbs, 'The "Grasses" of the Big Scrub District. North-eastern New South Wales: their recent history, spatial distribution and origins", Australian Geographer, Vol. 32, No.3, pp.295-310, 2001.

'You tell a Finn about timber work?' I laughed. 'Back at home we shunt timber on the water. Water moves fast in spring with the melted snow.'

'In 1849 Terania Creek rose to forty feet in one night. Men have been caught in it, John Meanley and young Simes were drowned in a block.'

Forty feet? Thirteen metres? Surely an exaggeration.

For some weeks they told me we had loud thunder, but I slept so deeply I didn't hear it.

Then rains began to pour down. We sat by the campfire waiting for the creek to rise. Soon the flood came rushing and roaring downstream. We leaped to our feet to shove the logs into the flow, jumping into the chill water to ride them like horses, easing them past snags and blocks, clinging to vines and branches. I was too cocky or showing off Finnish *sisu* when I tackled a block of timber wedged tight into a heaving mass, hundreds of metres across.

Big Dan leapt in with his handspike to free the chock. The logs shot forward with a crack that jolted me down onto the mass of bucking timber. I was sucked under, my leg stuck between them. I remember little after that lightning strike of pain except that Anders grabbed me to safety.

'Hold on, KJ, I have you. Sanna will never forgive me if I lose you so soon in this country.' Then I blacked out.

Did I hallucinate? Or did Kerstin give me mouth to mouth resuscitation? I woke alone.

Recovery

I decided to abstain from hard work to some extent and try to improve my knowledge.
K.J. letter, 1 December 1913

When I came to, Big Dan and Anders had laid me on the bank. I gasped out water and vomit. As pain shot along my leg, Anders passed me a bottle of rum. Through a haze I heard them argue what to do with me. O'Meara hauled his bullock dray close and men hefted me onto it. The next jolting hours were a blur of pain.

'Where am I?' I muttered, little caring. Calico sheets reminded me of home after my rough blanket at camp.

'This is the hospital at Lismore—such as it is,' a voice said, 'and we must set your leg. It's broken in several places so will need time to heal.'

A nurse brought broth and after our camp damper and Johnnie cakes that was a treat. But a Swede misses *potatis*. I regained strength and called for books to read.

Letters awaited me at the post office, pleading for news. The doctor supplied pen and paper to write home, but I delayed. How could I describe my experiences in a way that would not make Mamma worry and Pappa write more lectures?

I fretted through weeks of inactivity. Would my boss O'Meara lay me off? He was a fair man and had called me a hard worker before the accident. But my leg would take weeks to heal; how could I eat, unless I worked? If only Pappa would send me more money I could buy my own land and not need to work for another person. Write I must.

Bangalow, 20 June 1900

To all of you at home, forever in my mind.

Now that I have time I will write to you. I left the hospital on the

16th. I hoped to move to the camp straight away, but O'Meara said that it is inappropriate, as I could not get over stumps. I have been here three weeks. After another three weeks I shall travel to the hospital again and let the doctor take the cast off. He will see if my leg is strong enough to walk on. It is not at all sore. I think I can start walking by the time you get this letter.

But I sighed as I put aside my pen; never mind my accident, Pappa would berate me for not making sufficient income, say that I must be independent and not call on him yet again. He would ask why I had leased land instead of buying it. After the drought everything looked dead but land was still very expensive. It cost up to £40 an acre and never less than £25 per acre. How to convince Pappa that I am capable of making a secure future in this land? He had no idea of the costs settlers face on a daily basis, to buy potatoes at such a price, or flour.

I hobbled through the next weeks, unable to work save odd jobs like sharpening tools. Another letter from home had worries and advice but no money enclosed. I used my time to write a longer letter about the climate in my new land.

When I first came to the south coast area of New South Wales I thought myself deceived in my expectations. It was winter so it did not surprise me to see the ground dead. But then it came spring and summer and with drought little grew. Now it is mid-winter here but we haven't had a frosty night. It has rained for more than a week. The sun is warm, the grass is green and everything reminds me of spring at home. Plants don't grow so fast as they do in a Finnish spring. It seems as if nature there has learnt that one must hurry or be late.

Pappa urged me to buy land as soon as possible. I had looked around this area, even up in Queensland, when I met with Matti Kurikka before he sailed for Vancouver.[3] His Utopian commune in Chillingham tempted me but was too far north and my leg not yet strong enough. I must use my money wisely, and feared losing all in some bungle. I reassured Pappa that

---

3 There is no evidence that a meeting took place. But on 17 October 1900 he wrote home: 'Send me a letter to Brisbane PO Queensland.' On 13 September 1900 Kurikka wrote to his daughter that he was 'now leaving Australia.' On 3 December 1900, KJ wrote 'I decided to buy a bit of land in Queensland even if I didn't like the soil there as much as other places but then found out that it rained more there.'

I sought information about many areas and prospects.

Here, some settlers tried to grow tea and even coffee, but this and sugar cane failed. Fruit trees grow abundantly. Cows live free out in the fields all year round. The Sanderson ladies churned butter at Myocum but they lost business to the Norco factory built in Byron Bay in 1895. My neighbour, Stan Robinson ran a carrier to take the separated milk and cream early each morning on his horse and spring cart. Dairy farming was profitable but I had no mind for these beasts.

Timber I knew best from Finland, where trees grow in abundance. Cow cockies milked day and night, with never a break. If ever they took longer for a picnic and returned late they heard complaints from cows mooing in distress. The smell of those beasts repelled me; their manure always a soggy mess, a magnet for flies. These insects were forever buzzing around and into mouths and eyes.

I wrote to reassure Mamma that my leg began to strengthen.

Bangalow, July 2, 1900

Although it has been a little bit frost, we have eleven months to plant, not like in Finland where it's so short a time to plant. If you want to sleep later in the morning, it is not like in Finland.

There are no poisonous or venomous flies here. We have a kind of fly like the ones at home just not as big. You may think that it is not hard that they don't bite but you would think otherwise when you've had hundreds of them on your face in your eyes, ears, mouth and nose. Lice are so rare here that I haven't seen one since leaving Finland. If one at times must sleep in a dirty bed there is no need to fear them. I remember that there were even wall lice in older houses. Rats and mice are rare.

Mosquitoes attacked at dusk and disturbed my sleep, so hungry that our faces and hands swelled. I thought I should have been accustomed by Finnish mosquitoes and elk fly. But no.

Often rain poured down the hillsides. Dirt tracks were full of rocks and potholes in the dry, but soon became torrents of mud and slush. We slithered along. So fast did these creeks become torrents, a carrier lost his wife when his horses and cart capsized into a deep water hole on Wilson's Creek. These carriers were good company in lonely times. They welcomed a jug of beer or mug of tea and yarn; they told all the latest gossip, like whose cattle were infested by ticks. The people hated the 'tick dodgers' that inspected animals and enforced the dipping to keep animals clear of infestation.

No, cows did not appeal to me, silly passive and needy beasts. I loved the clean smell of cedar newly hewn and damp rain on foliage of the forest. I worked at a logging camp deep in the forest with a team of men. Eventually I would make enough money to build and plant on my own land, to grow those wonderful fruits. I drew plans to build a sawmill as tall as these huge trees.

Battling the elements

Adversity acquaints us of the necessity of gathering sufficient strength for a future storm.
K. J. Back, *The Concentrated Wisdoms of Australia*

Even Pappa should be impressed by my industry, if he could see how I struggle to clear thick scrub from around the land I lease. By 1901 I planted bananas and corn on the sunny side of the hill that overlooks the sea and Byron Bay lighthouse.

Orange trees grow with such speed I will soon enjoy an abundance of fruit. Passionfruit vines run wild over my lean-to. My tent feels homely, with a kerosene lamp and my gun hanging from a nail in a nearby tree under sprays of orchids. My swag now lies on a straw-stuffed mattress. A canvas safe holds provisions, shotgun cartridges, wax matches and enamel plates. On a cedar bench are my cherished books, pens, paper, and ink bottle. A cake of Sunlight soap rids the rich red earth from my hands so it does not soil my writing paper. Life feels full of opportunity and hope. Often I can believe I live in freedom. And wish it for my family.

> I shall have my photo taken soon, but must postpone it for a few weeks while we have beautiful weather; I must follow the rain with planting. If it is impossible for you to lend me any money I plan to sell everything I can, lease the land and borrow the rest of the money from the bank. I wish not to share this with my brothers as it would be futile for us three to start with a hundred acres together but I am willing to do everything I can to make sure that they get a piece of land themselves.

> PS. This letter is badly written because I'm tired. I fall asleep as soon as I have had my supper; it's because I am up so early in the morning, sometimes about four o'clock.

Pappa cannot realise that, however hard I work, the elements are fierce in this country.

Perhaps I should have read the signs. But I am more used to scanning Finnish skies for snowstorms. No warnings could prepare me for this onslaught. First, the sun boils such heat that rivers of sweat course through my shirt. My fair skin is ruddy from working long hours in the open but today it flushes from heat so oppressive I feel faint. My thermometer reads thirty-eight degrees but I know the humidity is greater than normal. In past weeks brutal storms have lashed at my tent and lean-to outhouse. Already the land is slippery with mud.

The broiling sun makes me lethargic or perhaps, as Pappa often says, I am lax from dreaming. The skies so fascinate me that I spend an hour on my back propped against the slabs of iron forming the lean-to next to my tent. A towering eucalyptus tree filters the strongest rays. I marvel at the kaleidoscope as colours evolve from wisps into clumps of fluffy white with tinges of gold, to indigo and into the deeper purples and greys.

Growls of thunder wake me from a doze. It is like a menacing troll hidden behind the purple banks of louring cloud. They turn midnight blue-black and so thick that my Gibraltar-like mountain is blanked from my vision. Jagged shafts of lightning crack through a greenish haze. Never have I seen such lightning—it snakes and sparks across the sky and plunges headlong over Devil's Lookout.

The storm hits. A wild banshee screeching of wind howls up and down the gullies. It hurtles massive eucalypt trees and even cedars like skittles across the valleys. Felled tree trunks fling despairing spindles of roots heavenwards like imploring arms. Debris flies helter-skelter. The outhouse ricochets down the gully. Its roof flips over, light as a playing card, and lashes around a giant cedar tree.

Water buckets against my tent. The canvas flies in all directions and billows into a raging creek, lashed with waterfalls. But this is nothing compared to the loss of my irreplaceable treasures. My stomach lurches to see precious papers and books sink in a mudslide. I skid on my backside in a futile attempt to grasp them.

Logs spill down the hillsides in a tangle of matted branches and trunks. There is no hiding from the flying branches. I huddle into a corner of my lean-to where part of the roof still clings to two sides. This shelter proves meagre against the wall of rain pelting into my body.

An hour ago I had cursed the infernal heat, now my limbs jitter with the chill of hailstones big as a man's fist. They bounce onto the shelter and even off my head. I pull myself upright, dazed and unstable on my feet—from the rocking of the wind or concussion, I am not sure. Blanka my horse is somewhere out there in the mayhem. The blanket of rain eases to a surly curtain. I must face the elements to bring him to safe ground.

In the event it is Blanka who saves me. The torrent of water rages so strongly that it drowns other sounds. As the wind's wailing drops, I hear Blanka's frenzied neighs. They lead me towards the gully where he huddles. I miscalculate the danger. In my haste to reach him I slither down the mudslide of the hill, topple against a protruding tree root and somersault the last dozen feet to land on my ankle—that same leg already weakened by my earlier accident. There is no time to think of pain. All that lies between me and the sheer cliff of Devil's Lookout is a fallen log. I must crawl backwards from the precipice without starting further landslides. For a few moments I lose all my senses until a whinny and snort of hot air wakes me to consciousness.

Blanka, bless him, has wrenched free of his hobbles and stands while I clutch one leg to pull myself upright. I scramble onto his back. Teeth gritting against the pain, it takes several attempts. He needs little direction to head back up the hill, for all his rearing and skittish baulking at flying branches. The wind blows away my words.

Somehow we reach the lean-to, which rocks back and forth, yet two posts still remain. I tether Blanka to one, hoping it will not blow down the mountainside and take him with it. I collapse onto a sodden blanket. In a blur, hours or days pass in delirium. I wake aware of a change. The roaring tumult is still.

I rub my eyes. Have my nightmares festered into fever? Surely I imagined that Armageddon of trees flying around the mountain? Dragging myself onto weak knees, I wince at a shoot of agony that runs up my leg from my ankle. I grasp a joist, pull myself upright and peer around the side of the wall.

My heart plummets. All my efforts to build a home and farm are tossed into a mess of trunks and roots, crowned with soggy blankets of leaves. A few crushed orchid petals tangle with tree roots, mocking their luminous fragility. My books, newspapers, diaries and notebooks, my pens and inkpot, how could I find them in the sludge of mud?

Yet even in this travesty of the peace I crafted, nature revives. Beauty shines. Between the joists of my lean-to a spider bravely weaves back and forth, its web glistening in the sunlight.

My stomach growls, reminding me that my hanging larder lies at the bottom of the cliff. I hobble to find hay for Blanka then sit on a log to ponder my prospects. There is nothing left on Devil's Lookout. The horns of fire-blackened trees that give it this name mock me.

I hope Blanka has the wits to carry me safely to the township of Bangalow for I have little sense to guide him. A length of rope lies in a mud pool. I loop it around my waist, and knot it to his bridle.

'Lycka till, Blanka,' I mutter as we head in the direction of the settlement. The journey is a blur except when freezing water jolts me back to consciousness. Blanka ploughs through creeks now churned into raging rivers, the water froths over rocks into rapids. I arrive at Stan Robinson's door and slip from the saddle in a daze. My only awareness is of hands cramped from clinging to the mane through tortuous plodding. The claw shape of my fingers eases as Stan's missus puts a pannikin of tea into them. Its heat sends ripples of life into me. She sets before me a tin platter of bully beef and pumpkin, and I wolf some down so fast it burns through my frozen body. Yet I am too exhausted to eat much. I roll into a swag by their fire and sleep like a body in the cemetery.

Next day I fashion rough crutches from sticks. My leg is slow to mend and next week still keeps me hobbling. Stan shakes his head at my grumbles.

'You should see the doctor,' he says, offering to saddle Blanka to his sulky. A medic's services can be bought for some guineas, but I have few of them and urgent need to rebuild. For days I resist but the pain increases.

The stench of whisky on this doctor's breath is so strong I would have walked out if my leg allowed. I yelp like a dingo pup as he prods it. He wraps it in a plaster cast, tells me to rest and shoves out his grimy hand for my money. I wonder if my own crude splint of stick and rope might have sufficed. Unable to work, how long can I dally on these kind peoples' hospitality? My leg might take weeks to heal.

Stan supplies me pen and ink and paper to write a letter home. Somehow I must make light of problems, else Mamma will never consider coming to such a hazardous country. How can I describe my experiences in a way that will not set Pappa to telling me how I might have avoided such tribulations simply by building a stronger house?

Yet write I must. If only Pappa will send me more money I can buy my own land instead of leasing—and replace that tent with a cottage that will withstand the elements. Now, more than ever, I must persuade him to send money—and soon.

As for the money I have none in the bank and only an insignificant sum in my pocket. I spent almost all my money on the farmlands. It is my first priority to acquire some land of my own as soon as possible. If you could possibly lend me £200 I would be very happy.

PS. Please burn this letter.

Against the doctor's orders, I saddle Blanka to return to my land. I will begin again.

KJ the Settler

We have no seasonal extreme.
No vexing winters raw and wild;
But life is like a pleasant dream,
We live it like a smiling child.
Our country is, to young and old,
The home of happiness and health.
K.J. Back, *The Royal Toast*

Many months later I gaze over the valley. It has cost me much toil, for after clearing the storm damage, wild winds flung yet more destruction a week later. I wrestle with many setbacks. Yet in this warm climate ferns and delicate orchids grow lush. I replant bananas and oranges and look forward to the time soon when I can eat them straight from the trees. My potato patch thrives and corn grows tall in this rich earth. But how I long to grow Finnish trees! Much as I often write to ask for some seeds, still I wait.

> *Send me all kinds of trees and wine currant berry and gooseberry.*
> *You can put them inside a sheet so thin like a cigarette. Please post*
> *them as soon as possible to me.*

It is a hard life but I begin to live without furtive glances behind me. Mates accept me as a hard worker, though they laugh sometimes at my mistakes in speaking English. They see more good in me than my own father does.

I hitch Blanka to my neighbour's sulky. We hurtle licketty split down from Devil's Lookout to Bangalow, where I buy provisions and collect letters from home. These are full of judgments as harsh and mocking as the birds that laugh and ridicule from the treetops: jackasses and lorikeets.

I push Blanka so hard back up the ridge that the bandicoots and pademelons leap away from us, scared like we are trolls. The moon is just a sliver; my kerosene lantern sways, stabbing light through the gullies. Back in my hut I light a lantern and reach for the inkpot.

Coorabell Creek, 12 May 1901

I see from your letter that you are unhappy that I rented land in a clearing lease and did not buy it but this is because I took it more as a speculation. I can't see any danger in it because if I don't win anything in it I will not lose either.

You need to know that people are always willing to put the blame on others but on the other hand you have seen from my earliest childhood that I was very eager to leave home. If you had only given your consent I'm sure that I would have left many years earlier. In that case I would have had at least ten times more than I have now, even if I didn't get a thing from home. I might be a rich man today.

Laying aside my pen, I sigh. Letters hurt but it is a relief to have escaped Pappa's daily censure. His standards reach as high as heaven. I can never match them. Even at this distance he tells me what to do and judges my failings, with no idea of the hardships I have to surmount. He always expects more of me than I can give.

On whichever side of the world I stand, Pappa still finds me worthless however hard I work. He does not comprehend the complexities of making a new life in a land he could never envisage. He knows nothing of the terrain, of lashing tempests that inflict havoc. Of the bush I must clear in order to fashion a living, in spite of misgivings about future land erosion.

Here nothing is left as forest except some trees for animals. Often great housekeeping blunders are current. Many settlers buy coals for heating instead of using the cleared timber. Some claim that it will become dry here in the future as the forests are cleared.

The idea that felling forests changes the climate for worse is here so general that they sent a petition to the parliament and wanted a law made that all farmers must have at least some forest on their farm. The parliament asked the advice of an Astronomer. He just laughed at them. He argued that it is only temporary and that nature would come to order every now and then. He reminded them of old Egypt and how although it was dry sometimes for many years it got back to normal afterwards. It is possible to have drought next year but it is just as possible that it lasts for ten or twenty. Man does not know what will happen but our God no doubt has his pests for every area.

Pappa advises on what he cannot understand. My own father knows me so little—and thinks so inflexibly of me. It is easy to criticise, with a cocoon of family around him.

Does he not realise how I hack through the gargantuan forest? I chop cedars as wide as houses and shoot them down the hill. Soon I have established my own team of cutters who slit and peel back the bark, kick the timber out of its shell and send it off to thunder down the mountainside to the coast. I manage as best I can, alone in a strange and huge new land, in my makeshift shelter. As raucous jackasses and catbirds scoff at me, I long for the comforting soft calls of lark, cuckoo and nightingale. Sighing, I pick up my pen again.

When it comes to my house I don't know if I should say I have it or not. A few weeks ago there was a storm that broke my old tent. I tried to hold it together as well as I could. When the storm mellowed down a bit I thought it time to run. I had to go over a little creek where there normally is only a little water. It was so full that I could barely pass over it. The water rose fast, and everything got wet.

Now I have decided to build a hut but it's hard to believe that can be so expensive. I bought iron sheets for a roof for twelve shillings and it took me a whole day and many hours to build. My house is eight feet on one side and nine on the other. The roof rests on four posts. Walls are made of old bags, which are little by little being covered with short saplings, which I cut and carve with an axe. I won't build a better house because we have eternal summer and I could not get the money back that it would take to build.

At night as I fall into my swag, my body aches from hefting massive logs and dodging those that might crush me unless I move quick-smart. New words rattle helter-skelter through my exhausted brain. Yet my legs jerk and tangle in my swag. Sleep is restless. I am alone in a forest with crackling noises as strange animals run up and down trees. Dingo howls lift the hairs from my neck.

Especially I miss those feather-light caresses of that angel Kerstin who loved me. Questions tease me through restless nights: does Matti Kurikka lure her to his Queensland utopian commune at Chillagoe with his fiery dark eyes and claims to rebuild *Kalevala* in the Antipodes? Has she already discovered that this leader woos other women with his ideals? As dawn breaks into chill reality I huddle into my blanket; they were but dreams that Kerstin joined me in my shack.

At times I wish myself back in the familiar bustle of life in a village. There everyone's nose is stuck into their neighbours' lives. Marriages and business affairs so interweave families that no one can keep his thoughts to himself. Tiny plots of land like pocket-handkerchiefs are allocated to each parishioner for hay or potatoes or corn or cows.

When I was there I longed to be alone, away from intrusions. I dreamed of my own land, far from other peoples. On board ship, there was no space for privacy—not even in sleep.

Now, in my wide expanse of virgin forest, it is a lonely life, far from family intrusions. I find myself loose in this enormous continent.

Do I regret that I attained my dream of freedom?

Loneliness

However fate may cast our lot
A land, a homeland, we have got.
Johan Ludvig Runeberg, *Our Land*

Knots of trees twist and interlock and twine around each other in their efforts to reach higher. So much they crave the sun's blessing—as I had done in Finland. My private space spreads so far that I seek companionship by talking with the trees—nature shows more sense than humans—and the possums that frolic along their boughs. They twitch and peep at me, their inquisitive pointy noses remind me of neighbours back in Munsala. I name these creatures after them: Katarina and Kajsa and Brita. Small wallabies called pademelons are my friends. I share corn bread with them.

At nights I doze, jolting often when the wind throws tantrums around my shack. My flimsy canvas walls billow and heave, giving scant protection from dingoes that forage for food. Their malevolent eyes fix on my canvas safe nailed to a tree and I shiver at their howls. I track a mocking cat sound to a bird.

I dream of Kerstin's breath warming my cheek, long for her warm arms around me. Should I send my savings for her passage? But how would a woman survive in this rough life? Was she serious about joining Matti Kurikka's Utopian community?

I tell myself that her arms would cling like the strangler vines that encircle trees and engorge their trunks until they are empty shells. She has not written to me, she has surely forgotten me.

Pappa's letter tells that Wilhelm is going to school and intends to study to become a priest. But I will entreat my brother to join me here. Why would a student of the church not be called to the Russian army? The Queensland government seeks workers and offers free tickets. Wilhelm can bring a friend and they might work there together for a year; I know places where they could get a job staying with good people.

So I write to Wilhelm:

> It would be wise to come here immediately, still in your youth to learn the language and customs. It's stupid to stay in Finland; the longer you stay the harder it will be to move which you will have to do sooner or later. If you don't you will become a slave. Try to mention this to Pappa.
>
> If you so want I will write to the Queensland government for a free ticket and send it to you. You just buy a ticket to England where you pay £1 for bedding that you can take with you in the boat. This way will be about £14 cheaper. Don't worry about hard work; we use oxen to do the heaviest jobs. I will end my writing with lots of greetings to you.
>
> PS. Destroy this letter as soon as you read it. Don't tell anybody about it.

Yet Wilhelm is young, he cannot think beyond his life in Finland. While I struggle, he has the nerve to ask my assistance to buy a bicycle, of all things! My answer is blunt.

Coorabell Creek, 23rd July 1901

My brother, always on my mind, be well!

It is impossible for me to send you any money. Even if I could afford it, I wouldn't since my father is against it. It would hurt him terribly. The summer in Finland is so short that a bicycle is unnecessary.

Don't think that I would begrudge you a bicycle, because I would not. If our father would write and ask for money on your behalf then I would send some, even if I would have to go and work for others to afford it. When you get here, and learn to think ahead, we will be able to help one another in our strivings, and try to live as brothers.

Loneliness tears at my innards. I play Finnish melodies on my mouth organ to fend off the silence. Alone on my mountain, I think I am hallucinating when I hear them repeated, followed by the sounds of a saw and then a didgeridoo.

It cannot be Jacky Too or his tribe for they have gone walkabout. The grasses that they cultivate on the ridge behind my hut are all eaten.

For days I puzzle over this strange Finnish echo until I discover the tease is a lyrebird nesting on the hill nearby. Albert, as I call him, is hungry for new sounds to mimic. Soon he bids me *'God dag'* clear enough to fool me I have a visitor. He sings *'Our land, our land, our fatherland'* with a fine accent. I train him to compete with the crow caws that startle me out of nightmares at the break of dawn. The cuckoo call is quickly mastered and he even copies my laughter at his version of nightingale song.

Such sport wanes and gives way to worry when my beloved horse Blanka—that cost so much of the money Pappa loaned—develops a limp. It spreads from his front legs to all four limbs over a period of just a few weeks.

He slid into a pademelon hole on one of our wild scrambles down Devil's Lookout at night, a lantern swinging from the sulky. Between Goonengerry and Wilson's Creek the bullocky tracks over the range are so steep that even a bush wallaby might sprain an ankle. A cedar limb bounces behind as a brake. Blanka enjoys these escapades as much as I do and needs little urging. Yet one black night he stumbles and never regains his balance or strength.

My foolhardiness caused his fall. I apply poultices to his leg but the swelling spreads to his hind legs. He winces and neighs when I attempt to feel it, snorts, froths and pulls away from my touch. It hurts me as much as it agonises him—Blanka, my dearest friend in all this country.

Yet to maintain his life is self-indulgence. My head tells me this even as I wrestle with the urge to prolong his friendship. He is all I have to love in this great land and endless forest. He possesses as fine a feeling as any human being. I swear he reads my mind. Always before I lift the bridle from the hitching post he knows from my purposeful tread that I intend a ride. Wherever we go, he sets his nose homeward even before my hands pull the reins.

Alone on that mountaintop, I must take my rifle and shoot a bullet straight between his eyes. I see his resignation as I lift my gun.

~

The trees hush and sigh with my loneliness through misery-filled days. I long for a friend to share my sadness. Anders, my only kin, often travels far afield on projects. Jacky Too returns from walkabout, yet communication is too basic. I cannot tell him about my loss and be understood. How I miss Blanka's quiet acceptance.

I search in Lismore's auction yards for another horse. My eyes find only white-coloured beasts, of similar size. And what do I do? Do I not know well the expectation it spells for man or beast to replicate a name?

So my instincts cry against such a move. Yet I name my new steed Blanka, imprinting on him all my expectations and hopes for friendship. Just as surely I sing through a cracked voice, 'Rida, rida Ranka, Hasten heter Blanka'—'Ride, ride, horse called Blanka'—until he responds, knows this to be his song. His whinny at night outside the hut comforts me.

Evenings are lonely except for the apparitions that chase through my mind, grasping my throat and wrestling me to the ground. I carve another soul-bird figure from cedar to protect me when I am vulnerable in sleep. Yet even that taunts me. I huddle deeper into my swag but the terrors follow me there.

Once when Anders stays in my shack, he pulls me awake from such a phantasm. 'KJ, calm yourself, you are safe here.'

Bleary, I clench my fists. Anders holds me at bay.

'Leave me be,' I cry, writhing from his hands. 'You cannot take me, I will jump in the ocean and take my chances with the Arabs.'

'There is no danger here, KJ. Wake up!'

As my mind and eyes come to focus, I see his kindly face and the dreams fade. Anders boils a billy and brings a pannikin of tea to me as I huddle under my blanket.

'These terrors came with you to your new land,' Anders says, 'but you are safe here. You do not need to hide in that treehouse. Yes, you think it well hidden but I saw you scuttle up there when the tick inspectors visited. But would Russians still follow you to the end of the world, to a mountain top forest?'

My sleeping mind does not know sense or distance. But I must guard my hard-won freedom.

The vision still hovers. I long for the comfort of that angel Kerstin who loved me.

The Lighthouse

I throw my eyes across the sea,
I watch and wait, I think of thee.
I think of thee as mine,
My heart is wrapped in thine.
K. J. Back, *The Concentrated Wisdoms of Australia*

Always the ocean has soothed me; each afternoon, my walk down the ridge to Byron Bay is a rebirth. This is the most easterly point that Pappa pointed to on the maps that sailor Erik brought from Australia.

The Pacific Ocean is not peaceful at all. The name is nonsense. Foam pounds rocks into a constant froth of white, roars day and night. Restless water surges back and forth, unlike the Gulf of Bothnia, still in summer and frozen solid in winter. Goats leap across rocky outcrops, mindless that the ocean dashes into froth below. The sea whips spume, the wind bends trees over like frail grandfathers.

When I think of eternity I see this ocean, always seething, always bringing yet more waves to shore. It teems with abundance, fish of all brilliant colours, sea snakes, turtles and dolphins. Whales breech and flip their tails in sheer delight. Sandpipers strut their spindly legs along the shoreline. They feast on crustaceans that will sustain them for the long flight back to the Arctic. Their instincts draw them back to coasts I will never see again.

Perched high on the promontory is the new lighthouse. I have watched it to completion. Now it reaches new-born silver arms out to my vantage point at Coorabell and enfolds me in pulsing arcs. Its beams ease the bleakness of keening winds that howl around my ridge. The great heartbeat comforts me that I am not alone in this southland; a lighthouse keeper tends the glow to protect and bring solace to sailors—and myself.

I will never again see Northern Lights that sweep across Finnish skies.

But here every night this radiance cheers my lonely existence as I remember my family at the other end of the world. Do they spare a thought for me?

Family—that would warm my heart. Imagine, sharing these experiences with one of my own blood! I urge Wilhelm to join me before Russians ensnare him.

> *Please burn this letter after you read it. It was sad to read from your letter that your land had frozen. It would be best if you all come here as soon as possible. You wish that I tell you whether it was smart or not to come. I do not regret anything even though I made some mistakes and have done some foolish things. One would think that it is cheap to live in Finland but that is not the case, there are very few countries in the world where you get so little from your work and few so expensive. Don't worry about the trip; you should be able to make it on your own.*

Letters crisscross the world as plans progress. Mamma worries it is too dangerous for such a young lad to travel across the world, even with friends. Pappa decides to escort Wilhelm to safety.

Anders Hopes

Väinämöinen, old and steadfast
Now resolved upon a journey...
Kalevala

Anders Back sits on the ship deck, a large hat protecting his fair skin. He pulls from his pocket several letters from his eldest son. He frowns as he reads of the mixed fortunes that have befallen him. A year ago KJ wrote that his crops would not bring income:

> *It has been six months since I last earned anything. It will be another year before I expect to get something from the fields. My hay harvest didn't turn out good so I had to lease 90 acres of cattle grazing land and got £90 for four months. Grass seeds cost me £50 last year but it was profitable because I got a higher return for four months' lease compared with what anyone else got in twelve months around here.*

Soon Anders will arrive and be able to sort out his son's business. First the voyage allows some relaxing after the hectic months at home, fighting against the crop failures to save every last ear of grain. Thomas Cook and Son booked him a passage on this fine ship, *Ophir*. To leave the family in Finland and travel across the world gave him many concerns. He had rushed to finish the late autumn haymaking, always looking behind in case any Russian officials wised up to his plans. It was imperative to leave as soon as possible after Wilhelm's birthday on July 29. They slept little, planting potatoes and shearing sheep. He could not have left this heavy work for seven–year–old Edvard and three women.

Wilhelm soaks up advices as if they were ink into blotting paper. His eyes fix on the horizon as he paces the deck, pulling his ear in that habit he has developed while thinking. Anders has great hopes for his future, for all that he's so young. Not like Karl Johan. And he travels with his friends Mats and Otto, they will support each other.

But Anders must not dwell on the past or the grief and anger his eldest son brought; after all, he was merely a lad at the time of the accident. If only he had been less preoccupied. Is KJ still such a dreamer?

Anders shakes these thoughts aside; he must block memories of those dark days or anger will sully their first meeting. He realises that when he shakes his eldest son's hand—no, he will embrace him, even—he will see an adult, not a fifteen–year–old boy. This is a fresh start for a relationship. They will speak man to man, and ease the pain of that dark time. Anger will be left behind at the other end of the world.

Karl Johan writes that he seeks to purchase good farmland and forests. Three years is enough time to build a worthwhile farm. The patch of land that he leased gave him a good yield of corn, over £500 the first twelve months so 'I got 250% on the money that I supposedly spent in vain.' Anders compresses his lips.

> *I had to work hard but it turned out to be very profitable. When I cultivated two hundred and twenty–one acres at once their faces changed and many say that I will earn more than £1000 the coming year. If I can work for money to buy seed I will plant the biggest and best in all this area, close to three times as much as I had this year.*

He wrote helpful advices about funds for the journey, suggesting that in case no banks in Finland could exchange for Australian currency, they should first go to England. There they could put money in an account at the Bank of New South Wales.

Karl Johan sounds as if he may have matured. He refused Wilhelm money for a bicycle (the boy was but fourteen years of age). This promises well for improved relations during the visit. Almost Anders wishes he had not booked such a speedy return passage, for it would gladden his heart to develop a deeper communication with his eldest son. Who knows if the good Lord will grant him another chance in this life?

KJ will encourage Wilhelm in his settling. As adults the nine–years age difference might be less of an issue, if Wilhelm resists telling Karl Johan how to improve his farm. Isolation will bring them closer together in a unity that will reap prosperity.

Many times Anders feels God has revealed such promises as he thumbed his Bible while sitting on the bench by the church, near the wood carved *Fattigubba*. The Poor Man reminds that our blessings come from above. Yes, we work hard for our profits, but the Lord provides for our needs. When larrikins, fuelled on brännvin, thrust bottles under his nose and laugh, 'Hej, Anders, you know it says in *Ecclesiastes* to eat and drink and be merry?' he ignores them. He reads aloud from the book of *Proverbs* that 'strong drink leads to poverty'. They tire of their jests and stagger away to sleep off their headaches under a haystack.

He is grateful KJ missed the worst of Bobrikov's Russification in 1902 and 1903. Thankful to God that he was able to take Wilhelm away before things worsened. The lad was more circumspect than his older brother, always willing to do Anders' bidding. No mixing with radicals. No shameful *congerichuchins*. Wilhelm followed in his father's footsteps, even thought to become a priest. He shared an inclination for a life devoted to the Almighty. Anders longed to preach the gospel, not sweep the church; to give the bread and wine direct to the communicants rather than prepare it onto platters and into the chalice.

Often as he walked up the hill to the church past the wood carved statue of the poor man, Fattigubba, Anders had thanked the Lord that his enterprises, farms and crops provided funds to support the family. As he entered the grey granite church dominating the village, he praised God for the opportunity to serve in such a place decorated by the fine wooden sculpture of Bishop Henrik. While dusting the organ, he ran fingers across its keys and imagined playing Lutheran chorales to lift voices high into the white–washed ceiling. The organ, built in 1736 by Ericus German, is the oldest and finest in use in the country.

Now with time to walk together on the ship deck, Anders broached his concern about Karl Johan's antipathy for Christian faith. 'Try to persuade Karl Johan to attend a church sometimes, so he may be challenged to think of heavenly matters.'

Wilhelm is wise for his years. 'KJ had reason to lose respect for the church.'

'Why would that be? I blame his humanistic philosophy. Your mother and I raised our sons to fear God. "Work out your salvation, in fear and trembling" as St Paul said. With my example as churchwarden, why does he turn away with such a haughty attitude?'

Wilhelm shakes his head. 'It is not so simple, Pappa.'

'Reason with him, son. I dread that a son of mine should suffer hell–fire.'

Wilhelm arrives in Australia

Dearest friend and much–loved brother…
Let us now begin our converse,
Since at length we meet together,
From two widely sundered regions.
Kalevala

The *SS Ophir* sailed into Sydney town on 17th January 1903. Very grand the harbour was, a little like Finland with so many inlets and islands. Its blue green water shimmered in sunlight so hot that it burned Wilhelm's skin.

Anders calculated the best use of his *markka*. The captain assisted to change the money into Australian pounds and check swindlers didn't take advantage of their limited English to line their own pockets. He sent a telegraph to KJ notifying him of their passage north to Byron Bay on a coastal ship to Lismore on the Richmond River. A railway line, operating since 1896, would bring them to Bangalow, near to Coorabell where KJ had his clearing lease.

Sydney town had many Victorian–style buildings like England. It was rough compared with Helsinki or even Vaasa, though St Mary's Cathedral had the grace of European cities. Trams and steam trains carried people and produce from town to town.

Tweed vests and coats prickled in sweat. They flinched from the smell and sanitation of small outhouses. A guesthouse proved to be of a reasonable standard and the travellers looked around Sydney town. They spent an evening at the theatre, baffled with their limited language. But they sensed the excitement of the Commonwealth of Australia, proclaimed in January 1901.

Anders tried to understand how this federation of six sovereign states grappled for supremacy, as arguments ensued about where to site a government house. Isolation gave some protection but also the land needed defence from invasion—look how Russia had treated Finland. Since the

133

British imperial troops left Australia in 1872, the new federation should create a unified defence scheme.

At last both sons were safe in the Promised Land. Karl Johan was twenty–two when he arrived in Australia. But even though Wilhelm was only sixteen, he could follow in his brother's path, like on a ski track. It would make it easier to avoid stumbles. And he came with friends, on a good ship, the bestest ship, like a big holiday at sea. They were well rested for any rigours they might encounter in northern New South Wales.

The train from Lismore slowed into Bangalow station. Wilhelm could see Karl Johan beyond the platform. He was waving his hat and dancing in a sulky—his horse frisked. He threw the reins over a hitching post and ran to pull open the compartment door. '*Välkommen till Australien!*' His smile faded to a frown. 'Where the blazes will we put all this luggage?'

Anders swept an arm at the green hills and pronounced: 'This is surely the Promised Land. May de good Lord grant some of dis to my descendants.'

But a new land needed tools and equipment. Wilhelm, Mats and Otto made a chain to offload the luggage before the train departed. They tossed portmanteaux from the carriage onto the sulky. It was soon crammed full. There was no room for the boys.

Pappa nodded that KJ put his money to good use in a horse and sulky.

'I borrowed the sulky from a neighbour, Mr Newberry, he has been most helpful,' KJ replied. 'But the horse Blanka is mine. You boys can walk.'

'How far is it? How will we know where to go?' Wilhelm asked. Now he found a brother after three years, he must not lose him in this strange country. Or himself.

'Ten kilometres, straight up St Helena Ridge.' KJ pointed. He helped Pappa up onto the sulky. 'Follow that straight clearing up the hillside, called Possum Shoot.'

'Shoot? Soldiers here?'

KJ laughed at him. 'That means logs are shot down the mountain. Do not walk on the wide track or logs will crush you. They weigh tonnes. They fall down so fast you have no chance to jump aside. Stay on the path. I'll meet you at the top.'

'But what is this possum?'

'It is a small animal that leaps in trees at night.'

Pappa waved his hat to make some breeze; he sweated in his big fur coat as if he were in a sauna. Wilhelm had tried to persuade him to take it off on the trip up, but to no avail. KJ had no better luck: 'You will cook in that, Pappa. I know honest people, where we could leave your coat until the winter.'

'But I must return to Finland in two weeks.' Anders shook his head. 'At least it will keep out the mosquitoes,' he shrugged, 'they even worse than a Finnish summer.'

'So soon, Pappa?' Wilhelm quivered.

'You know I must return for the spring planting.'

KJ led the way along the 'main' street—there was no other—past a general store.

'Wait, Karl Johan,' Anders ordered. 'Do you have hens? First we buy some so my boys have eggs and flesh to eat.'

'No, Pappa, for I have no fowl run. Should they sleep with us, or out in the forest where snakes and dingoes eat them?' Only a half hour had gone by and already they were arguing. Pappa would insist on his way. He jumped from the sulky and pushed open the slab door of the store.

Eyes popped. The woman behind the counter cackled. 'Strewth! Look what just blew in here. A bear. I reckon I could use a bit of that coat round me shoulders come winter!'

Anders ignored her, pointed to the fattest hens and held out a fist full of notes for the man to take from his hand.

KJ frowned. 'You must learn English, and the currency. You have been several days in this land.'

Anders scowled. But Wilhelm knew KJ was right. He spoke easily to the locals in English, and slower like people here. He knew which v's should be w in words.

The boys tramped up a mountain each with a squawking 'chook' struggling in its sugar bag. They pecked through the jute. Wilhelm stumbled over rutted tracks steep as ski runs. Raucous birds laughed and made nightmarish whipping noises. A call like 'Cooee!' guided the boys to a clearing in the forest where KJ and Pappa stood facing each other off as if they'd been fighting.

To divert them Wilhelm pointed to a tree. 'Look at the bear, Pappa.' It was not fierce, ignored the pebbles they threw to wake it.

'Bear?' he said. 'The book told of kangaroos that leap but that there are no dangerous bears and wolves.'

He muttered to himself. 'How can I leave Wilhelm in this wild place, with strange animals and birds that laugh and screech at us? Do natives with spears hide behind the trees?'

'This bear is sleeping,' Wilhelm said. 'KJ, if you start a sawmill you will make a fine business; many people need to build houses in this new country, so much land for settling. Shipyards pay much money for this strong timber.'

'Wilhelm, I know this country,' he grumped, 'I been here three years, you don't tell me how to make it work. And I am nine years older.'

It was time to keep quiet. For the moment. Wilhelm stumbled when a fierce large scaly lizard reared up from the ground and threatened. He shivered at a howling sound. His blisters ached. 'How far is your house?' he asked, impatient of so much forest.

KJ pointed up the hill as he tethered the horse.

After an age KJ said, 'Here we are, you can rest.' A bird cackled.

'Rest?' Wilhelm repeated, staring. All around were trees, that smelled tangy.

Pappa's eyebrows beetled down towards his nose as he stared at KJ. 'Where is this house you have built with the monies I sent, son?'

The Snake

A simple hut may be considered a happy home if love and sympathy unite all the members of the family.
K. J. Back, *The Concentrated Wisdoms of Australia*

KJ pointed to a hollow tree he called 'black butt'. He pulled open a rough iron door slotted into it. Inside was a space barely bigger than the privy at home. Over the top was fashioned a corrugated iron roof of sorts; a bucket underneath to catch rain. He saw their blank faces and boasted, 'Fresh rain water right to my house, I don't carry buckets from the creek.' He straightened. 'Home, sweet home. And in a storm it keeps as dry as any fancy house.'

Pappa's mouth sagged open, so flies buzzed in and out. Wilhelm thought perhaps it was a joke. Did KJ suggest they sleep in a tree? With spiders inside?

'This gives as good a shelter as anyone could wish. I don't know where we shall fit all these ports,' KJ muttered, 'but stack them in the corner as best you can.' He took Pappa's big coat and hung it on a rusty nail.

Leeches fell off dead from Pappa's arms. He pulled up a trouser leg. Ugly black creatures clung to his legs.

'Leave them, Pappa,' KJ advised. 'We will remove the leeches with kerosene.'

Mosquitoes were huge and attacked in swarms, but leeches were worse. KJ wrote untrue that insects were not problems here!

Pappa was quiet, too quiet. His neck turned red like when he was about to roar at sons for a transgression. He swallowed and breathed deep. 'So this is all you have to show for the money we sent you from home, did you fritter that away?'

'Pappa, living costs are so expensive; everything must be imported, hauled long distances by bullock dray or steamer. I needed money to buy tools and grain to plant.'

'You have been three years in this land and this is the best you can show for it?'

'Remember, I wrote that storms damaged my first huts, it costs much to rebuild.'

Pappa glared at the newspapers and books stashed around the floor, under the table, beside his bedroll. He clenched and unclenched his fist.

'You put my hard–earned money to buy those books, didn't you? To import them cost many markka, yes?'

'Pappa, I used money from my corn crop to buy books. A man must feed his mind as well as his belly. You have said that. And newspapers—imagine how it is living at the other side of the world, and worrying how you suffer under Bobrikov? The Scandinavian Sailors Mission sends me papers to keep apace with the world.'

KJ nodded towards Wilhelm who bit the inside of his mouth. 'And I read English books. You must learn the language if you are to get ahead in this country, Wilhelm.'

He shrugged. 'Whatever I speak, I will become rich—with my wits and hard work.'

'You must establish your future,' Pappa roared at KJ, 'before you fritter away *my* money on books and newspapers. Many times you wrote asking for more money to buy nails and timber; do you not realise what a sacrifice it cost me to send?'

'Pappa, you are tired from the journey. We have shelter and soon we will have full bellies. Wilhelm, help me light a fire and boil the billy. We have bully beef—save the tin for your cup, I only have two—and also I shot some meat of the Wonga pigeon. All will look better by light of day.' A water bag and meat safe swung from nails. He lit a fire and poured water from a hanging canvas bag into the kettle that he called billy.

'Just like me? Australian people call me Billy,' Wilhelm said.

KJ laughed. While the water heated, he showed his notebook where he was writing in Australian words, whole pages of them. He threw in a fistful of tealeaves, unthreaded the billy and swirled it above his head. The boys scrambled away. KJ swaggered like a magician performing tricks for their welcome. Even Pappa's long face loosened.

Dusk fell quickly. The newcomers were glad to drink hot tea and cornbread tasted good though Wonga meat was tough to chew.

KJ said, 'Eat it all, tomorrow we shoot more, also scrub turkey.' He pointed to birds with funny long wrinkled necks that poked through the bushes for scraps. They snatched the bread from hands and looked fierce.

Wilhelm was thoughtful. 'KJ, they might eat our fowls?'

He laughed and shook his head. Mats and Otto agreed the hens were safer inside the 'humpy'. They would not stay in a corner, with planks, hessian bags and a branch for nesting. They escaped to forage in the food.

Pappa set his tin pannikin aside and started again: 'But you wrote how you made good profit planting maize on the steep hillside near that Chincogan hill—'

'Yes, in a dry season when others said there was no hope of a good harvest and I confounded them by reaping a bumper crop—'

'—What happened to all my money?' Pappa banged the table so it fell.

Karl Johan shuffled his feet. 'The next season I planted double, and the crop failed. So I had no income at all from that season.'

Mats propped the table upright again.

'You lost all your income? Worse, mine?' Pappa's face turned from pink to red.

'Yes… But this country is a cruel one for seasons, there is no telling how much rain will fall or whether droughts will shrivel all the crops. It's not predictable like in Finland where seasons are ordered. I am still learning to understand this land, the soil, the crops, what grows and what won't.'

Wilhelm was attentive as KJ outlined the world demand for corn and insisted he would become very rich because he planted more acres than other pioneers.

But he lost interest when KJ pointed to the flora. 'See, these orchids thrive, and so easy.'

In the moonlight they shone with bright colours. Pappa sniffed.

KJ fidgeted with his tin cup, started to ask a question, then turned aside to stir the pot. 'What is news of the village?'

Otto described their sister Anna Sanna's marriage to his brother Erik Johan. Wilhelm lowered his voice to whisper about how badly their sister Sofia was treated by that merchant from Vaasa. All Ostrobothnia knew that he was a lady's man. Sofia tossed her head in the air and did not heed.

KJ stoked the fire so hard that sparks flew everywhere.

'What of others in the village,' KJ asked, 'have there been more babies born in the village, these past years?' He bit his fingernails.

Wilhelm said: 'Kerstin Matsdotter—you remember her? She had two babies, a little girl then a boy—'

'—Two illegitimate brats and to two different fathers,' interrupted Pappa.

'Did she say who the fathers were?' KJ's frown was as black as a storm cloud.

'She shut her mouth about the first one. Now that next man, Lars, went to the mines in South Africa.'

'So, she was abandoned again, poor woman.' KJ prodded the fire so it roared.

Otto poured more bully beef pannikins of tea. Pappa brought out a bundle of letters. KJ laughed to read Edvard's childish hand, but nodded at his efforts. He saved till last a letter from Kerstin. When Pappa snored and the other boys dozed by the fire he asked Wilhelm questions about her. But he could only shrug, for she lived now in Vaasa. KJ smoked his pipe and stared into the flames. Wilhelm wondered why she left with barely a farewell. KJ roused and smashed his fist on the table, setting the pannikins clattering.

'She hid away, she left without so much as a word. Yes, she thinks it was her fault and carries the stain of guilt. I would have helped her, would have sent her money for the voyage and taken in her children too. But she was stubborn, too proud.'

Mats lifted his head. 'That howling noise, is it wolves, here in Australia?'

But KJ didn't answer, just shoved his letter into his jerkin pocket and muttered that he must tend his horse. Hooves thundered as he rode off into the forest.

Pappa roused from his snores to wonder where they might lay blankets to sleep. It was cramped with books lined up against the walls. They feared to go outside in the dark to relieve themselves as the howling grew closer. They sat in a tree far from other peoples. Weary to the bone all curled up near the fire, elbows digging into ribs.

They jumped upright as hens squawked. Feathers flew all around. The fowls flapped around the shack.

'Light the lamp, Wilhelm,' ordered Pappa, pulling on his trousers.

'But I don't know where KJ keeps kerosene.' As he groped around his hand touched something thick and scaly. Wilhelm stumbled on ropes that crawled around his legs. Terror choked his breath. He leapt away, knocking over the stool. For all Wilhelm's sixteen years he screamed shrill like a girl. Righting the stool Otto jumped on top of it. Mats prodded light from the lamp. A huge snake—just like the sailors warned of—had its wide mouth open around a hen. He swallowed it down. Bulges along its scaled body was another fowl.

'Chase it out the door,' cried Pappa, grabbing the tongs. The boys threw books so pages flew like hen feathers. They prodded it with a stick but kept wide distance. It slithered away crackling over twigs.

Wilhelm peered around the door; a thin moon skittered dark shadows all around. 'It's climbing up that tree, all coiled around,' he squeaked.

He slammed shut the door and pushed the table against it. All huddled under their blankets but kept open eyes. When birdcalls told that dawn neared they heard horse hooves. As KJ punched the door open, the stools keeping it shut flew backwards.

Wilhelm clutched at his feet so he stumbled and cursed. They rushed outside to relieve ourselves.

'You were too afraid to go out?' KJ scoffed as boys lined against a tree, all pissing.

'Outside we heard howls like wolves. We saw mangy dogs with mean eyes.'

'There are no wolves here. Those are dingoes, aboriginal dogs what run wild. They may take my hens, but *you* are too big for them.'

It came out in a rush. 'But the snake *has* eaten the hens. It would bite us also?'

Wilhelm had never seen Pappa fearful, even when he stared down that bear in the barn. Anders muttered 'This is a wild country. Soon as my sons are settled with land, I go home to Finland.'

Anders Back Returns, 1903

Your heaven cannot exceed the size of your heart.
K. J. Back, *The Concentrated Wisdoms of Australia*

Anders Back stayed only two weeks in Australia, according to our oldest relative. My father's cousin, Wally Holm, was born in Finland in 1914 and migrated as a boy of six with his parents, Anna Sanna and Erik Johan Holm and four siblings. His mind and memory were sharp; he told that my great–grandfather Anders bought three blocks of land for his sons then caught the same ship back to Europe.

But did he? My eyes are red from a day's straining over microfiche screens in the state archives at The Rocks, Sydney. A printout of the passenger lists for *SS Ophir*'s voyage to Australia shows two lads accompanied Anders and Wilhelm, not six as Wally said. But such is the stuff of stories passed down family lines. The return voyage eludes me; there is no Anders Back listed for *SS Ophir*'s next two journeys homewards. On 6th March a 'Mr Bock' sailed on *SS Wyandra*, possibly it was misspelled? The Finnish parish records show that he received communion on the twenty–first of May in his home church.

As I plod through three months' shipping lists an inner voice rebels. This is a waste of time: perhaps Anders sailed to Europe from the closer Brisbane port? Does it matter when he sailed and from where?

At the end of a microfiche reel, I stretch my aching neck and shoulders. I decide to visit the Mitchell Library to see if I can discover any response to KJ's challenge in literature. At Circular Quay, I imagine the steam ships departing in 1903. How did Anders Back feel to leave his two sons in this strange land?

Anders was deflated on the return journey to Finland, his feelings the polar opposite to great hopes on the voyage south. Then Wilhelm and the lads had rollicked about, rivals at the deck games. They had chattered of their wins, insisting that he join in also. They demolished strange food with enthusiasm.

This voyage was more reflective. There were few Scandinavians with whom he could converse and his halting efforts at English frustrated others and himself. He had no taste for the frivolity of games but paced the deck to exercise and to shuffle his thoughts. He sat by the rail in a deck chair, a hat sheltering fair skin from the fierce sun, pondering that he perhaps would never see the sons left behind again. They must make their lives without his guidance. Yet Karl Johan was distracted by silly fancies.

It pained Anders that he could not right turmoils of 1892. He could not absolve his eldest son of blame. Often in these last few weeks his tongue sought to find words that they might part as loved ones. KJ called his father domineering. Yet one must be strong to raise sons in this precarious world.

Anders knew he mishandled that meeting. As he watched the waves bring him closer home he reflected on this visit to Australia. If only he had healed their relationship. Dark memories tested his faith.

～

Anders was horrified that first day. This primeval forest was not like he had pictured the Promised Land. Massive trees grew on all sides, twisted into ropes that twined and looped around thick trunks, some the size of the barn at home. He recoiled, 'Are those snakes?'

Karl Johan laughed. 'These do not bite humans but they do eat trees. They are called strangler figs for they choke the host tree. Like a parasite they kill it so it hollows and dies. This leaves space inside where we can shelter in storms.'

How could Anders leave a sixteen–year–old son with a feckless brother, at the other end of the world, far from his own influence and advices? Strange birds screeched and cackled. His eyes darted to either side. Fierce natives might throw spears, just as they took possession of this land. Misgivings grew when Pappa saw KJ's dwelling.

'What have you done?' he demanded. 'You frittered your time and my money?'

'You remember, Pappa, that in Finland I planted cherry trees which bore excellent crops? How my potato patch fed the whole family? Believe me, I am a skilled farmer. Who can counter droughts and floods and bushfires? It was not an easy time, twice laid low with my broken leg. In rough country, one easily trips over huge roots.'

'The leg is mended, I hope.'

It is a father's duty to guide his sons. With just two weeks before sailing home, Anders' advices were expressed straight, with no time for softening or niceties. The discussion became heated. Anders remembered to not let the sun go down on his wrath. He resolved to solve the matter in the morning.

Cackling birds woke him from a restless sleep long before sun was up so he could spend time in prayer. The priority was clear: to establish where best land lay and buy it for his sons. With this goal in mind they had little time for hurt feelings. They viewed land for some distance around. He acquired three blocks (of 640, 510 and 22 acres) at Goonengerry. Karl Johan became animated and drew plans for the huge sawmill he intended to erect on the smallest block, Devil's Lookout. (Perhaps there was hope for his eldest son?) This was adjacent to land bought for Wilhelm and Edvard. Their youngest must join his brothers here, though Sanna would grieve to lose another son.

When that snake ate the fowls Anders knew this country was not for him. At forty-four years he was too old to adjust. The land was thick with forest. 'You will have a big effort to clear this land sufficient to grow crops and run cows.'

'We will fell the timber and burn the stumps and plant maize and run some cows,' rattled Wilhelm.

Anders was torn with anxiety to leave the lad with a wastrel brother who still begged money yet grew exotic flowers. Much as he boasted of the corn crop, what had he to show for it a year later? Was this some tall story, to impress?

KJ mocked the church. Anders sought opportunities to ascertain the state of his soul but he flicked the questions away with flippant humour.

As they paced the platform at Bangalow railway station, about to separate, Anders' last efforts to speak of faith met a granite wall.

With a leaden heart he farewelled these two sons of his loins. He could only entreat the Almighty for their protection. Wilhelm threw himself into his father's arms. 'Pappa, please stay longer. Don't leave us!'

Anders could only shake his head and climb aboard. Wilhelm ran after the train. Before it turned the corner Anders' last glimpse was of Wilhelm slumped on a log as KJ patted his shoulder.

Anders Back didn't return as planned. Did he abandon his sons? But what else could he do?

~

Sanna took to her bed with a stomach ache, sick with worry for her boys. Her husband recounted his last words to them: 'Settle down, marry an Australian girl and forget Finland.'

'Better they marry there, than waste money returning to Finland to search for a bride. And safer.'

A thought made her pause.

'How can Wilhelm find a wife?' she scoffed. 'Who would marry him when he doesn't speak any English? He should return to choose a good woman here.'

'He will find a wife no trouble. What other sixteen–year old boy owns his farm already at this age?'

Still Sanna sighed and moped even though he told her the boys had safer futures than in Finland under General Bobrikov.

The Brothers, 1904–5

And I should give you that advise to sell all your land in Finland. I will try to assure you that <u>none of your sons will for their lifetime live in Finland</u>. It's nothing that I regret so much as that I didn't travel when I was 15–16-year old.
KJ Back, letter dated 31 October 1905

Letters from 1904 and 1905 show KJ as mentor and guide to his younger brother, who owned adjacent allotments at Wilson's Creek, New South Wales. Together they built a sawmill at Devil's Creek but Wilhelm eyes land elsewhere.

His later letter of 7 September 1972 looks back to his pioneering years of 1903-1905…

And particularly what I learned from brother KJ with his wonderful crop of corn and getting such a good price for it on account of the big drought all over the rest of Australia and other countries who were buying corn at £1 a bag, something that had never been heard of before in the history of Australia.

A close neighbour came to me and told me how fortunate we were to come from another country and hit it so well in falling the scrub. He thought we were very adventuresome to fall 200 or 300 acres in one year and to be favoured with such a wonderful corn crop. And then Paspalum came into existence, a new grass which thrived well in the new ground. This old man taught me a lot as he was saying how long he had been there in 10 or 20 acres and here was a big undertaking for him and his family to fall the scrub and grass. In his early days they planted buffalo grass by root, which they had to dig up from established paddocks. Here we had the good fortune of getting a much better grass and only to sow the seed. He gave me a history of his early pioneering and to him it looked as if we were greatly favoured by God to give us such a wonderful start.

I am sure now that God sent that old man to talk to me and to establish faith in my undertaking, as I started to look at things in a different light altogether.

Photographs show the brothers in that era, wearing natty bowler hats and neat suits.

I imagined KJ in dungarees potting orchids as Wilhelm's sulky creaks up.

'*Hej, bror.*'

'Hello, William. Practice English—you speak good Hindi, from bossing my workers. Yet English is easier. How will you get a woman, unless you speak with her?'

'Plenty time for *Engelska* words when I have a fine house for a bride. A farm near to townships and the railway line is best. Women like tea parties with ladies.'

'Such land is expensive now that the rail connects Byron Bay and Murwillumbah to Sydney and Brisbane.' KJ led Wilhelm into his cottage, stoked the fire and set a billy on it.

Wilhelm smirked. 'Now hear my news. New South Wales State Savings Bank have written papers to mortgage my land here at Goonengerry. I convinced the bank manager so I can buy between Burringbar and Mooball. Land with rich soil, it will grow grass good for cows. The train takes it to market cheaper than the cream run.'

KJ threw a handful of tealeaves into the billy, then rinsed the pannikins. 'So you will move further away from the forest; what of our plans to build a sawmill?'

'*Ja visst*, we make the sawmill. But this one will function, better than your monstrous pillars at Goonengerry that reach to the sky but no one hews timber there. I work hard; I can also build a farmhouse. I will find a wife for company in the nights when dingoes howl.' Wilhelm strained the leaves in his pannikin.

'Brother, I am family for you, you are not alone.'

'Yes, KJ, and you helped me put my feet firmly on this new land. But a man needs a wife, yes? Have you no interest in a woman?'

KJ shrugged. He won't tell Wilhelm about the beauty Christina Hart he noticed at the local concert. She's new to the area. 'Have you brought the mail and papers from Bangalow?'

'You spend so many monies on papers and books! It could buy a good farm.' He relents. 'Indeed, here are newspapers.'

'We must be informed of world events, what is happening to our people. Our family writes so little. Or their letters are intercepted.'

KJ pulled the string from the bundle wrapped in brown paper. 'I hope Mats has not sent those government–subsidised papers, full of propaganda, a waste of postage.' His eyes gleam: 'This is an underground paper that circulates since Bobrikov has forbidden Finnish newspapers. Konni wrote to me that between 1899 and 1901 twenty–three newspapers were suppressed.' KJ glanced at its headline. He sprung to his feet and clasped Wilhelm in a bear hug. 'That monster is dead!'

'What is this, KJ?' Wilhelm reaches for the paper.

'Dear God, that this comes at last! How many times we wished for this!'

'BOBRIKOV ASSASSINATED!' announced a headline in black thick typeface. The brothers laughed and whooped and danced around the cottage. 'But how?'

'It says a student nationalist Eugen Schauman shot Bobrikov three times and himself twice. Schauman died on the spot and Bobrikov later that night in the hospital.'

'When? This paper is months old!'

'Back on June 16, 1904,' KJ read. 'All this time Finland has been free of him and we did not know. My nightmares were for naught.'

'For years I hated that man, hated and feared him! His Cossacks stole our horses and crops; if anyone dared complain they were lined against the wall and shot. We wrote you as much as we dared—did many letters arrive?'

'Yes, bearing Russian stamps instead of the Finnish lion.' KJ sniffed as he reached to read the latest news.

Six months later, with shaky fingers, KJ pulled the string from another newspaper.

'Will, read this! On 22 January 1905, Father George Gapon led a peaceful procession of two hundred thousand people through the streets of St Petersburg to present a petition to the Tsar.'

Wilhelm looked over KJ's shoulder. 'The protesters behaved in peaceful manner, singing the Tsar's own hymn *God save thy people*—others repeating the desperate cry, "Death or freedom!"—and carrying religious icons and portraits of the Tsar.'

'This is terrible! As they knelt in the snow outside the Winter Palace, Cossacks fired into the crowd, killing and wounding hundreds of men women and children. Even children who had climbed into trees to watch the proceedings were shot in cold blood.'

'It truly was Bloody Sunday. This unrest will spread. People will fight back.'

'This fate could have been ours if we had stayed home and been sent to fight for Russia.' Wilhelm grips KJ's shoulder. 'When the Conscription Edict was introduced thousands left Finland. When we got our passports in November 1902, already seventeen hundred passports were issued in Vaasa province alone that year.'

'You are lucky to have a passport—surely they realised what you planned.'

Wilhelm shook his head, thinking of all the paperwork. The birth certificate from the church records was easy enough to falsify, but they gave a cow as a bribe to get the certificate of non–objection from the police authorities.

'Officials have become rich from peoples like us wanting to leave.'

KJ unravelled another newspaper. 'Here is Father Capon's first–hand account, quoted from his book *The Story of My Life*:'

> At last the firing ceased. I stood up with a few others who remained uninjured and looked down at the bodies that lay prostrate around me. I cried to them, 'Stand up!' but they lay still. I could not at first understand. Why did they lie there? I looked again, and saw that their arms were stretched out lifelessly, and I saw the scarlet stain of blood upon the snow. Then I understood. It was horrible… Horror crept into my heart. The thought flashed through my mind, 'And this is the work of our Little Father, the Tsar.'

Wilhelm swept an arm towards the green hills. 'Brother, we are blessed to live here in freedom, far from Russia.'

KJ pursed his lips. 'This will spread to Finland. There will be demonstrations and strikes in Russia and at home. If only I could be part of them.'

KJ Meets Christina; 1908

When marrying, bear in mind that there is no one infallible on this earth. If you marry the woman you may have the pleasant surprise of finding that in some ways your wife is an angel, but if you marry the angel, you may find to your annoyance that she is only a woman.
K. J. Back, *Concentrated Wisdoms of Australia*

Ah, my, the drama, with Wilhelm courting Christina Hart, new to the district. The neighbourhood was a–buzz. He was cagey that his reprobate brother's rough manners might scare away his little treasure. Wilhelm soon squared off other swains; he impressed her by driving an automobile to Wilson's Creek to visit. Locals tut–tutted that it would frighten horses and cause accidents. The tracks were scarcely wide enough. When the wheels jarred in deep ruts the lady was jolted and bruised just as much on fancy leather seats as in a sulky.

Now he was sure of her affections and they talked of a wedding, she must meet his only family here in Australia. He brought her to visit at KJ's farm.

He puffed out his chest. 'Christina is her name.'

'Mamma will approve that you found a girl with a good Swedish name.'

Will spent much effort to groom his brother for the meeting. KJ countered with aphorisms but he didn't listen.

Doubtless Will warned her to not be offended by his wisecracks. KJ could act the gentleman. He changed into a clean shirt, a decent necktie and coat and dusted off his bowler hat. He thought of wearing his frock coat, but the weather was steaming. KJ cleared dirty plates from the cedar–hewn table and pushed papers to one end.

They rolled up, as flash as can be in the Model T Ford. Will made a great show of the fancy gentleman rushing round to open her door for her dainty foot to alight. A veiled hat shaded fair complexion. Yes, it was indeed the woman KJ saw at the concert. If only he'd had more courage to introduce himself.

Christina's blue eyes were fetching. They were of similar height: both around five foot five, a year younger than Will. They looked a likely pair. No wonder Will was smitten.

An uneasy silence settled after the introductions. KJ put the billy on the fire and brought out cups instead of the pewter pannikins. Will inspected them to be sure they were clean, but he had no reason to be ashamed of his brother on that count.

'So, you're from the Clarence River?'

'We were. From Maclean.'

'And your father is a farmer?' John Hart, of English stock in the eastern fenlands. Will had told KJ often, touting his conquest of a true lady.

'Seven days after he married my mother Harriet they sailed from Plymouth on SS Durham, on 29 October 1881. They came past Cape York and set foot on Australian soil at Cooktown on 17 December, then disembarked in Brisbane.'

So Christina had an interest in history. She talked about some uncle who died soon after her parents arrived in Australia and about their move to Billinudgel. Words flew over KJ while he feasted his eyes on this angel.

Christina spoke in a whisper; he realised that this was not just shyness but that she did so when excited. Smiling, always smiling and with a tinkling bell of laughter. That was a good thing for a wife of a Swede, who tend to bleak moods. If she found Wilhelm pushy at times, she had the knack for getting round his forthright ways. She talked straight and kept him on track when he ran away with ideas. 'That's Wilhelm for you, always wheeling out new projects.'

'Do you read much?' KJ asked by way of small talk.

She could read and write; many cow–cocky daughters had some schooling. She did domestic duties in the home, like most girls of this age.

Christina chattered away like a magpie, bright as the sun. She accepted KJ just fine, so Will's fussing was unnecessary and condescending. Indeed she smiled often at him.

Her eyes lit up to see KJ's orchids. He listed their names while she nodded and tried to remember. Christina loved flowers; they had that in common. KJ promised to strike cuttings for her new home in Mooball farm. Will put all his time into building this so it would be ready when they married.

Will tried to whisk her away. But Christina was interested and said, 'Wait, Will, these are so beautiful though their names so complicated.'

'This one's an *Arachnis clarkei*, I ordered that in from India last year; it took a while to accustom to the climate after its journey. You see how it resembles a spider? This is *Paphiopedilum faireanum* from Siam, it will bud continuously through the year. I went in my sulky to pick these up from Brisbane port.'

Christina stroked their petals while Will scratched calculations in his note book about a deal he planned. She promised to visit again to collect the plants. KJ would tell her the best ways to grow them.

Will finally drew her away. She placed her foot on the running board and he helped her into the leather–bound seat, cranked the engine with a flourish. KJ waved until the car snorted out of sight and sound.

The humpy felt lonely. But next week she visited to gather cuttings of plants for her new garden. While Will loaded flowerpots into his car, KJ showed Christina his notebook of poetry. Her attention emboldened him to express his dream: 'I plan to publish them.'

Now her bell laugh rang a knell.

'Oh, Karl Johan, don't be silly. Who would buy such books?'

KJ shrivelled.

Then clutched at *sisu*, rallied.

'I will show you all,' KJ vowed.

Highs and Lows

Happiness is everlasting. No sorrow is so bitter that it can kill it entirely. It is like a fire in a stack of sawdust— always smouldering.
K. J. Back, *The Royal Toast*

After Wilhelm's marriage, this busy younger brother overshadowed KJ. It would be a decade before KJ's voice was heard in his published books and half a century before I located and translated letters from this time that revealed he had more success than credited. Photographs of the 1910–decade show KJ as a dapper, well–presented man wearing a bowler hat. In another he poses with six workmen, fellow–Finns. (Fourth from left)

My research found snippets from The Mullumbimby Star:

June 30, 1909: The Back brothers are building a large sawmill on their property at Devil's Lookout...surrounded by inexhaustible forest of splendid hardwood.

November 3, 1910: Mr Back has his sawmill in complete working order and some splendid stacks of timber are in evidence.

October 10, 1912: Mr Back's mill narrowly escaped being burned down last week. The sawdust caught fire, making it difficult to extinguish. No damage was done.

A local historian assisted me with maps and aerial views for my exploration of KJ's first land, near Whipp's Crossing, now known as Pioneer Bridge. It's overlooked by a massive mountain bluff, ideal for rolling logs. Yet a steep gorge separates this land from Devil's Lookout where KJ built and operated the earliest sawmill in the Wilson's Creek area. Apparently this was successful even though my Uncle Eric's memoir was dismissive of KJ's earlier efforts at nearby Goonengerry:

He stood a lot of huge logs up as the framework of the mill, and people wondered how he raised them without modern lifting gear. Well, those big logs stood out against the skyline for forty years but not a stick of timber was produced, and eventually bushfire destroyed the lot. Later, Uncle built and operated a sawmill at Wilson's Creek, concentrating on the beautiful red cedar then growing there. Three of the mill employee's houses were lined and ceiled through with red cedar, and most of the cedar in Dad's 'Cedarholm' came from there. Like so many other mills at that time, Uncle's mill and cottages were destroyed by fire.

With a helpful local, I set off to search for the site of KJ's sawmills.

An expert indicated on Google maps where he found aboriginal grasses and artefacts near the cottage that KJ reputedly built. Before Goonengerry hamlet, we turned right along Mill Road. My car lurched in protest at gullies and potholes in the dirt road.

A charred ruin pulled me short; maybe this was part of an old mill? Did KJ's hands fashion that crumbling cottage where hippies now live?

He wrote to Edvard in 1921 of his desire that their parents should emigrate:

I myself have five cottages and they could live in whichever they want. But I won't try to get them here against their own desire. If they would die on the travelling over everyone would blame me.

The foliage was so thick by the side of the track that I nearly missed a rusting steam boiler. Was this the one that KJ wrote of in 1921: 'Last Saturday we had a huge crowd on my property for the grand opening of the steam saw'? Yet in 1913 he wrote:

My steam saw is giving me a lot of unnecessary trouble and it hasn't been very profitable. I succeeded in leasing it until my forest's wood is cleared out, to a company named 'Queensland Company'. They have a lot of money so I may profit from this.

As dappled light filtered through strangler fig trees festooned with orchids, I felt close to my great–uncle. You, KJ, might have planted those orchids, bananas and that mango tree. I poked around a derelict barn, wondering if he built this. Did you huddle under its shelter from torrents of summer downpour? Did you sit on this rock by the creek to write poems? Did you see a platypus?

Were you content in your Garden of Eden?

Always the elements challenged. Research from the historical society prompted my next pictures of KJ's struggles.

The worst drought on record began in 1910 and malingered into the twenties. KJ's decision to focus on timber and growing fruit proved sound as dairy farmers struggled to maintain their butter production. The government imported butter from America, giving local producers but a penny per pound, rather than thruppence. KJ never shirked a protest against unfair rule, so joined their indignation.

During his few years there, Coorabell had grown into a bustling little hub with a general store, a blacksmith and a butcher. One small wooden church served most religions. In 1906 a School of Arts hall opened for social meetings on the Wednesday night closest to the full moon—so people could travel safely home afterwards. Roads were steep and perilous, especially after a few jugs of beer. As hills drop sharply to either side KJ anchored a log for a brake should the sulky wheel ease over the edge. Others fared worse. The Coorabell Project Association petitioned Byron Shire Council to improve the road.

1915 capped a disastrous year with one calamity after another. The ground was arid and riddled with huge cracks into which a man or horse might fall and break a leg. The few sprinkles of rain soaked down the fissures leaving little impression on parched land. Wilson's Creek normally gushed with fresh water. Then it was dried up under the sun's onslaught. Eucalyptus trees crackled with oil that evaporated but hung in the air. All it needed was carelessness to snap into fireballs from the scalding of the sun on pieces of broken glass. Often in the spring, banana growers lost control when lighting fires to clear space for the suckers.

In October, fires burned around Cooper's Creek and Wilson's Creek. They decimated pastures, orchards and homes. Sometimes leather beaters were brought in from Mullumbimby to fight the fires. Locals attacked flames with canvas sacks day and night, eyes red–rimmed from the smoke. They earned a flash name—the Wilson's Creek–Huonvale Bushfire Brigade.

Gusts of winds whirled up and down ridges, they scattered tinder and coals that multiplied into yet more brush fires. Stan Robinson's horse–drawn cream carrier brought women and children from the top farms down to the safety of Byron Bay and Brunswick Heads. KJ's neighbour Percy Whittall lost forty acres, others even more. One weekend, KJ helped save Cecil Russ's home. So when the wind turned and chased a wall of fire up the valley towards the brothers' sawmill and KJ's house, he was nowhere nearby to rescue it.

From the ridge, KJ stood helpless to see his work, sawmill and home reduced to charred sullen embers within minutes. The tender petals of the orchids were turned to black ash. All was lost. Now what did he have to show for all his years on this land?

~

KJ knew Wilhelm and Christina would welcome him in their Mullumbimby home. Wilhelm drove his Model T Ford up Mill Road, a slow trip with charred logs blocking the rough track. He picked a path through to the burned mill. The thriving enterprise they created together was a rubble of embers. All was quiet. 'Karl Johan, where are you?' No response.

A tent was pitched under a blackened gum tree.

Wilhelm lifted the flap. A huddled body lay tight in the swag, wrapped close like an Egyptian mummy.

'KJ, it's me, Wilhelm.' The bundle was still. He laid a clumsy hand where the shoulder might be.

'Wake up, KJ, the sun is high in the sky, a new day. We will rebuild this together.'

One thin sound at last: '*Nej!*'

'*Kom, KJ, stig up.*' Wilhelm lapsed into Swedish also.

'*Nej, jag vill inte!*' (I will not.)

His brother sighed. 'KJ, you must. You must keep going.'

'*Varfor?*'

Why? Because life goes on. But how could he persuade a bundle of blanket?

'KJ, get up so we can speak of this together as brothers. Let us boil the billy and drink some tea while we put our minds to rebuilding.'

KJ pushed himself upright and glared at Will, as if it was his fault he lost all, not the forces of nature.

'How many times do I have to tell you to bang on that sheet of tin when

156

you visit? I hate people creeping up on me.'

'I'm not just any people, I'm your brother! You can trust me.'

'Go away, Wilhelm, go off and earn all your filthy money, clear yet more land, sell yet more blocks! Leave me in peace.'

'I will not leave until I see you on your feet, taking your first steps to start again. You must snap out of this *sorg*.'

'*Varfor?*'

'Because we live in our Promised Land—even if it deals cruel fate at times. We have a rich future here. You squander that lying in bed. Don't let the Devil grab you by the neck and infest your mind. Look forward. Go forward.'

But KJ would not be moved.

There was bread in his hanging safe. Will set a pannikin of tea near his elbow.

'Remember, brother, you will always have a welcome with us.'

There was no answer. Wilhelm shrugged. A land auction awaited.

Revolution

There will be a single great rule of Finland.
Its Lion Flag will be carried by
the strong arms of Jägers,
over the roaring fields with blood
towards the shore of the rising Finland.
Jäger March, Dr Wilhelm Zilliacus

Karl Johan slithered down the mountain to the flat land and headed towards the Bangalow general store. Two newspapers and a letter were addressed to him. He unravelled the string and brown paper. His eyes widened at the headlines.

'Some problems back home, Jacky?'

'It's full–blown revolution! I must tell my brother.'

KJ gathered his papers and galloped the twenty kilometres to Mooball.

'Wilhelm,' he huffed, pushing the newspapers at him. 'Listen, I have great news!'

His brother signed a document with a flourish and laid down his pen. 'Call me WA now, it is safer.' He shakes a finger. 'You could buy more farms with money you waste on papers.'

'Listen, there is revolution in Russia.' KJ wiped sweat from his face.

WA covered a yawn. 'Again? People suffer all the more after uprisings are suppressed. Put Finland and Russia behind you, KJ, Australia is your country now.'

KJ pushed newspaper under his brother's nose. 'This time it is serious. They have deposed the Tsar. The Romanov dynasty is finished.'

'After centuries of Tsars? Pigs might fly. Spies and Cossacks will quell that, they are everywhere.'

'Such protests will spread all through Russia and to Finland.'

WA frowned. 'But that is far away. We must go forward and not look

158

back.' He swatted a fly on the windowsill.

'Read it!' KJ thumped his hand on the desk. 'How can you shut your mind to this? You saw Russians steal our horses. You were…'

'Oppressed. They tried to change my faith to Russian Orthodox. So I feel blessed to worship freely here. This is a good future for my wife and children.'

KJ clutched his arm, frustrated. 'Wilhelm, was it for naught that workers and peasants rose up against the Tsar to strike in St Petersburg in January 1905? Then at home? That I helped collect all those signatures for a petition against the February Manifesto in 1899?'

'The Tsar did not listen. Brother, you missed the worst repression from 1901 what showed us Finns just how little the Tsar heeded.'

WA sighed and reached to peel a ripe banana. 'Put Europe behind you. Even when serfs are free, they live no better. Imagine their faces to taste meat, as we do!

'People starve, weak from famine. They slave fourteen–hour days in hard winters—'

'Finns are tough, we endure hardship with little complaint. Remember *sisu*!'

'—Eating bread made from husks, pounded straw and fir bark.'

KJ sighed. If only Wilhelm would listen. 'Rebellion will soon ignite Finland; the revolutionary Social Democratic Party need little excuse to fight. You ignore all that is happening in Europe while you chase around the country buying and selling land. Yet your own people back home live in poverty as the Russians cream off their profits.'

WA noticed an envelope. 'Here's a letter from Anna Sanna. She so rarely writes. Is this Martha's hand?'

As KJ tore it open, he remembered how in 1892 he tried to teach his sister to read and write. How sad that, since that black time, she shut her mind to learning. 'She writes that the revolution spreads to Finland. She hints that her man is caught up in it.'

WA looked over KJ's shoulder. 'No doubt, living near Udden, they make their home a safe house for revolutionaries.'

'She fears she could have become a widow with five children. But she gives no reason except a mention of Monäs Pass and her husband's plough horses. And that there is hope of independence for Finland.'

War and Aliens

O who can reckon up the tale of trials this folk withstood,
When battle raged o'er hill and dale,
When frost brought famine in its trail.
Johan Ludvig Runeberg, *My Land*

World War curbed all plans to travel either to or from Finland. But the brothers still hoped to be reunited with family.

By 24 June 1917, KJ's letters were a mixture of English words, with 'well' crossed out, and changed to 'väl'.

> *Jag mor well. It is a long time since I heard from you and I would be happy to get some news from home. It seems to be an unwritten law that I always have to write at first to you, that you never write first to me, which means that if my letters don't reach you I have to write twice to you, to receive a letter from you although I am one and you are so many.*
>
> *Write and let me know me know how Mamma and Pappa bear their years, how old age has left its mark on them … I hope you are all well and that your pains and repercussions from the war will be over soon. I hope that I once could see them before they or I will die. It was my idea to come home to visit you in 1915 but I didn't expect the war and my plans weren't realised. And if I didn't come before, I hope to come in 1920 and then we can go together to see the European battlefields. You have perhaps not still realised that I am settled here and I have lived in almost the same place about 17 years.*
>
> *Life here is in some ways going on as usual with the exception that everything is more expensive because of the war. I am now rather well with the exception of my arm, I had a little accident with one of my horses but it will turn out well after some weeks.*

He wrote with 'Usual greetings' from Mullumbimby on 25 October 1917.

> *Some time ago we got two telegrams, the first told us that you meant to come here and the other that you couldn't make it here until June. I'll try and meet you in Finland in the beginning of June and maybe spend a large part of the summer there. If all goes well, I'll head back as soon as possible after Christmas. I'd like to travel first to California and head from San Francisco to New York. It is possible that Wilhelm and his family would like to come and meet you.*

News of the war filtered through, doubtless heavily censored. How did the family reconcile differing allegiances? Blood thirst was rife on both sides. The Germans were saviours to the Finns, smuggling in weapons on the ship *Equity* to sheltered bays in Ostrobothnia, training the Jäger troops. To Australians they were enemies. On 6 May 1919:

> *I got Edvard's letter and am happy nothing had happened to them during the war in Europe. In my opinion the fall of Germany in the war was unavoidable. I was surprised to see that such a 'civilised' nation could let itself be led into such a dangerous business. There were many things I would have liked to write to you during the war but I feared you would be punished for my sins, so I thought it best to write as little as possible.*

The Back brothers came to the right country. Of all nations, Australia was the only country to hold a referendum—twice—that allowed men to choose to fight rather than accept conscription.

Did free will ease KJ's pacifism? He wrote on April 16, 1916:

> *Great Britain has begun National Service so it is possible that we get it in Australia before long. If that is the case I would give my life happily for mankind. I have not yet seen in the papers if Finland has been forced into the war and I guess that brother Edvard won't participate in the war, as he is too young. Russia will probably select older men for their forces.*
>
> *The war has not yet had any great influence on our way of living but I expect that the taxes will rise soon. Australia could probably carry its burden better if we could all start saving.*

Yet in Australia, life was difficult for migrants during wartime; many were interned. In country towns during WW1 people were suspicious of those who spoke with an accent. When the brothers' sister, Anna Sanna

Nyholm, joined the brothers in Australia, she anglicised her surname from 'Nyholm' to 'Holm'.

–So Granddad, is this the time to make a decision about what I call you? It seems odd to keep you as Wilhelm as you integrate into Australia. Billy seems flippant, so what do I do?

–*My business name is W. A. Back. Call me WA. Then nobody can link me to Germans.*

Perhaps WA asked the local newspaper to publish articles to quell the suspicions about him held by the locals?

WA made conspicuous donations to the war effort, second only to the mayor's. He raised money by driving people in his new automobile to farewell soldiers—for a fee.

WA in his Model T Ford drove people to the Showgrounds to farewell soldiers off to
World War 1.
Photo courtesy Brunswick Valley Historical Society.

Locals suspected that KJ spied for the Germans, for he tended his bananas on the ridge by lantern light. But what is night to a Finn?

KJ protested his patriotism by writing two books and numerous articles. This first–published Finnish–Australian wrote in English that he had learned only on the voyage to Australia.

Did the pacifist KJ feel ambivalent for all his relief to have found freedom in Australia? Did he long to join in the overthrow of the Tsar and Romanovs? That his fellow citizens rejected conscription must have warmed him all the more to his adopted land. But I wonder how would he have reacted to later conscription and demonstrations against the Vietnam War?

Red Flag Riots

While hearty despots swing their rod
And bid defiance to their God,
A simple hermit in a den
May rule the nation with his pen.
K. J. Back, *The Concentrated Wisdoms of Australia*

In Brisbane on May Day 1918, two hundred Russians celebrated the fall of Tsar Nicholas II and the Bolshevik Revolution. Supported by a crowd of Greeks, Germans and Poles—and fifteen Finns—they marched up Adelaide and George Streets, singing *The Red Flag*. They cheered a revolutionary tableau '*Breaking the Chains of Bondage.*'

Pacifists called for immediate peace. War and high unemployment meant that many were disillusioned and so supported a Stop–the–War crusade.

Police attempted to suppress the rally, but it went ahead in Brisbane's Centennial Hall. Speakers called for the 'bloody madness' to end. Loyalists blocked the Bolsheviks from entering. They rioted against radicals in many towns. In March of 1919 seven thousand returned soldiers and conservatives marched across Victoria Bridge to attack the Russian community in South Brisbane. They chanted, 'Hang them!' and 'Burn their meeting place down!'

–KJ, knowing your hatred of the Tsar, I guess you were in the thick of all this?

–*Tom Sergeev formed the Union of Russian Workers; he was a confidante of Lenin and imprisoned in Siberia for his part in the 1905 uprising. He escaped through Korea and arrived in Brisbane in 1911.*

–Here in Queensland! So, were you a revolutionary, a communist?

He peers suspiciously at me, refuses to answer.

–This story is exciting. What was your part in the riots of 1918 and 1919?

–*Would I not support those who threw out the Romanovs? Tom transformed a rag–tag group of Russian immigrants into the activist URW. After the February*

Revolution of 1917, he returned to Russia and became one of the fifteen members of the Bolshevik Central Committee that planned the October coup. This rally was to commemorate the first anniversary of the Russian Revolution—

–Which you would celebrate! Yet looking back, was the Tsar a mere kitten in comparison to later monsters like Lenin and Stalin?

KJ folds his arms, picks up his newspaper.

–Don't interrupt or I won't tell more. Yes, it was banned. Of course, the newspapers blamed the Bolsheviks—not those who picked the fight. There were attempts to censor Hansard!

–There was rioting in the streets? In sleepy provincial Brisbane?

–Bloodshed, even. Some carried guns; many made do with jam–tin bombs against police with bayonets. Bottles, stones and bricks were thrown. Troopers charged their horses into the crowd. It was mayhem for over two hours. Just like the Cossacks back in Finland.

–Were you part of that riot? As a pacifist did you join the actions of a lynch mob?

He dodges that question. I wait. Soon his memories flow freely:

–I oppose all war. I resisted pressures to be sucked into that 'war to end all wars'— which of course didn't end anything. Issues festered to ignite again and decimate the next generation of young men.

–There was propaganda about 'aliens' in Mullumbimby? Against you?

Locals tattled against me for not enlisting, pointed fingers at me, even called me a spy. After all these years proving myself as a hard working upright citizen! Did I clear my land of that scrub, thick like jungle? Did I erect a sawmill that stood so tall against the horizon many marvelled at how I lifted those tall logs upright? Yes, I spoke with an accent but so did all those other aliens, Greeks and Italians and Croats and Hindus.

–But your brother's connections helped you? I found this newspaper clipping in the Mullumbimby Star in 1915:

> *It has been said that Mr W. Back of this town is of German nationality. On Mr Back's naturalization papers, 18 Feb, 1908, the place of birth is given as Munsala, Finland, a Swedish part.*

–Other aliens paid for advertisements that protested their allegiance to their new country. Will's influence as a fine upstanding money-making citizen helped when locals sniffed around foreigners, calling for them to be interned. He cultivated friends in high places, impressed people with all his land and his fancy office in Mullumbimby. He was an official in the local Lodge.

–We have a photograph of Granddad driving people in his automobile to Mullumbimby showground to farewell the lads off to war, raising funds for the war effort. Yet they accused you, KJ, of signalling to foreign ships from the hillside. Some muttered you were a spy.

—All I did was tend my bananas by lantern light. Yes, it was the dark at night, but what of it? I lived twenty winters of endless night, where the sun barely crawled above the horizon for a few hours each day before it slunk back.

—Yes, what is night to a Finn?

—Back in Finland, if we waited for those few meagre hours' sunlight to do our work our bellies would shrivel. Often I read far into the night, engrossed in Plato or Nietzsche, or penning my books. But I am a hard working citizen, so I roused to tend my corn and bananas. Why would I fight, a pacifist? Let them send their white feathers anonymously, sneer behind my back; I determined to wield my own sword—of the pen.

Letters Home

Whilst here on this island I dwell
My soul is a snail in its shell.
K. J. Back, *The Royal Toast*

Spanish influenza had reached Mullumbimby. KJ wrote that the doctor was the first to have died:

> *He was a heavy drinker and as far as I can understand it is almost impossible for a drinker to overcome that disease. Many die also because they leave bed way too early. I also think that we got a milder form of the disease than other parts of the world. I'm as healthy as ever and so are Wilhelm and his family.*

In June 1919, Mayor Joe Hollingworth died of the Spanish flu at the young age of 54. In his last year he had expressed interest to buy KJ's land and sawmill. His executors used money from his will to make a firm offer.

KJ waved them away. 'Indeed, you can buy the timber rights, I have less time for sawmilling now I am a published author. But I will keep the land. Discuss with my brother Wilhelm, he has a head for business.'

Grandson Nicholson Hollingworth revealed family considered they over–paid, as both a promissory note and cheque were presented. But he was gracious in suggesting more blame rested with the Hollingworth in–law who brokered a deal with WA.

Now KJ had no excuse to delay a return to Finland. He wrote to Edvard in 1922:

> *Thank you for your kind words concerning the selling of my forest. I got a pretty penny for it but sadly enough all of it went to pay off my debts, it wasn't enough to pay them all but it left me in a far more safe position. Had I gone home earlier as I meant to do I would probably have lost this opportunity and perhaps as a consequence lost everything I own.*

KJ continued with his usual mantra to sell up and come here, praising Australian life. He wrote about his dreams to bring his parents to the Promised Land.

> *Last time Pappa was here I didn't even have a cabin to live in and now I have four farms of my own and you could live in whichever of them. It would be so much easier for you to live here than in Finland where the long winters makes work on the farm such slavery. If you were here we could go to town any time in an automobile and come home any time you wanted as Wilhelm lives in the city and we are always welcome there.*

Did the brothers comprehend the impact of Finnish Independence, the struggle to achieve and maintain it, after two decades at the end of the world? KJ did not appear to share the euphoria when he wrote from Mullumbimby 26 June 1919:

> *I'm happy to hear that Finland got its independence. (I saw in the papers here that France, England and the USA have given their recognition). That Finns would have the view point of live and let live is too much to expect because it is in human nature to oppress other humans. When it comes to equality I think that Australia has a higher level of it than Finland… In truth the Finnish political sky looks dark indeed and the best you could do would be to move here: Mamma and Pappa, Sofia and Helmi as well as Erik Johan and Anna Sanna and their children. You could buy a home here for the price you'd get for selling your home there, if you sold it now. But if you wait until everything is back to normal you will lose more than you lost with the Nykarleby Bank, since if the banks in Finland lend money on the current land prices there will be many bankruptcies there at home and many people will lose their savings.*

As Hollingworth's estate bought the Goonengerry timber rights for £2000, plans hatched for KJ to go to Finland and bring the family back with him. WA sent a telegram advising them to sell everything and migrate together. On 26 June 1919, KJ wrote:

> *I cannot stay for more than a week or two in Finland so it would be best if you are ready when I arrive. It would be pleasant for us all if we could stay a week or two in London or in Paris. Myself I have a lot of land at the moment and my brother has nine properties. When you come here we could live in my house in Goonengerry. It has five rooms and if that doesn't work I have my own sawmill and timber so it won't be hard*

to build a new house. Erik Johan and his family could live in another of my properties where I have a good house. We'd like to see Edward and Erik Johan have their own properties and mother and father and Sofia and Helmi could live with me. You must all come together and sell everything you cannot bring with you so that mother and father can live unconcerned for the rest of their lives.

But he could accept their parents age and increased frailty. To Edvard, April 15, 1922:

My brother, forever in my mind, I got your letter yesterday and I want to respond. I was sad to hear that Mum and Dad have been sick and hope they will be well soon. I think it is very important to get them on their feet as they have worked all their lives and hence it would be dangerous for them to be in bed resting all the time.

You're still young and so is Australia and if you use our experiences wisely, you should be able to have more than Wilhelm and I have today when you reach my age. The best patches of land in Australia are mostly uninhabited and it's larger than all the present kingdoms in Europe. The worst thing is that the older you are when you get here, it's getting harder to get used to the new circumstances, especially concerning the language.

But he had plans for his money. This sale allowed funds to afford the printing of his second book, *The Royal Toast*. He wrote home on 22 June 1920 Sydney:

I sent 2 pound of tobacco and coffee. The tobacco is for Pappa and coffee is for Mother, and two black ink pens for Anna Sanna. I will take care that you have coffee and tobacco as much as is possible. It is my hope that Pappa will not have to smoke the Hokan in his old days. It is now June and I should have already been in Finland if it went as I meant.

KJ wrote that he planned to travel via America, spending some months there. He may have envisaged an author tour.

Between Australia and Europe you have to buy the tickets several months before. I still haven't bought the ticket. I hope to be ready soon perhaps in two months. There will be dark winter when I come to Finland, but perhaps that will be the best if it is winter, it is now 20 years since I saw snow last time, and that would be something to see a real winter again. If I could hear it's very cold and frozen and the house will creak then perhaps I will appreciate the Australian summer.

Still KJ procrastinated, absorbed. He never returned to Finland. He wrote in 1931 to apply for a new certificate of naturalisation because he supposed that termites had eaten the original. He needed this to renew his passport so he could travel back to Finland. As he had escaped with a friend's passport, perhaps he never had one? This may be the main reason why he didn't return to Finland in his lifetime. That, or fear of the Russians. Locals told me that he built tree houses on his properties where he could hide if threatened by those who held official positions.

By July 1921, KJ realised that Edvard should stay home 'until the old ones are dead which perhaps couldn't take very long in Finland, as the percentage of people dying is very high.'

But KJ was engrossed with marketing his books. He who the Board of Censors had silenced.

KJ the Author

There on that shelf my tiny compilation
Appears so unimposing to my sight,
Yet on and off, whilst it was in creation,
I had a tiresome day, a sleepless night.
K. J. Back, *The Royal Toast*

Since I became a publisher myself, the tasks of producing, marketing and distributing my books overwhelm me. It has been a fulfilling journey but such aspects consume my creativity. On this, my treasured writing day, I sit on my deck amongst the trees. An orchid blooms nearby.

–*What is it?*

–An *Oneidium*, with a burgundy coloured flower.

So why, in all this fresh air and beauty, is my brain like cotton wool? I've walked by the creek and enjoyed waterfalls splashing over the rocks after rain. Green has sprung up. I sat and thought of KJ and scribbled a few sentences on a yellow 'post–it' note—

–*What is that?*

–Coloured paper that I carry in my pocket on my walks to write ideas. Often I forget them and so they turn to mulch in the washing machine, lost forever.

–*So you also tend to muddle. Like your father, like me, they would say.*

–Sometimes. KJ, how did you do it, publish books?

KJ pulls out a pile of pages closely written with black ink:

–*I persevered in spite of weaknesses. My first book starts: 'As an introducer of this, my first offence to a reading world I am coming just as I am, a poor sinner, with no great expectations, yet no trembling fears—'*

–Sounds like the revival meeting hymn that we were dragged through, all ten verses. But I heard you avoided such meetings, were a free thinker. (He glares.)

–*You interrupt. 'My work is bristling with faults and its merits are few, if any.'*

–KJ, you put yourself down so! You were in the prime of life, about forty years old when you published your first book in 1918. You had successes, built a sawmill and produced that stunning red cedar I've seen in Granddad's house 'Cedarholm'—

—I had my failures also. The mill burned down.

—And you're writing this book ten years before your bankruptcy—

—Don't talk of that, or I'll go away, leave you to write your book by yourself. Mistakes all through, I'll be bound. Serve you right for baiting me. Like the rest of them, you doubtless think the sun shines out of Wilhelm's backside, because he was a dealer of properties and became so rich that folks idolised him while they laughed at me. He was often close to bankruptcy but wriggled out of it.

KJ beetles off into the forest so fast that I huff as I run after him. Holding a stitch in my side, I conciliate:

—Truly, KJ, you have the more interesting story; I'm impressed that you wrote in your second language without formal schooling. How did you learn it so well that you could even write whole books? Please, can we sit down on this log? And did I hear you had articles published in *The Bulletin*? (Thinking, how can I access them? Are they digitised yet or must I plod through microfilm?)

Poor man, he had so few accolades, living in the shadow of his brother Billy Back. KJ folds his arms but settles back onto the log—cedar, of course.

I bring out from my backpack copies of his books, open *The Concentrated Wisdom of Australia* and prompt him to look back to the *Preface*.

—Where were we? Yes, you were berating yourself.

—Why would I do that?

—I mean you were being too humble. There's a saying that we should not give people ammunition to fire at us. As you wrote, 'I regret that this should be the case but I find consolation in the conviction that perfection is unattainable to man. Perhaps someday I may bring out a worthier production.' And if you don't mind my posthumous editing, in the preface of *The Royal Toast* it was unfortunate to apologise with an excuse about the typos, because you'd been ill.

—Typos? What do you mean?

—It's a colloquial expression meaning mistakes.

He shoots a fierce look from under a lowered brow. I read on.

—Let's jump over the stuff about the patriotic gathering—

—Certainly not! That is the whole point of writing, to show my patriotism when neighbours were suspicious of all aliens during the Great War.

—Sorry, I diverted you; let's read your rationale.

—'In an effort to illustrate to the world—'

—I just love your world vision while living in a small insular hamlet.

–'*The public feeling in Australia at the outbreak of* THE GERMAN UNIVERSAL WAR—'

–If I were you, I'd go easy on the caps, KJ, they're considered pushy, called shouting when we use them in emails.

He slams shut the book. (Pest. Why don't I learn to edit my mouth?)

–*Caps? Emails? What do you talk about? You are not really interested in my book. I hoped you had more sense but you waste my time.*

I clasp his wrist before he can leave, open the book and continue to read:

–'And during the continuation of same, I am writing a book, the name is to be: THE PATRIOTIC GATHERING.'

He nods at my fitting emphasis.

–*That also describes our public meetings arranged by the schoolmaster and myself to show patriotism. We read out compositions representing the real opinions of all classes of men and women. We rehearsed at the home of the composer—*

–'We' meaning you. For this was your baby.

–*No, I never have a baby. Maybe not. None peoples know about.*

–I mean you were the author. The parson recites a 'lengthy supplication to the Supreme Being'. Didn't he suggest that this title is a little generic?

–*It was my, how do you say, baby, so I have the decisions.*

–And in this paragraph you write of yourself:

> *He possesses no wealth of any description, nor has he any ambition to become rich. His mind has somewhat reached the standing of that of Solomon, for he maintains that "All is vanity, vexation and profitless labour under the sun, and that wisdom alone is worth going for."*

–An irony is that you were considered ungodly, while your rich brother quoted Biblical verses about receiving God's blessing.

As if on cue, Granddad rolls up in his Model T Ford, winds down the window and shakes his head.

–*KJ, are you just sitting around? You should spray these bananas.*

KJ ignores him, engrossed in his word self–portrait.

> *He has a few grape vines, some stools of bananas—*

–And you were fined for bunchy top disease on your farm at Goonengerry. The *Tweed Daily* printed that for all to see and be appalled by your slovenly farming.

KJ winces. WA tests the tension on a stooping fence. The brothers glower at each other so I draw the conversation into safer channels by marvelling how KJ would organise his challenge in literature, such a huge undertaking. He has written:

> *I would appoint a judge from a leading university of the civilized world, like Oxford. Contestants submit twenty poems of five hundred lines each and also one book of prose of three hundred pages; five thousand maxims, mottoes and proverbs—*

–You have that already, in your book *The Concentrated Wisdoms of Australia.* I recall it well: '*Five thousand lines to be written in his measure and five thousand in those of mine; both have to use the same measures, but each one can choose his own subjects.*' And what language? English?

–*In order to exclude no one I left it optional to write in any language. The only preference was given to Germany. I would take up the contest single-handed against ten Germans, provided that they (my opponents) were born and educated in Germany.*

–KJ, I think it's wonderful. All through the Great War, amongst the warfare of bullets and gas and mines, you chose to fight with words. For in your *Challenge in Literature,* you wanted to tackle a German and you expected to trounce him or her, didn't you?

A wolfish grin flashes across KJ's lean face. He writes a letter home.

> *Thank you for the congratulations about my pen fighting. I never intended to earn money from my writing I will not make much for it but also hopefully not lose. But if I could find something that I could live from it I could feel very much lucky to bring an income.*

Both KJ's books contain his *Challenge in Literature* to become the poet laureate of the world.

Did anyone accept his challenge? None of the 30 reviews I've located from newspapers around the country mention this but overall most are positive:

'No Australian should be without a copy of *The Royal Toast.*'

'It overbrims with patriotism added to which are many gems of philosophic wisdom.'

'It is a publication that should appeal directly to the heart of every true Australian.'

Others inform: 'Twenty years ago he could not speak a word of English... Now he is a fluent English speaker. He has absorbed the ideas and the ideals of Australia.'

Some noted that KJ was no Tennyson and advised against printing further books.

'It should rank as one of the curiosities of Australian literature.'

KJ's Pinnacle

One of the surest ways to consecrate your own name to fame is to add a worthy
slab to the literature of your nation.
K. J. Back, *The Concentrated Wisdoms of Australia*

The white feather galvanised KJ into print. It arrived in his post box in a plain brown envelope, so he could not guess the sender. Perhaps a woman who rolled her eyes and giggled as he read his poems at the benefit concert in the Goonengerry hall. He tried to speak with her later but she turned her back; her friends pursed their lips and sniggered. They would not laugh if brutal soldiers invaded their country, if it were occupied by officials who stripped them of their rights. In Australia, citizens all worship as they please, not as dictated by a Russian Tsar. They can read or write what they choose, in their own language.

They thought him a coward because he had not enlisted to fight the Hun. They refused to dance with those men who had not volunteered to fight.

What did these small village misses know of his valour against the Russian forces of the Tsar? Of the battles he fought back in Finland? Not with a gun, but with words. These ignorant women would not have heard of *Kalevala*, of the hero Väinämöinen who waged war with words. But KJ was in the elevated company of mythological heroes who waged war through words and music.

He wrote many poems and articles and sent them to the editor of *The Bulletin* and *Mullumbimby Times*. They published most about banana diseases and the progress of the war. At this bottom end of the world, far from combat, they had little idea of the terrors and strictures ordinary folk endured when a battle raged over their land.

Even now in 1917 it would not be safe to tell them how Karl Johan Back risked his life to bring enlightenment to people who struggled under the Russian rod. Those silly girls, who laughed at his performance in a village concert, would not believe him if he told them how powerful were his dramatic productions in Finland. So potent that those Russian officials instructed the police to watch out for subversion at his performances. The Finnish constabulary respected him; they were on his side, and that of the people. They attended that concert on Runeberg's Day, to celebrate the great poet from the region. The concert was so long, how could they last till the end without coffee? Just before KJ stood up to sing that item, the police went next door.

They heard the melody of the Marseilles, a good rousing tune—but not the words KJ put to it. So when the Russians grilled him next day, the policeman shrugged. We enjoyed the concert, yes, but it went so long we became tired and needed to drink coffee and smoke our pipes outside.

KJ the pen–fighter wrote articles, he even type-set the words onto paper, one letter at a time. He would have been shot if the Cossacks checked the loft in Munsala farmhouse for a bench covered with paper and racks of small metal letters, or behind the sacks of potato in the barn at Tjitton. With so many small barns scattered across the flat fields, why would they look?

Here in the Promised Land of freedom, KJ brimmed with new energy. He pulled out his note books, pen and ink. An excellent solution; KJ would not be pushed to enlist for war; he had faced a lifetime of conflict in those two decades before he fled to Australia.

The whispers rankled him. All 'aliens' were viewed with suspicion. WA had convinced the *Mullumbimby Star* to support his Swedish nationality in 1915. KJ would not rely on another person's words; his own should speak for his patriotism. All the better that they were contained between red bound covers. And what better to express his love of his adopted country than to display an embossed gum tree on the cover, with a kookaburra in it. KJ scribbled a rough design. Mrs Newton on a nearby farm was handy with her pen, she could make this eye–catching.

He would publish a book of his patriotic writings, showing the depth of his thought and patriotism. His concentrated wisdoms would reveal for the world Karl Johan Back, the upstanding citizen of Australia. And in it he would issue a challenge to other writers, a pen–fight. In *Kalevala* Väinämöinen fought with words. KJ would do the same. He would mount a contest and his book would be emblazoned: '*By the man who Challenges the World in Literature*'.

But what if Russians should hear of this challenge? They might trace him in his haven at the end of the world. A *nom de plume* was wise. *Australianus* had a literary ring, and spoke for his patriotism. Of course he must reveal his own name and address, for how else might contesters apply? But the initials K. J. Back gave no suggestion of his foreign origins.

Already he had written many poems and stories. He shuffled papers all over the cedar wood table. He collated a section of aphorisms about various topics, some from Finnish lore, others of his own imagination.

He would end with a flourish: the *Challenge in Literature.*

At the front of the book must come his plea: *give all men their due.* As those flibberty–gibbet women did not. He dipped his pen in the inkbottle and blots spluttered onto the paper to mark his emphasis:

THE GROUND WORK

Here is the Australian version of the scriptures:

GIVE ALL MEN THEIR DUE.

This is the busy man's bible. It is a long sermon in short words; none too little and none too much. It is the key to heaven and to all true earthly greatness. It is one of the few rules to which there are no exceptions, being equally well–suited to the high and the low, the rich and the poor, and to all circumstances wherein man may be placed. I place this as the first commandment and not only as the first commandment, but as the sum total of all commandments, as the essences of all true moral law, of all noble thought and of all good literature, for it contains all our duties to ourselves and others, God included.

'Hello, KJ, are you home?' a voice called from the verandah. The schoolmaster, Bill Uptin was a good friend. Since Herr Svedberg mentored him all those decades ago, KJ had sought and enjoyed the company of such learned people.

'Just the person I need, Bill. I'm writing a book. Would you check the manuscript for grammar and spelling?'

They emptied the teapot many times while Bill read through his pages and offered suggestions.

'How will you tell people about it, KJ? We need ways to find buyers for this book.'

'We could produce a dramatic presentation, speak the poems before an audience,' his words tumbled out. 'Like I organised in Finland for the youth group.'

Days blurred into long nights while KJ wrote and prepared his manuscript for the printer. When his lamp flickered out, he stirred himself from the flurry of pages to buy more cans of kerosene in the village. He strained bloodshot eyes until they watered. He survived on bread and jam and drank gallons of strong tea to stay awake. Never mind food when inspiration fuelled his brain and spirit.

All else was forgotten. Pumpkins needed no attention; they grew as huge as tubs without any effort on his part, the choko vine straggled over his outhouse. Oranges ripened in the sun. Production at the sawmill dropped, but he had good men like his old friend Ulf Bexar to maintain enough sales to afford the printer.

Bananas ran riot on the hillsides and he closed his ears to warnings about a disease called bunchy top. Anyway, his crop of bananas brought no income. As the war effort commandeered rail transport for troops there were no trains to take produce to markets. His bright yellow fruit turned to black, insect–ridden mush by the railway line.

KJ received a telegram that the books were ready for delivery by train to Bangalow station. He enlisted WA and his Model T Ford to retrieve them. As KJ mounted his pinnacle of authorship he needed some family, his own brother, to share the excitement. He capered along the siding as the train steamed to a halt. KJ rushed to haul off boxes filled with two hundred copies of red–bound books.

There on the platform, he tore open a box and pulled out his book.

'See, Wilhelm, what a handsome binding this is, how well the etched title and drawing look!'

WA took the proffered copy, flipped through some pages and returned it to the author. 'Yes, it is an achievement, brother,' he nodded. 'You must be the first published Finnish author in Australia.'

'Imagine, what will Pappa and Mamma say when they receive their copy?' KJ laughed. 'Will Pappa regret his words about my education being a waste of time? I will post a copy tomorrow. How I wish Herr Svedberg were still alive to see this.'

'Indeed, he would be proud.' WA helped to lug the boxes into the trunk of his car. 'Come on, I must auction land at Mullumbimby after I drive you back to Goonengerry.' He turned the ignition key, pulled back on the hand brake and got out to crank the starter lever.

WA carried a few boxes onto the cottage veranda, shook his head at a rickety fence and drove away in a cloud of dust.

KJ stacked some books on the mantelpiece. He set the billy to boil water over the fireplace and opened a copy, stroking the pages with shaky fingers. He sniffed the aroma of new minted paper. 'My own book! Who would have thought it back home, that I should publish a book? Twenty years ago I spoke no English and now here is a whole book of my writings.'

Next day KJ wrapped in brown paper a copy of *The Concentrated Wisdoms of Australia* and walked down the hill to Bangalow post office. He tried to interest the *Mullumbimby Star* to write a review but news of the war took precedence. He gave away more copies than he sold. But he revelled in his achievement. Until the printers sent a second reminder that their bill must be paid or else it would be placed with receivers. The red–covered books brightened his shelves, rather than those of his compatriots.

Armistice Day of 11 November, 1918 was a flurry of whistles, bells and sirens rejoicing that the Germans had been trounced. Euphoric people jammed the streets, dancing and singing the National Anthem, *God Save Our Gracious King*.

For Karl Johan, it brought relief that the white feathers and hisses subsided. Now he opened his post box with eager fingers. If only there were more envelopes stuffed with bank notes to order copies of his book.

The Prince of Wales Visits

We meet with joy our Royal guest,
The prince who shared our smarts and sores,
And bid him welcomed, wish him blessed,
Upon our sunny Eastern shores.
K. J. Back, *The Royal Toast*

The end of the war brought new problems. Discharged soldiers flocked home to eager arms. The euphoria burst like a balloon. They slumped into disillusion in a struggle to find work and eke out an existence. Many were wounded in body and spirit; they had been maimed or gassed in trenches. Their lives, whether awake or asleep, were nightmares of a bare survival existence. The streets were noisy with protests by bands of soldiers in shabby uniforms with a letter A for Anzac over their battalion colours. Many were disabled and others blind. *The War Precautions Act* was still in place and many demonstrated against its continued strictures.

KJ shook his head at the newspapers and sighed at the futility of war. How it crippled the lives of the people—whether they fought in action or grieved loved ones, or supported those who returned, all staggered with halting steps to rebuild their lives.

The sheer mess of it all frustrated Karl Johan. If only he could act to improve the situation.

Then an opportunity presented. In 1920, the Prince of Wales toured Australia and New Zealand to thank the soldiers and hearten the wounded that their sacrifices were valued. This was just the patriotism expressed in KJ's book. Could he interest the Prince of Wales as a patron?

But the title would not hook the attention of a royal visitor so much in demand.

The Concentrated Wisdoms might prove how he had integrated into his new land as a worthy citizen. But this regal visit needed a new book, a new title to catch the eye of a Prince amongst the madding crowd. One that might cause him to raise a glass and…

Aha! He thought. *The Royal Toast* is a more apt title.

The visit to Sydney was planned for early June. That was not much time to put together a new book. Again the bananas and sawmills were neglected.

But though KJ had written fresh poems, inspired by the bloodshed of war, would that suffice? He would repeat the Challenge in Literature as a focal point. Perhaps someone would read it and respond this time. And the aphorisms from his first book offered sound wisdom.

KJ checked his bankbook. There was little in his account and a pile of bills shoved onto a nail on his wall. He would visit the bank manager to explain the situation and ask for a loan to pay for the printing. And give him a copy of his first book to show such visionary writing was worthy of an advance. He was an author with track record, capable of a worthwhile venture that may earn repute.

Then luck shone his way. If misfortunes like sickness and death can be termed such.

He even bought coffee and tobacco in Sydney to send as gifts home to his family. KJ had funds to publish his book, five hundred copies. He instructed the printer to bind one in the finest quality Moroccan leather, fit for a prince. He would present it in person so must travel to Sydney.

KJ cut from the newspaper the Prince's itinerary.

'Wilhelm, you have contacts in high places; can you put me in touch with the mayor or *aide de compte* so that I can book a meeting with the Prince?'

His brother shook his head. 'Thousands of people hope to meet the Prince. Even with my connections I cannot secure an invitation to the ball or dinner for Tine and myself.'

KJ consulted the royal tour schedule then booked his passage. There was no other way; he would go to Sydney a week before the Prince arrived so he could collect his books from the printer, days early in case a hitch delayed publication. With many boxes of books, he must afford accommodation in a hostel or guesthouse. He would gladly pitch a tent in a park, but there his books would not be secure. And what if it rained and his frock coat was crumpled? He scoured the newspaper for advertisements and chose a boarding house in Surrey Hills. He would stay the full ten days of the Prince's visit. What if the Prince wanted to discuss it with KJ after he had a chance to read his book? Yes, the schedule was packed, but how could he resist opening the covers of such an attractive book written in his honour? Imagine if the Prince should offer patronage!

Even a week before the royal party arrived, Sydney was at a fever pitch.

Shops and houses displayed bright bunting and flags danced in the wind. KJ opened his wallet to purchase these; they would display his patriotism.

He walked around the routes and venues where the Prince would tour to plot the best vantage points and where he might intercept the regal party. His letters to the Lord Mayor and Government House had received no response. But doubtless they were busy planning such a big event. If he could just catch the Prince's eye, wave the book...

Then news came that plans had been delayed by a week. After onerous engagements in New Zealand and Melbourne the Prince of Wales was exhausted and must rest. He would arrive on June 16 instead of June 9. KJ asked the landlady if he could extend his stay another week. He spent the days roaming the city planning his tactics, and the evenings musing by the harbour, entranced by the illuminations reflected in restless water. Sydney was a blaze of lights for ten successive nights.

On the morning of June 16 KJ rose, wide-eyed before dawn. He jogged to Farm Cove and claimed a spot on the hillside close to the dais where the Prince would be welcomed to Sydney. The harbour and city were drenched in sparkling light.

'To think I sailed into this harbour twenty years ago, terrified for my life. I struggled to piece together a sentence in English and people laughed at my efforts. Now I hold under my arm a whole book written in our language. What a difference freedom and opportunity have made to my life.'

The Prince disembarked *HMS Renown,* bright with bunting, and came to shore on a launch that danced over the waves. Even before it docked KJ was hoarse with cheering. After the speeches and presentations the Prince was to meet many people; the queue stretched all the way up the hill. If only he could slip into that line!

Eagle-eyed, all week KJ stalked the Prince. He was no closer to his quarry. Personnel surround the regal party and fobbed off any attempts to push in. They refused KJ entry to the Government House grounds for the induction of Victoria Cross winners and Boy Scouts. When the Governor-General hosted a dinner for His Royal Highness, followed by a ball in the Town Hall, KJ pushed to the front of the crowd that lined the gates, but the Prince was quickly ushered inside. Perhaps there would be an opportunity at the races, a more relaxed setting with many people attending—but there were too many people. And so it went on.

At each venue, thousands of people milled around. They waved flags, threw their hats in the air and shouted, 'Digger! Teddy!' to tumultuous ovations. Choirs sang, children performed gymnastic displays.

On Saturday night a display of fireworks added to the illuminations in the city. On the harbour the warships were silhouetted by the light. Vessels danced with the waves and their lights shimmered with excitement. Searchlights crisscrossed and swept across the sky, playing with the clouds.

He found time to write home to Finland, but how to capture the excitement of this city? Pappa might sniff at the outlay of a new publication so he did not share that with him. On June 20:

> I am still in Sydney and may perhaps be here for 2 or 3 weeks longer. There were so many people, more than I ever saw in one place. The masses have gone now and everything is as it was before.

Two days later he described the scene:

> I am here for business but will soon return to Mullumbimby. We have the English Crown Prince here for a visit and hordes of people are sweeping along the streets, there has been a big effort to spruce up the town. I could hope that you would be here by now and see our electric light. The beauty of it could be unbelievable for you. I hope you are all well and to see you in a few months.

Yet KJ would never return. Issues would fester unresolved. And then it was too late.

On Sunday, KJ arrived before dawn at St. Andrew's Cathedral to ensure a place inside the packed congregation. It was the first time he had set foot in a church since that day when he arrived in Sydney. But again he was thwarted. The Governor–General and the State Governor, and their wives and staff, formed a phalanx around the Prince. KJ was too distracted to listen to a long sermon preached by Bishop Long of Bathurst.

He caught a train to Parramatta where the Prince was feted in a huge field at Harris Park before boarding a launch for a private tour of the Hawkesbury River. It was dark when the Prince returned to a spectacle of Chinese Lanterns and electric light. KJ was waiting at the landing stage near Hawkesbury railway station. Always KJ carried his book, wrapped in brown paper, tied with string. The days were warm for mid–winter; his armpits sweaty with the throng of close bodies. His cheers rang in chorus with the mob of flag–waving enthusiasts, to no avail. KJ shivered in the June night and plodded back to his hostel.

He had two hundred copies of the book stacked in boxes. On days when the Prince visited Canberra or rested, KJ used the time to post a hundred copies to newspapers around the country.

183

The day before the Prince would sail for Hobart, KJ was in despair. It is his last chance. By now the *aide de compte* knew him, so often he had pushed KJ away.

'Sir, it's my last chance. Could you please arrange a meeting? Just for a minute?'

The man shook his head. 'Sorry, but that's the protocol. Leave your package with me—a book, you say? I must check it. I will promise that he receives it.'

There was no other way. KJ couldn't follow the royal party to Hobart for his wallet was empty. The landlady insisted he pay the account today. He counted out his remaining note. All that remain were a few coins to buy bread. Not enough to afford a passage home to Mullumbimby.

But what is 800 kilometres? He had strong legs and always walked.

KJ packed his corn bag sack with the crumpled frock coat and dozens of books. But more boxes remained, and he couldn't afford shipping costs.

A wheelbarrow. He located an ironmonger, bought steel and asked a blacksmith for use of his forge.

The Prince had sailed south. KJ loaded his books into the wheelbarrow, wrapped in the frock coat to protect them from the rough tracks ahead.

He adjusted his hat against the sun, checked its angle and calculated due north. As long as he kept the sea to his right, there was little need of his compass. He crossed the Hawkesbury River, dotted with boats and oyster farms. Piles of soggy streamers and flags lay desolate in parks, like his dashed hopes.

But Karl Johan, published author, still had his land.

He gripped the wheelbarrow handles and headed home.

TIMELINE

Year	Event	Year	Event
1535–1635	Munsala church built.	1894	24.6.1894 KJ first communion; didn't attend 1.12.1895–8.8.1897.
1809	Finland became Grand Duchy of Russia with own laws, language, religion.	1894	Nicholas II became Tsar.
1832–1889	Anders Svedberg 11.3.1832–25.1.1889.	1897	January 1897 Youth Group play.
1848–1936	Betty Hällsten 22.5.1848–13.4.1936.	1898	KJ gained sailors' permit 4 June. Bobrikov became governor.
1862	Svedberg school opened 31.10.1862.	1899	Petition signatures presented to Tsar in March.
1871	Anders and Sanna marry 21.2.1871.		*Osterbottningnen* issue 27.4.1899 lists KJ among those conscripted for military service.
1866–1868	Famine.		*Osterbottningen* issue 69, 8.9.1899 calls men including KJ to active service.
1876	Munsala family home built.		Four newspapers shut by Board of Censors.
1877	Karl Johan Back born 20.10.1877–20.6.1962.	1899	Family Bible notes KJ fled 26 May.
1878	Conscription Act.		First dated letter from KJ letter written from Scone, 9.12.1899.
1881	Tsar Alexander II assassinated; Tsar Alex III increased repression.		
1886	Wilhelm Back born 29.7.1886–2.4.1974.		

1899–1905	Konni Zilliacus (13.9.1894–6.7.1967) submitted petition to Tsar demanding a constitution.	
1900	Finn army strike. Seven newspapers shut down. Konni Zilliacus founded Fria Ord (Free Word). Youth Group performance halted 5.2.1900. 20.6.1900 KJ letter: 'I left hospital on 16th... and stayed in Bangalow three weeks'.	
1902	2 March KJ letter asked loan of £200 to lease Coorabell land. 'I have none in the bank.' KJ sent £20 to Backlund for travel. Anders Back passport No. 4190 dated 7.11.1902.	26.11.1902 Anders, Wilhelm, Otto Nyholm and Wilhelm Backlund departed Hangö on SS Arcturis to Hull.
1903		Anders and Wilhelm Back arrived in Sydney 17.1.1903. Anders bought 3 blocks at Goonengerry. KJ and WA building sawmill on Devil's Lookout block. WA bossed 20 'Hindoos' for KJ.
1904		17.6.1904 Eugene Schauman assassinated Governor General Bobrikov. General Strike, 12-19 November. Leo Michelin (24.11.1838–26.1.1914) organised petition against conscription.
1905		KJ: 'I have now three separators working and milk 125 cows. I have others milking for me.' 22.1.1905 'Bloody Sunday' led to Russian Revolution.

	8.9.1905 Konni Zilliacus brought weapons on SS Grafton to Jakobstad, a centre of Finn resistance. Unrest until Tsar complied with November Manifesto. Michelin founded Senate with equal voting and human rights. End of First Oppression. Clash of Red Guard & White Civil Guard.
1906	KJ sought approval land board, sp1059 (21.3.1906 Tweed Times). Finland first European country to give women the vote.
1907	KJ conditional lease 06-2 at Lismore (Tweed Times). Russification resumed.
1908	WA naturalisation Certificate 5555 4.11.1908: WA married Christina.
1909	'The Back brothers are building a large sawmill at Devil's Lookout' (Mullumbimby Star, 30.7.1909). 15.10.09 KJ naturalised, Certificate 14006 .
1910	Russian PM Pyotr Stolypin persuaded the Russian Duma to pass laws that ended most Finnish autonomy. Russian plan to take over Finnish railway. 'Mr Back has his sawmill in complete working order'. (Mullumbimby Star, 30.11.1910). 3.11.1910 KJ letter suggests that Russians might banish them to Siberia.
1912	'Mr Back's mill narrowly escaped being burned down last week' (Mullumbimby Star). 1911–12 Drought; also 1915.
1913	WA bought a Model T Ford. 'By end 1913 I had safe income' (KJ letter, 15.4.1922) Finland ruled from St. Petersburg as a subject Russian province. Finnish press published secret Russian plans for complete Russification. Finland looked to Germany.

1914	KJ Back testified for Mullah, a 'Hindoo' underpaid for wages, 21.4 and 28.4.
	Hughes' War Precautions Act.
	WA opened office in Mullumbimby. Subdivided Jasper Hall, Rosebank, Morrison Farm.
1915	Built 300 houses, created 30 dairy farms.
	Russian military stationed in Finland created discontent.
	Rumours of anti-German riots Lismore, shop windows broken.
1916	Dairy slump, fixed butter price. Necessary Commodities Commission.
	Moves to intern all enemy aliens whether naturalised or not.
	14.10.1916 compulsory registration males aged 21-35.
	First Conscription Referendum rejected.
1917	February Russian Revolution. 15.3.1917 Tsar abdicated, assassinated 16.7.1918.
	1.10.1917 SS Equity shipped arms to Vaasa. 6.12.1917 Independence declared.
	1917-18 KJ writing Concentrated Wisdoms, published March 1918.
1919	Second Conscription Referendum rejected 20.12.1919.
	1919-20 Hollingworth executors negotiated purchase of Goonengerry timber rights.
	3-24.3.1919 Red Flag Riots Brisbane.
1920	KJ letter dated 20 June, in Sydney 'for business.' Published The Royal Toast.

Thank you for reading my stories.

For indie authors like me, reviews are like gold.

If you enjoyed this book, please take a minute to leave a review
on the website of your favourite bookseller or a review site such as
Goodreads.com (as did these readers—thank you!)

Reader Reviews:

This lovely book touches my heart deeply. It is a history of lives disrupted by famine and wars at the beginning of the twentieth century. Through the colourful painting of history that Ruth so vividly creates in this book, I glimpse into my own great grandfather's struggles in the land down under. —Annika Wicklund-Engblom

I found myself pausing, absorbing the lyrical qualities of this work as it drew me into the author's years-long wrestle to unravel the mysteries of her family's past. These historical identities came alive for me, staring back from the pages, conferring their fears and despair, dreams and determination. K.J. is a likeable dreamer, introspective, yet passionate about his family and country. I was inspired by the quoted passages from his work, and enjoyed the 'exchanges' between the author and her great uncle. —Adele Jones

Beautifully told with occasional photographs and diagrams, this is a rich treasure trove for future generations... blends creative non-fiction with a dab of magic realism to bring to life an absorbing story. —Anne Hamilton

It is an intriguing story and a rather quirky book…a fascinating read.—David Bennett

An excellent, challenging book. For anyone not only interested in European history but Australian stories of refugees who arrived here years ago, this is a must read. —Mary Hawkins

I thoroughly enjoyed this book.—Jeanette Grant-Thompson

There is nothing dull about this historical search, from the start I was drawn into the story, entertained, amused, challenged and moved. —Jeanette O'Hagan

A charming blend of well-researched narrative non-fiction and creative imagination.
—Mazzy Adams

Part memoir, part family history and part Finnish-Australian history of the late 19th and early 20th century, Midnight Sun to Southern Cross is a stirring story of courage, hope, opportunity, strength in adversity and enduring family

connections across years and latitudes. This is not a dry family history, but a tale of adventure and momentous historical happenings. Ruth brings the past to life with her evocative descriptions, her dialogues and dramatic retellings, her imagined conversations with her ancestors. —Jeanette O'Hagan

Books quoted or consulted

Australianus (pseud of K. J. Back), *Concentrated Wisdoms of Australia*, Sydney, 1918.

Australianus (pseud of K. J. Back), *The Royal Toast*, Sydney, The Kingston Press, 1920.

Åkerlund, Bror, *Munsala Socken Historia*, Munsala kommuns förlag, 1972.

Back, Eric, *William Andrew Back, Esq. and Mrs Back, from his arrival in Australia From Finland in 1902 until his death in 1974*. Compiled 1991. Unpublished memoir.

Comettant, Oscar, *In the Land of Kangaroos and Goldmines; A Frenchman's view of Australia in 1888*, (translator: Judith Armstrong), Rigby, 1980.

Condon, Christopher, *The Nineteenth Century World*, Melbourne, Macmillan, 1990.

Cormick, Craig, *Kurikka's Dreaming; The true story of Matti Kurikka, Socialist, Utopian and dreamer*, Simon & Schuster, 2000.

Daley, Louise Tiffany, *Men and a River: Richmond River District, 1828-1895*, Melbourne University Press, 1966.

Hassam, Andrew, editor, *No privacy for writing: shipboard diaries 1852-1879*, Melbourne University Press, 1995.

Hollingworth, Nicholas, *The Mullumbimby Sawmill*, Brunswick Valley Historical Society, Mullumbimby, 2012.

Koivukangas, Olavi, *Sea, Gold and Sugarcane: Finns in Australia 1951-1947*, Turku, Institute of Migration, 1986.

Linna, Väinö, *The Unknown Soldier*, Collins, Putnam's New York, 1957.

Under the Northern Star, Impola, Richard, Aspasia Books, Beaverton, Ontario, 2001.

MacKinnon, Neta, *What They Did: Families of the Brunswick 1890-1950*, Brunswick Valley Historical Society, Mullumbimby, 1998.

Tsicalas, Peter, *Mullumbimby: Boom and Bust 1908-1928*, Brunswick Valley Historical Society, Mullumbimby, 2012.

Tsicalas, Peter, *Mullumbimby: Foundation Events 1848-1908*, Brunswick Valley Historical Society, Mullumbimby, 2011.

Tsicalas, Susan, *A Century of Schooling in the Wilson's Creek, Huonbrook and Wanganui Valleys, 1908-2008*, published 2008.

Skrivargruppen, *Mellan Lojlax och Åkvarn, Berättelser ock hågkomster från gången tf. samlade av Munsala byaforskare*, Munsala, 1997.

Lönnrot, Elias, *Kalavala*, (translator: W F Kirby), Everyman, J M Dent, London,1907.

Olin, K-G, *Grafton-affären*, Olimex, Jakobstad 1999.

Oja, Niilo, *Corals and Spinifex*, unpublished manuscript in John Oxley Library, Brisbane.

Polvinen, Tuomo, *Imperial Borderland: Bobrikov and the Attempted Russification of Finland, 1898–1904*, (translator, Steven Huxley), Duke University Press, 1995.

Rayner, Richard, *The Cloud Sketcher*, HarperCollins, 2001.

Rundt, Dennis, *Munsalaradikalismen: En studie i politisk mobilisering och etablering*, Turku, Åbo Akademis förlag, 1992.

Runeberg, Johan Ludvig, *The Songs of Ensign Stål*, (translator: Clement Burbank Shaw), New York, G. E. Stechert & Co. 1925.

Wall, Marketta, *To America America; Hanko as Port of Departure for Emigrants*, Hangon Museo, 2013.

Westwood, J. N., Endurance and Endeavour; Russian History 1812-1986, *The Short Oxford History of the Modern World*, Oxford University Press, 1973, 1987.

Acknowledgements

Professor Olavi Koivukangas whetted my interest in family research by sending me his book Sea, *Gold and Sugarcane: Finns in Australia 1951-1947*. As former director of the Institute of Migration in Finland, he mentored, encouraged and commented on the manuscript. Helpful and enthusiastic Institute staff include Dr. Elli Heikkilä, Krister Björklund, Jouni Korkiasaari, Ismo Söderling and Elisabeth Uschanov who supplied shipping records.

Gretchen, Rolf and Karin Back generously shared information; much is recorded as audio and video. Thanks for research assistance from Birgit Dahlbacka in Munsala for Munsala village history and genealogical charts; Jakobstad Museum's Director Guy Björklund and Jan Ehnvall; historian authors Bengt Kummel and K.G. Olin. I have drawn on articles at sydaby. eget.net by June Pelo.

Carl G. Friedner, Dr. Tiina Lammervo and Marie Campbell gave invaluable help to translate letters, books and theses.

Alice and Wally Holm recounted memories; cousins and brothers supplied me with letters, photographs and memories. Thanks to the Brunswick Valley Historical Society, Susan and Peter Tsicalas, Ruth Fox and Nicholson Hollingworth for land searches, information and for putting me in touch with old-timers from the region. Ian Fox shared research and photographs of indigenous artefacts.

Dr. Peter Fenoglio designed the luminous covers; Stuart George, Nigel Holmes, Michael Bretherton and Martin Barry enhanced visual and digital aspects. Thank you Dr. Paul-Antoni Bonetti for encouraging me to crowdfund and for editing its video. Thanks to Book Whispers for handling the left-brain pre-press intricacies.

How to thank those who supported through this book's long gestation; writing buddy Debbie Terranova who travelled this story with me through countless drafts and edits; Anne Hamilton for insights and editing; Laura Back and Robert Nicholls for further edits; proof-reading by Bob Hunter. This saga came to fruition thanks to encouragement, support and feedback from Omega Writers Inc. colleagues, Bob Johnson and my sons.

Sandy McCutcheon mentored, endorsed my magical realism path and shared Finnish insights. Thanks for saying 'This is the book you must write!'

Special gratitude to my husband Antoni, who shared my journeys of discovery.

About the Author

Ruth Bonetti grew up in the arid Queensland outback, intrigued by the strange-accented relatives she met on holidays near Byron Bay. She preferred Mozart to hillbilly music, books to horses. Ruth's gift for classical music became a passport to the world.

Destiny led her to live in Sweden, directly across the Gulf of Bothnia from her grandfather's birthplace in Finland, where she researched this story.

Ruth is author/editor of a dozen publications about music, education and performance, five through Words and Music and two with Oxford University Press.

Ruth Bonetti is a Fellow of the Migration Institute of Finland where she presented a conference paper in 2014, published in *Participation, Integration*, and *Recognition: Changing Pathways to Immigrant Incorporation*. She has published in the Institute quarterly journal, *Siirtolaisuus-Migration Quarterly*.

Burn my Letters was short listed for the 2017 Omega Writers CALEB Award and won the Non fiction prize.

Connect with Ruth Bonetti

Website: ruthbonetti.com
Email: ruth@ruthbonetti.com
Facebook: facebook.com/RuthBonetti
KJ Back has his own Facebook page: facebook.com/BurnMyLetters

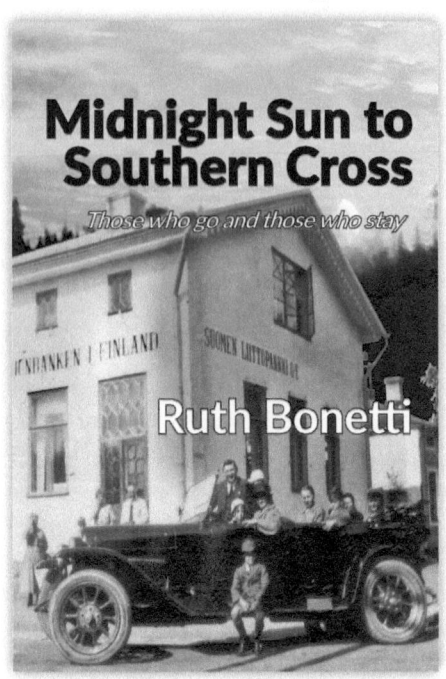

Midnight Sun to Southern Cross:
Those who stay and those who go

ISBN: 978-0-9875442-4-7

What challenges did Karl Johan encounter after arriving back on his land?

In the tradition of great family migration stories, Midnight Sun to Southern Cross continues the saga of the Back brothers' flight from Russian-occupied Finland to Australia as the nineteenth century turned into the twentieth.

From frozen Finland to the lush rainforests of northern New South Wales, to the dry and dusty sheep country of western Queensland, you follow the highs and lows of their new life under the Southern Cross.

It is an extraordinary tale of success, failure, hard work and dreaming. What drove the wheeler-dealer Wilhelm Anders Back, known as WA, to become in his time Australia's richest Finn? And what stirred his eccentric writerly elder brother Karl Johan, KJ, pacifist and political dissenter? What of those who stayed behind in Finland, and bravely struggled to oust the Russians from their homeland? This book, and its predecessor, Burn My Letters, are timely in the centenary year of Finnish Independence.

WA's granddaughter Ruth contrasts his and KJ's formative years in Finland with her own upbringing in outback Queensland. Her voyage of discovery and self-discovery uncovers research in Finland and Australia, and interweaves her own transformation from shy bush girl to speaker and musician.

Available at www.ruthbonetti.com